W9-CNI-915

I WAS AIRBORNE.

That's the closest word I can find, other than webborne (which is not, according to Mr. Webster, a word at all) to describe that exhilarating feeling somewhere between free fall and flying—when he showed up. He actually slammed into me in mid-air, which is an unusual feat in itself, more so in this instance because my spider-senses didn't give me any warning at all. He wasn't there and then he *was* there, in a flash of light, and the collision was instantaneous. I caught a familiar whiff of sulfur and death.

Knocked off my trajectory, I plummeted like—well just about anyone would if they were falling from two hundred feet above the city pavement. By the time I'd dropped a couple dozen feet I was able to regain my balance and shoot webbing out to the buildings on either side, stopping my fall. Hanging over the streets, I caught a glimpse of my assailant in the ambient light from below. He hovered, suspended as if on strings, up above me where he had first appeared.

I recognized him right away.

NORTH DEARBORN LIBRARY

Read these other exciting Marvel novels from Pocket Books!

FANTASTIC FOUR®

War Zone
by Greg Cox

The Baxter Effect
by Dave Stern

What Lies Between
by Peter David

Doomgate
by Jeffrey Lang

SPIDER-MAN®

Down These Mean Streets
by Keith R.A. DeCandido

The Darkest Hours
by Jim Butcher

Drowned in Thunder
by Christopher L. Bennett

Requiem
by Jeff Mariotte

X-MEN®

Dark Mirror
by Marjorie Liu

Watchers On The Walls
by Christopher L. Bennett

The Return
by Chris Roberson

WOLVERINE®

Weapon X
by Marc Cerasini

Road of Bones
by David Mack

Lifeblood
by Hugh Matthews

Violent Tendencies
by Marc Cerasini

The Nature of the Beast
by Dave Stern

Election Day
by Peter David

THE ULTIMATES®

Tomorrow Men
by Michael Jan Friedman

Against All Enemies
By Alex Irvine

SPIDER-MAN®
Requiem

A novel by
Jeff Mariotte

Based on the
Marvel Comic Book

POCKET STAR BOOKS
NEW YORK   LONDON   TORONTO   SYDNEY

The sale of this book without its cover is unauthorized. If you purchased this book without a cover, you should be aware that it was reported to the publisher as "unsold and destroyed." Neither the author nor the publisher has received payment for the sale of this "stripped book."

Pocket Star Books
A Division of Simon & Schuster, Inc.
1230 Avenue of the Americas
New York, NY 10020

This book is a work of fiction. Names, characters, places, and incidents either are products of the author's imagination or are used fictitiously. Any resemblance to actual events or locales or persons, living or dead, is entirely coincidental.

MARVEL, Spider-Man, all related characters and the distinctive likenesses thereof are trademarks of Marvel Entertainment, Inc. and its subsidiaries, and are used with permission. ™ & copyright © 2008 Marvel Entertainment Inc. and its subsidiaries. Licensed by Marvel Characters, BV. www.marvel.com. All rights reserved.

All rights reserved, including the right to reproduce this book or portions thereof in any form whatsoever. For information address Pocket Books Subsidiary Rights Department, 1230 Avenue of the Americas, New York, NY 10020

First Pocket Star Books paperback edition November 2008

POCKET STAR BOOKS and colophon are registered trademarks of Simon & Schuster, Inc.

For information about special discounts for bulk purchases, please contact Simon & Schuster Special Sales at 1-800-456-6798 or business@simonandschuster.com.

Cover art by JH Williams III

Manufactured in the United States of America

10 9 8 7 6 5 4 3 2 1

ISBN-13: 978-1-4165-1078-9
ISBN-10:   1-4165-1078-8

This one's for David.

ACKNOWLEDGMENTS

The greatest thanks to all those who've chronicled Spider-Man's exploits over the years, beginning with Stan Lee and Steve Ditko, and continuing to the present day. A special shout-out goes to Gerry Conway and Gil Kane, the two people who most explicitly shaped my view of the wall-crawler. Thanks also to the folks at R-Galaxy in Tucson for the research materials, and to Ed, Howard, Katie, and my family.

1

THERE WERE FOUR of them and one of me. Not what I'd call even odds, but I didn't want to give them time to round up a dozen of their friends—not with the owner of the Washington Heights *bodega* they had just held up stumbling around the street with a shotgun in his hands and blood raining into his eyes from a cut on his brow. He held on to the weapon like a drowning man with an unexpected lifeline, but he was blinking away blood and trying to see which way his assailants had gone.

I knew where they'd gone. I also knew they had already put about a dozen innocents between themselves and the man with the cannon. Time to earn the big bucks . . .

. . . or it would have been, if anybody paid me for webslinging. Definite flaw in the business plan, there.

I executed a textbook swan dive off the roof of a four-story building. Halfway to the ground I shot a line of webbing to the building across the street and on the other side of the fleeing robbers, nailing it just beneath the roofline. I tucked my head, rolled in midair, and shot a bracing line back at the building I'd just bailed from. That one went taut instantly, slowing my fall and interrupting my trajectory, and then I used the longer one to aim myself at the fleeing felons. I had to shoot one more, back to the side of the street I'd come from, as a course correction, but then I rocketed toward them.

They were a racially mixed group, the perfect twenty-first century mob, with skin colors ranging from fish belly to coffee bean. What concerned me more was the fact that two of them carried .38-caliber automatics. As I swung in, one of them stopped in his tracks and aimed his at me, bracing his gun hand with his left. No matter how many times you do it, hurtling at high speed straight into the muzzle of a gun is a disturbing sensation. The barrel opening begins to feel like a tunnel, and you're a train, and because the track leads inside there's no way you're not going in. Only you also know that there's another train, small and steely and deadly, coming out at the same time.

One more course correction. As his finger tightened on the trigger I threw my legs up and followed them, letting my momentum carry me in an aerial backflip. The guy with the gun fired once but his bullet sailed past me. I hoped it would be spent by the time it landed, blocks away. But I had to make sure he didn't get off another shot.

Sailing over his head, I shot a quick burst of thick, gooey webbing onto his hands, enveloping them. Now he couldn't release the weapon, but he also couldn't budge his fingers to use it. The other gunman swung his pistol toward me—another quick blast of webbing, but this time I held on and plucked the piece from his grip. *Baby, meet candy. Now say bye-bye.* I launched it toward the rooftops, making a mental note to retrieve it before someone found it there.

"Scatter!" one of the thugs shouted. Best idea they'd had yet. Of course, he was the one carrying the paper bag that I presumed held the take from the *bodega*'s till, so it was in his best interests to divide my attention. He no doubt figured I'd go after the shooters while he slipped away.

"Guess you don't know my rep," I said, throwing disappointed-voice at him. He was already taking his own advice, and had made it almost four whole steps before I punched him in the middle of the back with a web-club. He flew forward, his legs splaying out, the bag of money still clutched in his greedy fist.

The fourth guy—no gun, no bag—had stopped and faced me with clenched fists. He looked like he knew what he was doing. Maybe he boxed at a local gym. "Think you're all that?" he asked.

"I know I am," I said. "And no matter how many wins you've had in the ring, you haven't faced anyone like me."

The thug whose gun I had flung onto the roof chose not to be part of our audience. He started up the street. I fired webbing around his ankles and he went down hard. I heard his teeth clack together when his chin hit pavement, and he lurched to hands and knees, spitting blood. The one whose hands I'd glued together swung them at me like a bat. I ducked easily and jabbed him once in the gut. The breath blew out of him, and he rocked back against the nearest wall.

Which left me facing Mike Tyson. He was a few inches taller than me, with long arms and fists about the size of holiday hams. For big families. He circled around me, stepping lightly on the balls of his feet, going up on his toes, keeping his heels off the ground. His right prodded the air in my direction, testing me. I ducked and dodged those big fists for a few seconds before I decided to quit playing and put these punks away. It had been a quiet night so far, but that could change.

"You're hot stuff at the gym, huh?" I said.

"I do okay."

"I'll just bet." I stopped weaving and put my hands on my hips. "Go ahead, then. Give it to me. Your best shot."

"For reals?"

I nodded instead of speaking. It felt less like a lie that way. I thought he might plant his feet, but he didn't. Instead he came forward, still light on his feet, and when he threw a punch at me it was like an uncoiling spring, driven from the shoulder. Had it connected, it would have hurt.

Not a lot. I am, after all, Spider-Man. Proportionate strength of a spider, yadda yadda yadda. Still, it would have rattled my teeth, maybe given me that shock up and down the spine that a powerful blow does.

What can I say? I cheated. I waited until he was off-balance, pistoning that massive fist toward my jaw, and then I twitched my head, ever so slightly. His fist flew over my shoulder. I caught the front of his baggy T-shirt with both hands and threw myself backward, curling my spine, bending my knees. I launched him off my legs. He slammed into a steel newspaper box about nine feet behind me.

The whole thing took maybe two minutes, tops. Not my fastest apprehension ever, but not bad. By the time the *bodega* owner caught up to us I had all four thieves upright, disarmed, and webbed around a lamppost, back to back to back to back.

The owner was in his fifties, I guessed, with salt-and-pepper hair and bloody smears across his forehead and the back of his left arm. Blood stained his sweat-soaked white shirt. He still held on to that shotgun, its twin barrels pointing toward the sidewalk. I held out the money sack, watching his hands. "Careful with that thing," I said.

"Oh, I never keep it loaded," he said quietly. "That would be stupid, no? So many people on the streets."

"Stupid, yes," I said. "Here, I think those guys took this from you."

He released the shotgun with his left hand to reach for the money. "Thank you, Spider-Man," he said. His accent was Latin American, but I couldn't tell from where. "Thank you so much, my friend."

"It's what I do."

"I must return to my shop," he said. "I am alone there."

"Of course," I said. "Go on back. These guys won't bother you anymore. If you could call the police when you get there, let 'em know where to pick up the package, that'd be just peachy. And get that forehead looked at as soon as you can."

"May I offer you a reward, Spider-Man? Anything you like, only name it."

A million bucks in small, untraceable bills? "Thanks, I'm cool," I said. He didn't look good for it. Besides, I needed to get back to that roof and snag the stray gun before someone happened upon it. Hardest part of the hero gig sometimes—disposing of random firearms safely without waiting around for law enforcement. I left him standing in the street singing my praises and webslung my way topside. The revolver was still there, much to my relief. I had already made a webbing backpack to carry the first gun, so I added this one to it. I'd have to haul them around until I ran across a cop, or else take the time to deliver them to a police station. Neither was ideal but both beat having someone point them at me again—or at anyone else.

Before heading home, I paused on the rooftop for a minute, wishing I had accepted at least a bottle of cool water as a reward. There are autumn nights in New York when you couldn't imagine why anyone would live anywhere else, when the evening takes on that perfect fall bite, crisp as a fresh apple, after a day that has featured clear blue skies overhead and the sun shining through gold and orange leaves like a promise that tomorrow, all will be right with the world.

This wasn't one of those nights. This was what Aunt May always called Indian summer, although that was probably no longer politically correct, and Native American summer had never really caught on. Anyway, nobody would want to claim such a sweltering, sticky day. Tempers flared and traffic jams seemed worse than ever, heat shimmering off the streets and the hoods of cars. Even the city's noise seemed louder on days like this one—and on the nights, when the miles and miles of blacktop and concrete, steel and glass released the heat they had spent all day soaking up, and a poor wallcrawler in a skintight head-to-toe costume could work up a sweat just thinking about a fight. Or even a friendlier tussle, like the kind I hoped to share a little later with Mary Jane Watson, my one-and-only ever-lovin' green-eyed wife.

MJ.

MJ had warned me not to dare come home without picking up coffee beans. The way she had phrased it, in fact, was "Doc Ock at his worst isn't half as scary as I'll be in the morning if I don't get some caffeine in me before I leave the apartment." She was working late into the night, rehearsing a play so far off Broadway that it was in Brooklyn, but in the morning she had a doctor's appointment so sleep would be fleeting and caffeine, apparently, required.

Back to the *bodega*, then. He had whole beans, three different varieties, near the back wall behind a donut rack with Plexiglas doors and greasy paper sheets lining empty shelves. His head wasn't bleeding anymore, but it would be several attractive shades of purple, blue, and yellow by morning. He smiled when I brought the bag of French roast beans to the counter. "For you, my friend," he said as he punched buttons on his cash register, "twenty-five percent off!"

"A bargain at half the price," I said. "I'll take it."

"Five eighty-seven. Call it six dollars."

So much for that million. "Six it is." I reached for my money.

And then remembered that I had no money. Not a thin dime on me. Nada. Zilch. A young couple stood behind me at the counter with a carton of milk and a box of cereal, waiting their turn. "I . . . ahh . . . I forgot to hit the ATM. I'm afraid I'm a little financially embarrassed at the moment."

"Oh, it is no problem, Spider-Man. No problem at all. For you? Take the coffee. Take."

"Well, thank you," I said. "That wasn't what I—"

"You can bring the six bucks tomorrow. Tomorrow night latest, right? I trust the famous Spider-Man. Anyway, you don't show up, I call the *Daily Bugle,* right? Spider-Man is thief?"

"No thief," I assured him. "You'll get the six bucks, don't worry."

On my way out I bumped into the woman behind me and almost made her drop the milk.

My costume is red and blue, with webbing threading all around it and white panels over the eyes. Bright, primary colors. Easily identifiable—basic blue, basic red.

At the moment, had anyone been able to look beneath the mask, they would have found my face even redder.

2

BETWEEN THE TOWERING peaks of the Andes range and the roiling waters of the Pacific lies a stretch of raw, arid land, some of the driest desert on Earth but irrigated here and there by raging rivers cutting from the mountains to the sea. Professor Marc Clevenger of Empire State University had been camped on those flatlands for the last three months, not far from the ancient, much photographed Nazca line drawings, leading an archaeological dig into a site that predated the Nazca and Moche civilizations that had once inhabited the area.

Clevenger had anticipated most of the problems that had arisen. He knew it would be dry, and all the water the little expedition consumed would have to be trucked in. The food had to be brought in on the same trucks. And the local labor pool was limited. On the positive side, he knew the winds would be mostly calm, the weather favorable, if warm. That lack of wind and rain had helped to preserve the ancient Nazca images for centuries. Those were fascinating—huge pictures etched into the earth, far too large to have been seen and understood by anyone on the ground. And the mountains were too far away for anyone to have seen them from there. The standard explanation was that the drawings were meant for the gods, to look down on from the heavens.

But those had been studied by Reiche and Hawkins, Woodman, Edgar and Aveni, among others. Clevenger's goal was different—reaching further back through history, into those who came before the Nazca, upon whose ruins the Nazca had built. They were called the Pechamenga, and their civilization had ruled the desert lands for five hundred years, centuries before the birth of Christ. They had built with mud and earth, so most of their structures were long since wiped out by occasional rains off the ocean, but they had dug deep into the hardpan for some of their most sacred buildings, and those remained. Clevenger's team had found six of them so far. On the surface they showed only as slight depressions in the desert earth, mounded on the west side where they had built higher walls to shield against the afternoon rays of the sun. The pit buildings had served as temples, noble residences, and centers of learning, judging by the artifacts found inside.

Clevenger was on the surface, sitting at a camp desk typing notes into a laptop in the shelter of an open-sided canvas tent, when Caroline Beck emerged from the pit with an anxious look on her face. "Professor C.!" she called, even though she could see him sitting there.

To be fair, when someone came out into the pale, bright sunlight from the depths of the pit structures, it took a minute or two for their eyes to adjust. And to be even fairer, Caroline was a perfectly adequate grad student but far from inspired. Her eyes were small, her nose pinched, her mouth always hanging open just a little. To be entirely unfair, Clevenger never quite believed that she could hold a thought in her head more complex than which celebrities were in rehab or one another's beds. She had proven many times that his snap opinion was untrue, or else he never would have allowed her on this dig. But he still couldn't bring himself to actually like her.

"I'm right here, dear. What is it?" *Dear,* he thought. *How demeaning. I'm a hell of an archaeologist, but I'm not a terribly nice man, am I?*

"Benny thought you should come and see!" She was breathless, and red circles rose on her cheeks.

"Come and see what?"

"Benny found a cache," she said. She sounded impatient, but that was just her usual tone, he had learned. "A little stash of magical artifacts, like. A human femur wrapped in sharkskin, a crown with five snake heads, and some other stuff. And a book!"

"A book?" The Pechamenga were a preliterate people—they had some writing, but mostly picture writing scratched on walls or the occasional animal skin. Nothing like books, though. "That can't be possible. You're mistaken."

"I saw it, Professor C. We all saw it."

"All" would include the other professional archaeologist on the expedition, Benjamin T. Silliphant, who in addition to being a dozen years younger than Clevenger was taking Caroline into his tent every night when he thought the others were asleep. As if anyone could stay asleep when she began her animalistic wailing. Three more grad students, Brad, Jessica, and DeWallis, made up the rest of the scholars, but the group also included some local men as guides and diggers—twelve to twenty of them, depending on what else they had going on at any given time.

"Who's we?"

"Benny, DeWallis, Brad, Jess, and me."

"A book."

"Definitely a book. Bound in leather, it looked like."

"Very well, Caroline, show me." Clevenger didn't want to believe it, because the easiest explanation for any mystery was usually the correct one, and the easiest explanation for the presence of a book inside an ancient Pechamenga pit structure was that someone else had found the building first and violated it. They had hid a book there, either on purpose or by accident; it didn't matter much which one, because either way it meant the integrity of the site had been compromised.

He heaved off the folding stool with a sigh, wishing he were still in his thirties, or even his forties. "All right," he said. Caroline was already starting down the ladder. Clevenger felt the sun on his bare head the moment he left the shelter. He always felt a little prickly here, like there was sand caught in the fine hairs of his arms and legs, dirt caking his neck, and insects crawling all over him.

The coolness of the underground enveloped him as he descended the ladder. There in the dark he was more comfortable, as if the chill air was a soothing balm. He followed Caroline down, then across the first chambers they had opened up, ducking through low doorways. Ahead he heard the urgent chatter of student archaeologists who believed they've found something interesting.

"Marcus," Ben said when he entered the final room. His name was Marc, not Marcus, and Ben—*Benny,* according to Caroline—knew it. "Marcus, you'll want to see this."

"Caroline says it's rather incredible."

Ben eyed him steadily. He had dark skin, baked by the Peruvian sun, and hair as blond and shaggy as an old-fashioned golf pro. "I know what you're thinking, Marc. It makes no sense, I'll grant you. But this nook I found—this place was sealed, man. Sealed up tight. Nobody's been inside it for a thousand years."

"Let's have a look."

The students parted and let Clevenger through. Clevenger examined the cut Ben had made, through three inches of baked mud wall. "Why did you go in here?" he asked.

"I was tapping the walls. This sounded hollow, so I probed it, got a light inside. I saw bone so I went in."

Clevenger knew one of the students would have photographed the whole process, while another would have jotted down notes every step of the way. He bent over and peered inside, at the hollow space Ben had found. "And it was just like this?"

"More or less, Professor C.," DeWallis said. "I took some pics and then Benny took some of the artifacts out for a closer look, but he put 'em back just as they were."

"And then I saw the book, Marc. Way in the back, with that five-pointed crown resting on it. The crown's been there for so long there's an imprint of it in the leather cover."

"But you understand, Ben, a book with leather covers, in a Pechamenga site—"

Ben cut him off. "I get it, believe me. We can try to date it, I guess. I can't explain it, I just know it was in there, and it's been there for a good long while. And everything around it looks genuine. If someone had gone in, don't you think it would have been to rob the place, not to hide something?"

"Ordinarily, yes, of course. But that doesn't seem to be the case here."

"Well, maybe not, but I don't know how it would have come to be hidden behind this wall."

"May I see it?" Clevenger asked. He half-suspected it would turn out to be a first edition Dickens or Twain or something—collectible, but so far from *right* that it would negate all the work they had done here. All the work *he* had done, even before this dig—his years of research into the Pechamenga. He had intended to get a book deal out of this, probably his last big book, and that was supposed to fund his retirement from ESU.

Now this. He frowned, his fingernails biting into

his palms, watching Ben reach into the space and draw out the book. Once Ben brought it into the light, a ball of bitter bile swelled in Clevenger's gut.

It was undeniably a book. Leather covers, paper pages bound on the inside. Everything people think of when they think of a book. And precisely what the Pechamenga had never seen.

"Pretty wild, huh?" Ben asked. He was smiling. He still didn't grasp what it meant to the expedition.

Clevenger was reaching for the book when the front cover came into the light. It was black leather, rough and large-pored, probably not cow skin, but he couldn't identify the hide. The only design on the front was a sickly green letter "d," lowercase. It wasn't quite the way he had learned to form the letter in Miss Jenkins's penmanship lessons in grade school, but it was close. One more indication of the modernity of this particular book.

And yet . . . as he stared at the cover, at the big green "d," his blood froze. Goose bumps rose on his arms, and he found himself shivering uncontrollably. Instead of taking the book in his hands, he quickly drew them away, hoping the students hadn't noticed the way they were quaking. Too late.

"Profesor C.?" Jessica asked. "Are you okay?"

"Put it back, Benjamin."

"What?"

"That damned book. Put it back in the hole. Seal it up and pretend you never saw it."

"You're joking, right?"

"I wish I were."

"Just a damn minute, Marc. I know this is your show, your dig, and I'm just the hired help. But if you think I'm letting you take all the credit for—"

Clevenger wanted to get away from the thing as fast as he could, and arguing with Ben only slowed that down. "It—it isn't about credit! Now for God's sake, just do as I say for once!"

"Marc . . ." Ben implored him silently. Clevenger didn't want to discuss it. Being in the presence of the thing was bad enough, but he didn't want to talk about it. He squeezed back out between the students and hurried to the ladder.

By the time he reached the surface, he knew he would have to talk about it at least once more, and in some detail. There was someone who needed to be alerted—the someone, in fact, who had told Clevenger in the first place that the book was more than just rumors and stories meant to frighten the gullible.

An hour later, Ben emerged from underground, his hands and arms caked with dirt. Clevenger was sitting on the folding camp stool with a rifle across his knees and the satellite phone by his feet. "What the hell, Marc?" Ben asked. His gaze wandered around the empty camp. "A gun? And where's all the local talent?"

He meant the Peruvian workforce. "I paid them off and sent them home, Ben," Clevenger said. "We're done here."

"What do you mean, done? What's going on? What is that book? I think you owe me some explanations, Marc. And the students, too. We're all invested in this dig."

"Gather them up," Clevenger said. "If I'm going to discuss this, I don't want to do it more than once, and I want everyone to have the same information so there are no rumors or misunderstandings. Bring them here to me."

"I've got to say, man, you're scaring me a little."

"That makes two of us then. In a few minutes, I suspect we'll all be scared."

He waited there while Ben fetched the students. As the sun danced on the watery horizon's edge, they gathered around, sitting in the dirt or leaning against trunks or rickety tables. They were filthy and tired, with bags under their eyes and grit in their teeth. Like working archaeologists everywhere, Clevenger thought, they didn't just accept the dirt and the minor injuries, the lack of decent meals and enough sleep, they thrived on it. It made them feel like they were sacrificing for something bigger than themselves, which of course they were. They reminded him of himself in his younger days, by which he meant every day before this one.

"Before I get into the details," he began, "I'd like to say how proud I am of every one of you, and how honored I am that you agreed to join me on this particular dig. The Pechamenga were a remarkable people, and the world deserves to know more about them—but you are also remarkable people, truly remarkable. As I told Benjamin a few minutes ago, this project is finished, and I've put in a call via the satellite phone. We'll be picked up tomorrow."

As he expected, the response was immediate and loud. He let the chorus of complaint and disappointment run for a couple of minutes, then shushed them. "I'm sorry, but there's nothing that can be done. The presence of that book that Ben found means the site's been tampered with. It's not the inviolate site we thought, and anything we find here will be suspect. The site should still be investigated, and I'm sure it will be, but not by me. Not by *us,* I should say."

"Marc, I get what you're saying, but it's just one book. Everything else seems untouched, authentic."

"*Seems* being the operative word. At any rate, Ben, it's more than that. It's what the book is."

"You didn't even touch it. How do you know what it is?"

"I recognize it. You should too. If you don't, I suppose that's my fault, because it means I haven't adequately prepared you for archaeological fieldwork."

"What is it?" Brad asked.

Clevenger knew he risked looking like a crazy man, some kind of conspiracy buff, but he couldn't help glancing around before he answered to make sure no one else might be listening in. Satisfied, he leaned forward (the rifle cutting uncomfortably into his thighs and belly) and lowered his volume. "It's called the *Darkhold,*" he said. "At first I thought the book was relatively modern— relative to the Pechamenga, at any rate—but it's not. It's incredibly ancient, or at least its text is. There have been various editions, all made by hand."

"It didn't look that ancient," Ben said. "Old, sure. But it's intact, the leather's not cracked, the pages aren't brittle—"

"That's because it wasn't published by any process we know today," Clevenger explained. "It was published by the darkest of magics, and created by the darkest of beings. I know this will sound absurd to all of you, but the *Darkhold* is the creation of an elder god named Chthon. It was originally a parchment, but Morgan Le Fey bound it into book form during the sixth century. At some stage, no doubt, a computer programmer will upload it all onto a disk, or, God forbid, simply onto the Internet."

"Professor C.," DeWallis said. "You do realize what this sounds like. Morgan Le Fey?"

Clevenger couldn't suppress a laugh, which came out more high-pitched and hysterical than he had intended. "Like I've gone completely insane. I do understand that. And now you see me with a rifle on my lap, having sent the locals away. I don't blame you for being a bit worried about my mental state. I assure you, though—when we're done here you can use the sat-link to go online and research the *Darkhold,* and you'll find much of what I'm telling you here. There is, of course, a lot of ridiculous rumor and speculation surrounding it, as well, but I'm telling it to you straight, as far as I know it."

"Straight." Brad shook his head. "If you had a bottle tucked away, you could have shared."

"You're not required to believe me, Brad, just to listen to me for another few minutes. The *Darkhold* has another name. The *Book of Sins*. It's a collection of Chthon's mystical knowledge—which, given his nature, is almost pure evil. I honestly didn't think it really existed until I saw that copy in Ben's hands, but that disturbingly modern "d" on it—which no doubt didn't exist on Morgan Le Fey's copy, but somehow magically inscribed itself there to identify it to our generation—convinced me. I no longer think some person broke into the pit structures and hid the book there. Maybe it hid itself. Maybe it was spirited there by someone in Tibet or Rome or Boston. If there's a way to tell, I don't know it. But I know I don't want to spend a minute longer than is absolutely necessary in proximity to it. So tomorrow we're leaving here, and I for one am never coming back. I advise you to make the same decision. Until we're picked up, I insist that you all remain on the surface. No one goes near that book again."

"Marc, no one's going to go down there and dig it up. I sealed the space back up, like you asked, with the book inside. But you need to put that gun away. Someone could get hurt."

"That is precisely what I'm afraid of."

"I mean by the gun. Since you sent our workforce away, there's probably not another human being within twenty miles of us. There's no need to hang onto that thing."

Clevenger lifted it from his lap, his finger resting lightly on the trigger. "You know what they say about cold, dead hands?"

Ben nodded, looking resigned. "Fine. When we get home, I'll be writing this up and reporting you to the university president and to Calvert. Just so you know."

Lucinda Calvert was the head of their department at ESU. "Be my guest. Most scholars in the field—the senior scholars, anyway, like myself, know of the book, and they would do the exact same thing that I've done." He lowered the gun again and waved dismissively at them. "Get some rest. We'll be leaving bright and early."

The students and Ben Silliphant gathered together around the fire pit, out of his hearing. He could make out anxious whispers, but not words. He didn't have to hear them anyway—he knew full well what they were saying. But he also knew what he believed, what he feared. He hung onto the rifle because he wanted to be able to enforce his decree that no one return beneath the surface. He didn't want anyone else handling the book, or having the foolhardy idea of smuggling it back home.

But more than that, he hung onto the rifle because he feared that people might be the least of their worries, during the long night ahead.

"Professor C.!" Caroline called from their little conclave. Someone had started a fire in the pit. Its heat didn't reach Clevenger. "Can I ask who exactly you called to come and get us out of here?"

"I suppose there's no harm in telling you that," Clevenger said. "Since you'll see when they get here. I called an acquaintance of mine, someone I met years ago at an archaeological convention. And he knows all about the *Darkhold*. His name is Dash Garrett, and he's an agent of S.H.I.E.L.D."

3

S.H.I.E.L.D. WAS, DASH knew, the most technologically advanced intelligence agency the world had ever known. The NSA thought they'd made great leaps forward when they convinced telephone companies to let them listen in on phone calls, but S.H.I.E.L.D. had had the ability, years ago, to beam a signal down from its Helicarrier or one of its linked satellites and listen in on any conversation taking place anywhere in the world.

But there were times when a good old-fashioned American-made helicopter did the job just fine. Dash had two of them under his command, at the moment, chopping through the night sky en route to GPS coordinates that Marc Clevenger had given him the night before. One of the copters was nearly empty, except for a couple of agents from S.H.I.E.L.D.'s Peruvian base, who would load on the expedition's gear. The extracted archaeologists would ride in that copter. The other held a special team of agents trained and equipped to extract the *Darkhold*. That was the one Dash rode in. He couldn't deny a certain unease, although it was mixed with the adrenaline surging through his system, increasing as they got closer to the point in the Peruvian desert where the book waited.

No previously unknown copies of the *Darkhold* had surfaced in years. Certainly the discovery of one was no banner day for humanity—but the fact that it had been found by someone who recognized it for what it was, and reported it immediately, was a good thing. It could be taken to a secure holding facility and kept out of the hands of any who might use it for the wrong reasons. Which would be just about anybody, Dash knew. Part of the book's sinister charm was the way it went to work on those who touched it, or even came too close, drawing them in and making them part of its innate evil. He hoped Clevenger had been able to keep the rest of his party away from the book, and had particularly watched the man who had unearthed it during the night.

He'd tried calling Clevenger's satellite phone before starting out this morning, but there had been no answer. That didn't necessarily bode ill—the battery could have run down the night before, or it might have been switched off, since Clevenger wasn't expecting a call, or they might simply have been busy packing up for the trip home. He'd find out soon enough—they were only fifteen minutes out, and closing fast.

The dangers the book—also known as *Shiatra, The Book of the Damned*—posed were legion and couldn't be discounted. Using it—hell, even reading it, he believed—

could open the user or reader to possession by Chthon. The indestructible book—in every form, and every copy printed, no matter by who—was Chthon's entry point into Earth, and even though he had long since been banished to another dimension, his connection to the *Darkhold* remained, as if there were a string tied around his wrist that alerted him every time someone perused its pages. Odd that a book created so long ago, and as a series of parchments, could continue to have such an effect on an Earth that Chthon had not visited since a scientific genius called the High Evolutionary had rebanished him in the 1950s.

The pilot's voice crackled in his headset. "Can't see 'em, Dash," Resenden said, "but the lines are below us now."

Dash looked down anyway. The desert was pitch black, but he had seen them before: the incredible geoglyphs of Nazca. He remembered some of them distinctly: a monkey, a human, a dolphin, a hummingbird, a plant. Others were simply straight lines—dead straight, running for miles and miles. Ancient peoples had scraped away rocks and surface gravel, exposing lighter soil beneath to make the images, and thousands of years later, the drawings remained. It was a sight that couldn't fail to inspire wonder and awe.

It also meant they were getting close. Dash's stomach lurched as the helicopter began its descent, plummeting toward the desert floor like its engines had been cut. The pitch of the blades overhead changed slightly, and it made his teeth ache to listen.

He peered out the window again a couple minutes later. Floodlights beaming down from the copters illuminated a scattering of tents and other gear. "There they are," the pilot said.

"Yeah, but they should have packed all that stuff up already. It's not like they didn't know we were coming."

"You know scientists," the pilot said. "They probably got involved in something else and lost track of time."

"I hope so."

Close by, the second helicopter kept pace with theirs. The pilot glanced over and gave them a thumbs-up, which Dash returned. But he didn't feel as confident as he tried to look. Something wasn't right down there.

That suspicion was confirmed a moment later, when they were almost on the ground. A form he hadn't quite recognized from the air became more distinct: Lying next to one of the tents was a woman's body. She hadn't gone to sleep there. A pool of blood had soaked into the earth around her head, tinting it a deep brown. Carrion birds peered up at the approaching helicopters, then flapped away, agitated by the prop wash kicking dirt into the air.

Clevenger, what the hell are you mixed up in?

He keyed his mic and spoke to the crews and passengers on both choppers. "Heads up, people. We've got a situation here. I don't know what it is, but it ain't good. There's a DB over by that one tent, and don't be surprised if we find more. I want the extraction time on that book stat, as planned. The rest of you, follow my lead."

His helicopter landed first, by a few seconds, about forty yards from the second. Dash threw his door open and raced out, his Heckler & Koch MP12 personal defense weapon—available only to S.H.I.E.L.D. agents, by special arrangement with the manufacturer—locked and loaded, ready for whatever waited out there.

But what waited wasn't doing any attacking.

He found Clevenger last, at the bottom of a ladder, down in a pit. Before that he found people he didn't know: the woman by the tents, another one sprawled across a smoldering fire that had burned most of the flesh from her body, a man with two bullet holes in his head, another man whose skull had been bashed in with rocks (still strewn around him, stained with black dried blood), and yet another who had been cut open with cooking utensils.

Clevenger's throat had been torn open before he was tossed down the ladder. Dash couldn't tell what weapon had been used, but he wouldn't have been surprised to find that it had been the claws of a jaguar or some other beast. There were no animal tracks in the dirt, though, only human ones, and disturbed spots that looked like fights had taken place there.

The *Darkhold*, he thought. *It got a grip on these people, and turned them against one another. All in less than a single night.*

"Find that book, people!" he called to the extraction team. "I know I don't have to say this, but I will— remember that it's extremely, extremely dangerous. You've been trained and you know what you're doing. Just be careful, don't touch it, don't look at it any more than you have to, and get it bottled up in a hurry."

"Roger that," one of the team members said. There were eight of them, five men and three women. They had all been through S.H.I.E.L.D.'s occult and paranormal training program, as had Dash, although more than a decade earlier. The program's high point was always the guest lecture by Dr. Stephen Strange. Four of them carried a specially constructed box, lead-lined and enchanted. They all wore enough protective gear to carry them safely through a nuclear holocaust. Dash had to hope that it was enough, because if his people went off on one another, like the members of Clevenger's dig had, then the book would win this round.

That, he didn't want.

"This is bad, isn't it?" Resenden had walked up behind Dash while he watched the extraction team.

"It's bad." He didn't know how much the pilot knew about the dual goals—people and book—they had come for. People, Dash could already tell, were a lost cause. He just hoped the book was still where Clevenger had described.

"You knew some of them?"

"Not well. I met the guy who called me, once. Clevenger. He ran the expedition. Met him at a conference, and—you know how it is, we have to spread the net pretty wide, make sure there are people in all walks of life keeping an eye open for things that might matter to S.H.I.E.L.D., and he came across one of them. So here we are."

"Little too late."

"Quick as we could make it here. They're in a pretty

remote spot, and it takes a while to put together an operation, even such a simple one."

"I know," Resenden said. "I'm not blaming anyone. Just saying. I'd have flown faster if I could have."

Dash blamed himself. Not that they could have made it much faster—could have come in jets, he supposed, and landed on the hardpan, but that would have been risky. They had taken hours to get here, not minutes. Would things have turned out differently? No way to know, but he doubted it. Most likely they would have wound up becoming casualties themselves.

While they descended the ladder (Clevenger's corpse having been brought up and zipped into a rubber-lined body bag, as had the bodies found at ground level) the others broke camp and packed the group's gear into the chopper's cargo hold. Dash supervised the loading procedure and waited anxiously for the underground team to wrap up. It only took three quarters of an hour before they were airborne. Dash had called in his report, and the Helicarrier would be waiting for them off the coast. It would fly them, and their precious, obscene cargo to rural northeastern Pennsylvania, where a state-of-the-art vault waited to store this copy of the *Darkhold* safely away from humanity. Forever, Dash hoped.

And may another copy never, ever surface.

4

". . . ARE SOME OF the purely theoretical—one might even say hypothetical—realms of science. Noted science-fiction writer Arthur C. Clarke told us that any sufficiently advanced science is indistinguishable from magic. And before you laugh, in this kind of discussion, the ideas of a science-fiction writer can have just as much validity as those of a scientist, because we're all pretty much equally in the dark. Is time a straight line, a meandering river, a Möbius strip, or an inverted sphere, with us standing at some point on the inside, able to point straight out there, or there, or maybe there, at the distant future or the ancient past or maybe the beginning of this sentence? Can time and space be looked at separately or are they different sides of the same coin—or the same side? Is every point in the universe connected to every other point by invisible superstrings? What would happen if you could suddenly see those strings, and yank on them? Are there three dimensions, or four, or eleven or more?"

I was distracted, riffing on things I could have discussed in my sleep. I practically was. I had made it back to the apartment late the night before, but MJ had been later, and her mood had been strange, kind of off-kilter. She hadn't wanted to talk about it, which was a relief in one way, because I really wanted some sleep, but not in another way, so what sleep I did get was disturbed and unsatisfying. Then in the teacher's lounge before classes started, someone mentioned that Marc Clevenger from ESU had disappeared, along with another ESU teacher and a group of students. I had never taken any courses from Professor Clevenger during my time there, but everybody knew him; he was one of those teachers whose presence was felt all over the campus, and I had seen him several times. They had apparently been on a dig in South America, and now they were gone, and no one knew what had happened to them.

So I wasn't at my best. Fortunately, the kids at Midtown High didn't know any better. Not that I faulted them. Midtown was a disadvantaged inner-city school that had gone downhill since I'd attended it. The kids in my science class came to it without the background they should have had, the background I'd had in basic chemistry and physics, earth sciences, even geometry and calculus. Catching them up was one thing, getting them grounded in Loop Quantum Gravity theory or Einstein's Cosmological Constant was something else entirely. I wanted them to know that there was an entire universe of cool, interesting . . . stuff . . . out there, that they would never learn about.

Unless they wanted to. Unless they needed to. Unless they made it a burning priority to find out. Because that's where scientists came from. I had wanted to be a scientist, and had been sidetracked by a bite from an arthropod. If I could encourage someone else to become a scientist, that would fill the hole I had left.

Failing that, I could always try building one from scratch. Doctor Frankenstein was a scientist too, right?

"The point is," I blathered on, "a lot of these things are considered fringe theories at first, and the people who first come up with them are thought of as crackpots or nutballs." That drew a snicker; they were awake after all, or some of them were. "That is, until they start to make sense to some other scientists. Then they become 'proposed theories.' When they're accepted by the bulk of scientists—like, say, gravity or black hole dynamics or global warming, they become 'mainstream theories.' "

"I heard global warming was a crock of—"

I interrupted Paco. "I've heard that, too." I graced the class with my smile. "A crock of bright, cheerful sunshine, he was going to say. And yes, some scientists thought so. Turns out most of those who did were paid to think so by oil companies who have a, shall we say, vested interest in keeping things running as they are. Abandoning fossil fuels, which account for a huge proportion of the greenhouse gases in our atmosphere, would cost them money. Not that they don't have money, but they like money a lot, as do you folks.

Not me—if I liked money, I wouldn't be a high school teacher." *Or a superhero.*

"Yeah, right," ShaReese said.

"Look, the point here isn't to debate global warming, although if you all want to do that, we can tackle it later this week. The point is to tell you that there is science and there is *science,* and some of it is so strange and foreign to anything you've ever imagined, anything you would ever have reason to encounter in your life, that it might as well be magic. In some cases, that's the best way to explain it. If you say, 'How does my computer work, Mr. Parker?' I might just say 'By magic,' because it's easier than trying to understand and explain how flipping around a series of ones and zeroes makes you able to post pictures of yourself on your MySpace page."

"I ain't got MySpace," Kendall said. "How 'bout Facebook?"

"Different ones, different zeroes, same idea."

Keaton's hand shot up. "Mr. Parker, are you saying that magic is real, then?"

An excellent question, that one. I tried to be scrupulously honest with my students—as honest as someone who wears a mask and keeps one of his two identities secret from the world can ever be—but I didn't think it would be a good idea to tell them some of the things Spider-Man had seen Dr. Strange do, for instance.

So I did what I do when I'm fighting someone like the Lizard or the Shocker, someone who can really pound the stuffing out of me if I let them—I bobbed and weaved.

"I guess what I'm saying is that it shouldn't be written off. What looks like magic today may be declared science tomorrow. Or what's presented as science today may be derided as magic by the time it's seriously investigated. As with most things in life, keeping an open mind is the best way to go."

"What's more important," Shelagh asked, "an open mind or a skeptical one?"

Another good question. Just when I started to think the country was doomed to a future in which the most critical questions would be "PlayStation or Xbox?" and "You want fries with that?" my kids threw these at me. "I don't think the two are mutually exclusive, Shelagh. An open mind means being willing to consider *all* the possibilities—including the possibility that not everything is as it seems."

She nodded thoughtfully, as if she understood what I was saying and would take it under consideration.

Sometimes the best moment of my day comes when I'm not wearing a costume. Usually, they're when I'm with Mary Jane, and not wearing much at all. But not counting those moments, ones like this, when my students were engaged and exhibiting genuine intelligence . . . well, they were about as good as it gets.

The other best moment of the day came during that brief time between my getting home from Midtown and MJ leaving for rehearsal. We had gone to a little bistro down the street from our apartment, a place cleverly called Le Bistro. We decided not to hold the owners responsible for the lack of imagination that went into naming it the first time we passed it and smelled the aromas wafting from it—fresh bread, rosemary, garlic, seared meats, strong coffee. I don't know about MJ, but not walking right in the door had been a struggle. Tonight we had enough time and just enough money for an early dinner. We sat at a small round table, flanking a *bifstek avec pomme frites* for me and a pasta dish for her, with an Alfredo sauce so light that it practically floated off the plate.

There are times that it's hard to eat with MJ, because I don't want to look away from those riveting green eyes. There are other times when she has me laughing so hard I can't force food down. There are still other times when realizing that I'm sitting there with—pardon the cliché—the love of my life ties my guts up in knots the way it did when we first started going out, or when I first realized that she really did love me and I wasn't imagining it.

This wasn't one of those times. The food was delicious. The lady was incredibly, improbably, impossibly beautiful, but catching her eye or seeing her smile or listening to her laughter (the chiming of angels' bells the only reasonable comparison I could think of) just made me happy that I was sharing such a good meal with such fine company.

The meal's only drawback was that when it ended, I'd have to go home alone while she went to Brooklyn for rehearsal. When I could slow down the *bifstek* input sufficiently to speak, I said, "Tell me again why *Luminous Blue* has to rehearse at night."

She had told me before, of course, but she was a

woman of nearly infinite patience—when she wanted to be—as one would expect of any woman willing to put up with me. Hardly sighing out loud at all, she said, "Because Sinclair"—that was his first name, she insisted, Sinclair. Also his only name. *Artists*—"insists that our biorhythms will be different at night than during the day. Since we're going to perform at night, he wants the rehearsals to take place during the performance hours."

"And also," I pointed out, perhaps not as graciously as someone else might have, "Sinclair hates to get up in the morning."

"Sinclair does hate to get up in the morning. 'Tis a fact."

"So in order to satisfy his desire to sleep in, everyone on the cast and crew has to drag themselves out to his rehearsal space at night."

She plucked a forkful of pasta from her dish and placed it into her mouth with surprising daintiness. Surprising to me, anyway, to whom eating involved more shoveling than grace or finesse. When she had swallowed—and not before, her aunt Anna had trained her well—she said, "That's correct. But really, he kind of has a point. If we don't keep a nighttime schedule during rehearsals, we might be sleepy, less sharp, when it comes to performances."

"That Sinclair, always thinking." He had written the thing, too. He had never won a Tony, which he dismissed as meaningless trinkets for the artistically challenged, but his plays got good reviews in the indie press and, while low budget, tended to run for quite a while and make decent money. Not that the money was important to him, MJ claimed—or claimed that he claimed—but he had financial backers and it was important to them. All he was interested in was the integrity of his words. *Writers.*

MJ had accepted the role of Sally Hawkins, a woman so brutalized by life that murdering her three children seemed like her only good option, because it promised to be the most challenging acting job she had done. Playing the part depressed her, but she was able to compartmentalize when she had to, to push that depression aside and enjoy life. On her way to the rehearsal space she would change, as if the character was growing up inside her skin, and it would take her most of the trip home to shed Sally and become herself again. Sometimes she couldn't even do it then, and I'd find her sitting up by the window, staring at the city lights, or worse, asleep but curled into a fetal ball, shaking and softly whimpering. I hated what it did to her, but loved the way she saw it through because she wanted to grow and stretch her talent.

"You going out tonight?" she asked. Changing the subject. Usually she was subtler than that.

"Don't I always?"

"Pretty much. Any special plans?"

"That I can talk about in a crowded restaurant? Not really. Let's just say same old, same old."

"Swingin' and slingin'."

"That's about the size of it."

She took another bite. A stalling mechanism. Or maybe the pasta was as good as my steak, which had already vanished from my plate. "I still worry some-times," she said.

"Yeah?"

"I do. I know, it's dumb. But there it is. You can take care of yourself. You've proven that about a billion times, right? How many days in a year? How many years have you been doing this?"

"Three hundred sixty-five, and more than I want to think about."

"Plus leap years."

"Plus that."

"So maybe not a billion. Just a few million. Still, every time you go out, there's that moment. It doesn't last long, but it's a moment. My stomach clenches. I think, what if it's this time? What if this is the night he doesn't come back? Or he does, but on a stretcher? What if my sweetie had to spend the rest of his life in a wheelchair or a hospital bed?"

"Mmm, you'd have to give me sponge baths."

"I'm not joking, Peter."

I had known she wasn't, but had gone for the cheap laugh anyway. She should have been used to it by now, but that didn't make it right. "Sorry."

"I worry. I'll always worry. It's the nature of things, the nature of our lives. I don't panic anymore, so that's good, right?"

"That's good."

"So that's all. I just wanted to say that. To let you know. I don't expect it to change anything you do."

"It won't."

"Good."

"Good."

"As long as you always do come back, that's the main thing."

"I will." Few promises in life had ever been easier to make. "Always."

"Always?"

"And forever."

"Good."

"Good."

She took another bite, and somehow it was her last bite, like she had been Hoovering the pasta in while I wasn't looking. Not that I had taken my eyes off her. Not that I could. "Science, or magic?" I asked.

"What are you talking about?"

"Never mind."

We couldn't linger, so I paid and we went outside onto the still-warm street. Dusk was settling over the city, but there was still a lightness to the violet sky, and the few stars twinkling up there were overpowered by the many electric lights coming on down below, and there were people out walking dogs or carrying groceries home or sitting on stoops laughing and whistling, and I had Mary Jane's hand in mine all the way to the subway stairs, and then we kissed, oh how we kissed, for a long time and no time at all, and even after the time it took to duck into an empty alley and strip away Peter Parker and sail skyward as Spider-Man, it was like I was lighter than air, like I was flying.

Magic.

5

SANDEN STURTEVANT HAD been part of many organizations over the years. Cub Scouts, Math, Chess, and Astronomy clubs, the Republican Party, the Association of Accounting Professionals. Pushing the professionalism part beyond its limit had cost him the latter membership and sent him to prison. There he had briefly joined the Aryan Nation, a membership he considered strictly defensive.

It was also in prison that he met Caleb Brewster, who—after many long, involved conversations in the yard—had confessed that he belonged to another organization that Sanden might be interested in, one that might benefit from Sanden's deft hand with numbers. So after they got out, Sanden went to his first meeting of the Cabal of Scrier.

He joined that night and never looked back.

He was good at accounting, but it was boring. Crime, he quickly learned, brought wealth, and wealth brought power. All it took was a taste to know that he liked that. Liked it a lot.

Within a couple of years, thanks to his facility with figures, he had become part of the leadership council of the New York chapter. He had taken part in decisions that had cost people their lives—he had a knack, as it happened, for reducing human beings down to dollars and cents, and when you looked at it that way, everyone had a price after all. Once that part was done, most decisions were clean and dispassionate.

Tonight an emergency meeting of the leadership council had been called. Sanden abandoned what he was doing—a blonde with long legs and wanton ways, the kind of woman who would never have given him a second's attention when he was an accountant but who now was so easily had that he could walk away from this one without an instant's regret—and reported to the deconsecrated church in Hunter's Point that served as their headquarters. In the car on the way over to Queens (he rarely went anywhere without a driver, and the Town Car's tinted windows offered privacy) Sanden changed into the hooded brown robe and white ghost-face outfit they all wore at official Cabal functions.

The church was a Gothic monstrosity, with steeply pitched roofs, a tower with battlements that always looked ready to collapse in the next strong wind, decorative trim and corbels and arches. Age and weather had blackened its granite exterior. Boards had been nailed up over empty windows. The building was surrounded by trees that seemed never to have leaves, regardless of season; bare branches reached toward the sky like imploring skeletal hands.

They met in the chancel, where the choir would have sat when church services had been held here. Above their heads, the roof arched to a point, and fluorescent light fixtures had been hung there—out of place in a church, but functional and cheap. Sanden looked at his fellow Scriers, all attired like him. Seeing the others, sitting on folding chairs drawn in an uneven circle, was like looking into five slightly distorted mirrors. Sanden tipped back in his chair, his back resting against the chancel rail—informal, but he had come to feel at ease in this company.

"I've called you here, fellow Scriers, because something very important has come to my attention," Scrier Everett said.

"What is it?" Scrier Leavitt asked.

Scrier Everett leaned into the circle, as if afraid the blank walls themselves might be listening in. "I've learned that a previously unknown copy of the *Darkhold* has turned up. Is there anyone here who doesn't know what the *Darkhold* is?"

No one spoke up. Scrier Everett continued. "The few known copies are closely guarded, of course. And this new one has been secured by S.H.I.E.L.D."

"Then what good does this knowledge do us?" Scrier Grant asked.

"My contacts are, as you might have already guessed, fairly extensive and knowledgeable in this area," Scrier Everett said. "I know of one of the designers of the supposedly impregnable S.H.I.E.L.D. vault in which it is stored, and I'm willing to bet that he can help us get into it and get the *Darkhold* out."

"Why would a S.H.I.E.L.D. agent help us?"

"He's not a current agent. He has no love for S.H.I.E.L.D., which he sees as having ruined his life. What was left of it, anyway. Also, he's dead."

"Dead?" Sanden—Scrier Sturtevant—echoed. "Then what good does he do us?"

"I've been putting a lot of thought into this," Scrier Everett said. "This man's death is not the biggest issue we have to face—we have the technology, in the basement of the Delany building, to bring him back to life temporarily. Then, I believe we can maintain his life and make him able to retrieve the book for us at the same time."

"Stop talking around things," Scrier Carson said. He sounded impatient. "Get to the point."

"Fine," Scrier Everett said. "Here it is. The dead man is named Stanley Carter. He was a S.H.I.E.L.D. agent and researcher who agreed to be the subject of an experimental drug. It was supposed to dramatically increase his strength and stamina, but it failed. Instead, he went berserk. All the drugs were supposedly purged from his system and his sanity restored, but he left S.H.I.E.L.D., angry at what they had done to him. He applied his intelligence background to a new career, as a New York City detective. That lasted until he saw his partner shot in the line of duty, and he snapped again.

"Carter was a deeply religious man, and under the

influence of whatever of the drugs remained in his system, alcohol he had begun to consume to excess, his sorrow over his partner's death—and what I believe to be an underlying madness that was what reacted so strongly to the drug in the first place—he became a costumed killer known as Sin-Eater. He murdered in the name of eliminating corrupt people from the city. His first victim was New York police captain Jean DeWolff. Unfortunately for Carter, DeWolff was a friend of Spider-Man's. Detective Carter was assigned the Sin-Eater case, which meant, obviously, that the investigation was stymied, until Spider-Man caught him in the act. The superhero beat him senseless, permanently disabling Carter. He never fully recovered, and he finally ended a life of agony and madness by threatening police with a gun. They shot him to death."

"So this Carter would have no reason to protect S.H.I.E.L.D.'s interests," Scrier Grant said. "And every reason to hate Spider-Man."

"And," Scrier Everett added, "when he was at S.H.I.E.L.D., he was involved in designing the security system for the vault in which the *Darkhold* is now held."

"But how do we keep him alive?" Sanden asked. "If your technology can only resurrect him briefly?"

"I'm getting to that," Scrier Everett said. "You all know that our ancient brotherhood is devoted to attaining power through any means necessary, including willfully breaking the laws of men and nations in order to pursue our own ends. Much of our fortune has been invested in technology, in ever more sophisticated weaponry. But a considerable sum has also been spent on occult research. With the *Darkhold* at our disposal, I believe we could use it to return the great god Chthon to his rightful place on Earth—and in exchange, Chthon would grant us essentially *unlimited power*. We would achieve that which the original Scrier sought so long ago when he created life on Earth—absolute domination over this realm and all its inhabitants."

Scrier Everett's voice rose during his oration, until it was practically shaking the eaves. The whole thing sounded a little corny to Sanden—but he couldn't deny a stirring of excitement, a *frisson* that raised the hairs on the back of his neck, as he listened.

"To answer your question, Scrier Sturtevant—you know that it was Scrier Fox who helped a certain Professor Miles Warren perfect cloning technology he had originally developed at the High Evolutionary's laboratory. Warren became the villain known as the Jackal, but his clone became the living dead man known as Carrion. The Carrion virus has infected several people since the first one fell to Spider-Man. Each time another Carrion dies, the virus is free to infect someone else. And one of Carrion's abilities is teleportation. By resurrecting Stanley Carter and infecting him with the Carrion virus—to which I have access, thanks to Scrier Fox's knowledge of Miles Warren's laboratory procedures—I believe we can keep Carter alive indefinitely, and certainly long enough for him to teleport into the S.H.I.E.L.D. vault and bring out the *Darkhold*."

"I have to admit," Scrier Grant said. "It's convoluted, but there's a certain twisted genius to it."

"There is still one sticking point," Scrier Everett said. "But that's being addressed even as we speak here. The Carrion virus can't infect a new host if there's a current living host."

"And is there?" Scrier Carson asked.

"There is," Scrier Everett replied. He steepled his fingers as if in unconscious imitation of the building's roof. "Yet another S.H.I.E.L.D. scientist, named William Allen. When he was assigned to study the virus, he deliberately infected himself and became the third Carrion, after the Warren clone and Malcolm McBride. He's currently in S.H.I.E.L.D. protective custody, where scientists are trying to understand and control the virus once and for all. But my sources tell me that because he hasn't been a real threat for some time, security has grown lax—especially since he has to be moved back and forth from a stasis chamber to S.H.I.E.L.D. labs for study. I've already pulled some strings with our cohorts at Hydra, and they're about to launch an assault on that particular S.H.I.E.L.D. facility. The assault will fail, and Hydra will retreat—but not before accomplishing its real goal of killing Dr. William Allen. That death will pave the way for us to use the Carrion virus on the resurrected Stanley Carter, and Carter will get us the *Darkhold*."

"And the *Darkhold* gets us Chthon," Scrier Grant said.

"There are a lot of moving parts, I grant you," Scrier

Everett said. "But I think once they're all in motion, we'll be pleased with the results. Now, we just need to vote on whether or not to proceed." He hiked back the sleeve of his robe and looked at a very modern Philippe Patek wristwatch. "If we're not, I have twenty minutes to call Hydra and abort the raid."

"Let's get to it, then," Scrier Grant said. "I'm in favor."

Scrier Winston had been silent throughout the proceedings, but she spoke up now. "It doesn't sound as if we have anything to lose," she said. "If any single element fails, we're no worse off, and if it all works then the reward will be spectacular. I say yes."

"Let's do it," Scrier Carson said.

"I'm in," Scrier Leavitt said.

They all looked at Sanden. "We haven't talked about expenses," he said. The financial end of things always seemed to slip past the others, unworthy of their attention. Not Sanden, though. He knew if you spent a thousand dollars to steal two hundred, you were playing a fool's game.

"Not significant," Scrier Everett said. "A million to Hydra. A few hundred thousand to my S.H.I.E.L.D. sources and the same to procure the virus."

"Less than two million total?"

"That's right."

"Then I'm in favor," Sanden said.

"It's unanimous," Scrier Everett said. His chalky mask distorted as he smiled beneath it. "Hydra will carry out the raid. Meanwhile, we need to get started on bringing Stanley Carter back to life."

• • •

The Delany building was a four-story office building six blocks away from the church. It had been built in the late 1920s, and abandoned by the early '70s in favor of buildings that included such modern amenities as working elevators, furnaces, and cooling systems. It was one of a half-dozen buildings owned by the Cabal in the five boroughs, a number that included a midtown Manhattan thirty-story office tower. None of that building's tenants, from the news vendor in the lobby to the multinational entertainment conglomerate that occupied five floors in the building's mid-levels, knew they were paying rent to one of the world's most secretive criminal organizations. The Delany building was occupied only by the Cabal of Scrier, although various dummy corporations received mail (sent by other Scrier chapters) and occasional shipments of office supplies and furniture, just to keep up appearances for the neighbors. Every Scrier chapter had two or three people employed full-time generating phony mail to send to other chapters just for camouflage. When Sanden first learned about it, he had been horrified, but he soon came to see it as just another necessary business expense, like insuring the fleet of vehicles the chapter owned.

The Hydra raid had gone as planned, according to the reports Scrier Everett received. A quick in-and-out with only a few S.H.I.E.L.D. casualties, but the nearly complete destruction of the S.H.I.E.L.D. lab studying William Allen. Thanks to Scrier Everett's source inside S.H.I.E.L.D. they had known precisely when to hit the lab in order to make sure Allen was inside. The Hydra team never made it back to its base, but Hydra had plenty of soldiers to spare. Sanden thought they probably would have done the job for free if Scrier Everett had worked them right. Still, if the rest of Scrier Everett's plan came to pass, the million dollars would prove a bargain indeed.

The recovery of Stanley Carter's body was also a simple matter. He had been buried in a cemetery in the Bronx. A crew of Scriers dug him up, broke open his casket, and found his body to be remarkably well preserved, probably due to the S.H.I.E.L.D. drugs that had clearly not been entirely flushed from his body after all.

The resurrection proved to be the hard part. It required a combination of the technology Scrier Everett had mentioned and ritual magic. Sanden thought it odd to see an alabaster-pale corpse with cyanotic blue undertones lying on a steel table in a concrete-floored basement of the Delany building, tubes feeding into his arms from IV sacks, electrodes attached to his head and heart, and the whole thing standing in the center of a pentagram with thick, sputtering candles at each point. Ten Scriers took up places inside circles flanking each candle, and they followed along with Scrier Everett's ritual chanting in a language that predated Latin. Meanwhile, from a nearby control room, other Scriers jolted the corpse with electricity and life-giving fluids at precise intervals, timed to coincide with Scrier Everett's ritual.

The first three attempts failed. Each time, Scrier

Everett began chanting again, his voice louder, with an angrier edge to it. The acolytes followed along, trying to match his tone. Sanden was one of them, off Carter's right leg, facing Scrier Canete, and when he heard his fellow Scriers mimicking Scrier Everett's growing fury and frustration, he thought it was silly but he followed along so as not to stand out. He repeated the chants syllable for syllable, utterly unaware of what they meant. As he chanted the fourth time, he started to think about the tequila he would allow himself once he got home from this wasted night.

He was so immersed in imagining that first swallow, the way the liquor would burn going down and its fire would spread, that it took several seconds for him to realize that Carter's foot was twitching.

When he did, Sanden's focus snapped back to the moment. He kept chanting because Scrier Everett and the others were, but he watched the formerly lifeless body on the table. Carter's fingers flexed, clenched, released again. His chest swelled, then collapsed. His lips quivered, parted, and he made a clicking noise.

Finally, his eyelids fluttered open.

The chanting stopped.

The machines surrounding Carter hummed and beeped softly. Robes rustled. Otherwise, the room was silent.

Sanden was gripped by a sudden urge to shout, *It's aliiiive!* He restrained himself.

But as Stanley Carter propped his elbows on the table and bent at the waist, groaning and rising to a sitting position, Scrier Everett left his spot within a circle and walked to the resurrected man's side.

"Welcome, brother Carter," he said. "Welcome back, I should say. We're delighted to see you."

He held out a hand, and a Scrier rushed in from the other room with the vial of the Carrion virus that Scrier Everett had procured. Carter was still wobbly, blinking and confused, when Scrier Everett dashed the virus—in the form of a red, powdery substance—into the recently dead man's face.

Carter inhaled deeply, suddenly, and then was wracked by a coughing fit. Plumes of red dust billowed from his mouth and nose. He teetered on the table's edge. Sanden thought he would fall off and die all over again. Instead he . . . he flickered, there one instant, then gone, then back. The red dust filled the air, drifting like smoke, and it grew thicker. When it dissipated, Stanley Carter still sat there, but he had changed, was changing right in front of them. He had been nude, a partially decomposed corpse. Now he didn't look much healthier, but he looked more whole. His skin went yellow, jaundiced. He was still gaunt, but with a stringy muscularity that the corpse-Carter had lacked. His facial features altered—Carter, in life, had been a reasonably handsome man, but now his nose and jaw elongated, his teeth shifting in his mouth, becoming uneven and yellowed, his eyes seemed to grow and sink into his skull at the same time.

Possibly the strangest thing, Sanden thought, was that he became partially clothed.

His clothes were rags, and they seemed to have been formed from molecules of air, because Sanden couldn't see any other source for them. On his bald head he wore a cowl and a short fragment of a cape, torn and ragged. A strap cut across his chest, holding a pouch at his hip. Shredded pants, not much more than a breech-cloth, covered his hips, and soft leather boots appeared on his feet. Strips of the same gauzy brown fabric were wrapped around his wrists, like bracelets.

Sanden realized, rather belatedly, that a stench had filled the room. It was sulfuric but unfamiliar, and he was surprised that he knew at once what it must be. For the first time in his life, he smelled actual brimstone. Recognizing it gave his heart a kick start, and he felt like the floor was tipping under his feet. What had they done?

And was it too late to run for his life?

When Carter rose off the table—levitating, not standing, Sanden realized with a start—he looked like someone who had just stepped from the grave.

Which, in a way, he had.

But he didn't look like Stanley Carter. That man—that corpse—was gone.

In its place was someone else. Some*thing* else.

Something that could only be called *Carrion*.

6

ONE OF THE greatest things about being Spider-Man is getting up a good head of steam and swinging along above the avenues, web to web, building to building. It only really works in Manhattan, where the concentration of really tall buildings is thick enough that I can be sure there'll be another one there when I need it. Still, although it feels incredible, exhilarating, the rush of air whisking past me, catching snatches of traffic noise and bits of conversation from open windows as I whoosh by, it's not quite as graceful as I like to think I make it look. It's really a matter of controlled disaster, since if I don't get the next web to the next spot at just the right moment, each swing has the potential of slamming me headlong into a wall of concrete, steel, and glass. Spidey-strength or no, even a spider can be smashed.

But there's no feeling like it on Earth, and I'm glad to be one of the only people around who get to do it. If everyone could, after all, the sky over Manhattan would be just as crowded as the streets are now.

Not that it was all fun and games that night. I swooped and swung, tumbled and tossed, keeping my spider-senses tuned for trouble, up, down, or anywhere else. After a few blocks, I heard some. A startled shriek, followed by a longer, throatier scream. Running footprints. A purse-snatching. Maybe not exactly front-page material—but then, I wasn't in the newspaper business anymore.

Anyway, the victim's voice reminded me of Aunt May's. I try to fight any kind of crime I can, because most crime means there's a victim somewhere, and if I'm not on the side of the victims, what am I doing in a mask and a crazy costume? But the two categories of victims that really make my blood boil are children and the elderly, and this sounded distinctly like a crime against the latter. I shot a strand of webbing at the building on my right, and let my swing arc me around the building. On the other side I sent a shorter length to another point on the same building, slowing me down, and landed on the structure's face, between two big windows.

From this angle I could see the sidewalk below, and the alley that ran between buildings. On the sidewalk, near the corner of Eighth Avenue, a gray-haired woman stood shouting and pointing toward the alley. And in the alley, the two creeps who had taken her purse laughed as they dumped its contents on the ground and scrounged for her wallet and credit cards.

This would be almost too easy.

An inordinate amount of my time is spent battling freaks with powers. Electro, Sandman, various versions of the Green Goblin, the Scorpion, and the good old many-limbed Doc Ock—these were some of the baddies who ate up my attention. I didn't mind. They could be dangerous, and their powers or technology made them hard for law enforcement to handle. And I had a certain grudging respect for them—they knew what they were, what they could do, and what they wanted. Their ideas were often grandiose, but that's because their abilities were outsized and they knew the world as it was couldn't contain them.

Punks like these, though—hale and healthy adult males who'd rip off an old woman's purse and laugh about it—well, they just plain ticked me off.

I dropped from my perch, a couple hundred feet above them, trailing webbing as I did to brake me before I hit bottom. When they heard the rush of my descent, the two losers looked up. One of them said something unrepeatable in polite company, while the other just threw the woman's empty purse at me.

I swatted it away, came to a stop over their heads, then performed a somersault and landed on my feet between them. The very picture of grace.

I *thwipped* webbing onto the purse and drew it to me. It was leather, but worn thin with use, like something she had bought a decade ago or more and used every day. "I believe you dropped this," I said. "And everything fell out of it. Time to pick it all up."

"Screw off, webhead," the profane one said. The

other started backing away, fast, hands up as if I might hit him.

Always that chance, I supposed.

"You seem to think I'm offering you a choice," I said. "Well, I guess I am. You can pick up the lady's things, give her back her purse, and apologize, or I can . . . well, I don't even like to say it out loud."

The guy with the potty-mouth started backing away, too. "We both run, how you gonna catch us both?" he asked.

I shook my head. "What, don't you guys read the newspapers? Nah, probably not. But I've been on TV, too. I'm kinda famous, even. A lot of people would want my autograph."

"Maybe another time," Potty-mouth said.

"I wasn't exactly offering it."

As if they had rehearsed it, both guys spun around and broke into sprints, heading in opposite ways toward the ends of the alley.

Really, they were making it too easy on me.

Just for variety, I crossed my right arm under my left and webbed them that way. One shot to each of their backs, and their feet flew out from under them. They hit the rough alley pavement simultaneously, their grunts of pain like happy music to my ears. I dragged them across the ground as they tried to scramble to their feet and break free of the webbing.

When they were back within easy reach, I hauled them up by their collars. "Okay, gentlemen," I said, "you want to try this again? The lady's things are still all over the ground, and who knows what people like you have tracked all over this alley."

"Okay, all right," the obscene one said. "We'll do it."

"That's what I like to see. Cooperation with the forces of order. You guys will earn those merit badges yet."

I released the men and supervised them as they went down on hands and knees, feeling in the alley's darkness for every coin, tube of lip balm, throat lozenge, tissue, and key they had scattered. Once those were gathered up and replaced, I made them empty their pockets and put all the cash they had—whether or not it had come from her purse—into her wallet, along with her credit cards. Then I wrapped my arms over their shoulders like we were old buddies and walked them toward the mouth of the alley.

The woman was coming toward us on the sidewalk. A small clutch of Good Samaritans had gathered around her, mostly women but a few men as well. Their faces were angry, their bodies rigid with tension. "Better speak up," I said quietly, "or I'll just let 'em have you."

The quiet one—or the smart one, depending on how one looked at it—held the purse at arm's length. "I'm sorry, lady," he said.

"Try *ma'am*. And make it sound sincere."

"I'm—we're sorry we took your purse, ma'am. We won't do it no more."

"Well . . . I'm sure you won't," the woman said. Close up, I could see that she was younger than Aunt May, but not by a lot. Stockier, too. She wore a knee-length dress, little socks rolled at the ankles, and sensible black flats. There was a Che Guevara T-shirt over the dress. A fashion or political statement, I was sure; the heat wave hadn't broken so it wasn't for warmth. "I'm sure you'll be in jail soon, where there won't be any purses to steal."

"Unless he's in cahoots with them!" one of the Samaritans said, pointing at me.

"Hold on," I said. "I'm the one who caught them."

"It could all be some kind of con. Lady, you better check and make sure your money's all there. And your ID—they could be doing, whaddya call it, identity theft."

"Ma'am," I said, "these clowns aren't smart enough to use their own identities, much less someone else's. But he's right, you should check and make sure everything's there."

Scowling, she took the purse and rummaged through it in the glow of a streetlamp, muttering to herself all the while. The Samaritans closed ranks around us. If I had to I could always go up, but they looked like they meant to make it hard for me to leave.

After a few minutes of counting and recounting, she smiled. "There's more money here than I had in the first place."

"Think of it as a thank-you gift," I said.

"Thank you for what?"

I still had my arms over their shoulders, so I shook the two men. Hard. Like a Doberman with a chew toy. "For teaching these two the error of their ways."

She closed her purse with a flourish. "I think you did most of that, Mr. Spider-Man." She pronounced it like a one-word proper name, *Speiderman*.

"Are you okay now, ma'am?" I asked. "Beyond the obvious fright you had, of course?"

She glared at the purse-snatchers like she wanted to kick them. Probably someplace it would hurt a lot.

"I suppose so," she said after considering for a moment. "What's going to happen to them?"

"I'll turn them over to the police, and they'll decide. Someone has called 911, right?" No one answered. "Anyone?"

Still no answer. "I have a phone," someone in the crowd said.

"Call, please," I said. I was aware that it was no longer strictly an emergency. But I didn't want to wait around all night with these two small-time felons, and I was afraid if I left them in the custody of the Good Samaritans, it might turn into an emergency for the bad guys. The crowd had relaxed somewhat, but there were still people there I worried might demonstrate the dark side of an angry mob if they had a chance.

I listened as the person with the cell phone called. "They'll be here as soon as they can," he reported. "Probably thirty minutes or so."

Great. A half hour wasted talking to the citizens, while who knew what might be going down elsewhere.

Unless . . .

The bad guys were cooperative now, probably understanding what could happen if I released them. The streetlight pole was eighteen feet tall. I hoisted one over each shoulder and hauled them up the pole, and webbed them to it. "You won't fall," I assured them. "If they try to cut you down, it'll take a while though. But the webbing will dissolve in an hour, and the cops'll be here by then."

More people had gathered on the sidewalk during all this, and some were leaning out of windows now. Spectators of New York's free street theater. They cheered when I left the two men dangling there. "Better call the cops back and tell them to bring a ladder," I suggested. The phone caller—surely not the only person in the whole group with a cell phone, but apparently the only one with free minutes—started dialing again. I left them there, the Good Samaritans standing in the light, with the thrashing, wriggling criminals suspended above their heads. Maybe not the most effective use of my time, but the name is Spider-Man, not Efficiency-Man.

Sanden was surprised to still be alive.

Stanley Carter had not reacted well to being resurrected. Or maybe it was the part where he was turned into Carrion. Sanden didn't know which, but something had seriously cheesed him off.

"Where am I?" Carrion had demanded. His voice was gravelly, as if he gargled with ground glass every morning, then washed it down with acid. He still floated several feet above the floor. "Who are you?"

"We are the Cabal of Scrier," Scrier Everett said. "We have brought you back from the dead, Stanley Carter."

Carrion's big eyes blinked. "I don't know any St-Stanley Carter. My name is Miles Warren. Or . . ."

"Yes, or Carrion. We know."

"Why am I here with you?"

"Because we resurrected you. We want to work with you."

"W-work with me? I wasn't dead. And I work alone."

"But you were dead," Scrier Everett insisted. "You don't remember, because, of course, you have no memory of that time."

Carrion lowered himself to the floor, his face twisting into a mask of fury. "Silence!" he shouted. "I need to think."

"Let me explain," Scrier Everett began. "We brought you back to go into a S.H.I.E.L.D. vault that you, as Stanley Carter, helped design. There you will procure for us a book called the *Darkhold*. With that, we will claim power beyond our imaginings or yours, and share it as equals."

"No! There is nothing equal about us!" Carrion then grabbed Scrier Sheehan, who was standing closest to him. He didn't squeeze hard, didn't seem to be crushing Sheehan's neck, but Scrier Sheehan flailed in his hand, kicking and gagging. A horrific odor filled the basement room, raw and primal, battling the brimstone smell. As Sanden watched, frozen in place, Scrier Sheehan's robes decayed, ashes to ashes, dust to dust, then her naked body did the same, flesh peeling away from muscle and bone. Her scream died in her throat as the muscles there atrophied and her tongue fell to the floor, thick and meaty until it bubbled and evaporated.

When he was done with her, Carrion threw her remains down. She looked like she had been dead for fifty years. Sanden's insides turned to ice water.

"Carrion!" Scrier Everett shouted. "There's no need for this—we're your allies!"

"I have no allies," Carrion growled. "L-least of all, you." He jumped toward the door, outflung hands brushing Scriers Canete and Milgrom as he passed them, but before he reached the door he vanished, blinking into nothingness. The two Scriers dropped, choking and mewling, their robes and flesh being eaten away in ghastly imitation of Scrier Sheehan.

Sanden had kept his position in the circle opposite Scrier Canete the whole time. Carrion's horrible hand had been just inches away from touching him. *That could have been me,* he thought, and his knees buckled, his hands trembling uncontrollably, tears springing to his eyes. He collapsed to the floor, barely managing not to touch Scrier Milgrom. *That could have been me.*

7

HE SAT ON a bench in Central Park, just down from Strawberry Fields, looking out toward the lake. The water reflected shimmering lights, and when it was still enough, the stars dotting the night sky. He knew he shouldn't be in the park at night—the police had told him that after he had been mugged a few years back, his wallet stolen, all his money and identification gone. ID theft is getting big, they told him, but hardly anyone on the planet paid attention to his identity now, so why would anybody want to pretend to be him? He was nobody. Not always—once he had been somebody, indeed—but even then, the identity that people talked about (usually in hushed voices, tinged with fear) hadn't been his real one.

No, in the 1980s New Yorkers had been afraid of the Surgeon. And well they might have been. Twenty murders had been attributed to him (although he had only committed eighteen of those, the other two had been well-enough executed that he didn't mind taking credit for them), over a seven-year period. A close call and a broken collarbone had put an end to that spree, and he had gone into retirement after that. Even the best of them—Lucas, Gacy, Bundy, and the like—were caught eventually if they didn't stop on their own. Since the mugging, he carried a scalpel again, so if anyone did try to accost him in the park at night, that person would regret it. Briefly, at least.

The newspapers had been full of the Surgeon in those days, and he enjoyed reading the articles, precisely because they were about him and yet not—him one identity removed, as it were. The police had never come close to finding him. He had never clipped the articles from the papers or videotaped the news reports about his crimes (although he had been sorely tempted by Court TV's reenactment special five years ago), because that seemed like a recipe for disaster if anyone got into his house for some reason and saw such a collection. For a guy with no costume and no press flack, he had generated a lot of headlines.

On this warm night, there were still people out and about. From the bench he could see a young couple sharing a bottle of wine on a spread-out blanket, four teenagers in baggy pants and untied shoes shambling along a path, probably looking for trouble, and six people walking or jogging around the lake. One of them, a slender brunette, especially caught his interest. Back in his prime, she would have been a definite candidate for the Surgeon's blade.

She couldn't have been more than twenty-five. His upper limit was thirty, although he preferred them between twenty and twenty-six or -seven. Old enough to have lived a little, to have seen some of the world, to have sinned and been sinned against. That was important—he didn't like to snuff a life that was utterly innocent, nor did he like to handle those who were too degraded. This one, though, was healthy and strong, with firm runner's thighs and a flat bottom, a chest that didn't swell out her tight athletic top too much, and all that lustrous brown hair tied back in a loose ponytail.

He would have begun by following her home. It was important to learn as much about a patient as possible before beginning treatment. At her place he would have found some clue to her identity—a name on a mailbox, an envelope pulled from the trash, something. That would be an important step, a kind of commitment to her treatment. From there it would be a matter of studying her life, learning her schedule, where she worked, what she did on her time off, who her friends were. The Surgeon had always been careful, thorough, not acting on impulse even when the impulses grew so pressing, so insistent that they could barely be ignored. The more he knew about a patient, the less chance he would be unpleasantly surprised when operating time finally came around.

All that time, the anticipation would build, the burning need for action and release would swell within him. Although it had been years, he still remembered the almost electrical sensation he felt running through him as the time approached, the tingle as if he were gripping a live wire. At those times the world seemed to swim into sharper focus, colors, tastes, and smells became more distinct; sounds seemed to pierce more deeply into his ears. He felt more alive in the two or three days before an operation began than at any other time in his life. During the operation itself, he was almost too alive and aware—the scalpel's cold steel burned his palm, any noise the patient made while she was still conscious ripped at his eardrums like hurricane winds through tissue paper, the metallic smell of blood and the sour meat stink of wounded flesh assailed his nostrils. At those times he was so alive he was practically godlike, and that's what kept him going back to the well again and again—that fleeting taste of the divine.

But that was all at the climax. Before that would come the weeks of buildup, of preparation. The learning, the studying, getting to know her as well as she knew herself. Finally, on whichever night seemed most safe, he would enter her home (having already learned the best route in, the traffic patterns, which neighbors might be up and about, and so on) while she slept, then drug, bind, and gag her. He would take her outside to his waiting van, which would look like a carpet cleaner's van, or a plumber's, or a carpenter's—different ones on different occasions so there would be no regular pattern. He would put her in the back, lashing her tightly so she wouldn't roll around and hurt herself, and then drive to his home on a quiet wooded road outside Tappan, New Jersey.

There, in the operating room he had set up, he would let the drugs wear off. She would awaken with a headache and cotton-mouth, but he would give her all the water she needed. She could scream and fight to her heart's content, but her bonds would not be broken, and no neighbors could hear through the soundproofing he had installed (not that there were neighbors within a half mile in any direction).

Finally, she would exhaust herself. The Surgeon kept waiting for a patient who didn't, but he never met one. She would tire herself out because she was sick, all women were sick; they carried the seeds of illness inside themselves and needed to have it cut out before they could be well. She would be soaked in sweat, her once-rich brown hair limp and lifeless, her nose and eyes red and swollen from crying. She had come in a beautiful young woman, and now the sickness inside her would have manifested itself—the first step toward being cured.

Using a tackle and pulley system he had devised, he would lift her (sometimes they struggled at this point, but to no avail) to a crossbar he had installed in the OR, and he would bind her hands to the bar, arms outstretched like a human crucifix, and strap her legs to the center post. Except it wasn't the patient who would be achieving divinity, it was the Surgeon, the only being on Earth who could drive her sickness from her and leave her cured forever.

Usually she would start screaming again, weeping, her nose running. This was the worst moment because her sickness was so visible now, so apparent that it couldn't be denied a minute longer.

And then the Surgeon would take out his scalpels and go to work. He cut through the clothing first. She would writhe and squirm, trying to avoid the blade, but there was nowhere she could go. He would talk to her at this stage, telling her he would cure her, that after the operation the sickness buried deep inside her body would be gone. His assurances rarely seemed to help.

When she was naked, he switched scalpels and kept cutting. Through the epidermis, through the dermis, through the muscle. By the time he brought out the bone saw, most of them were unconscious, and a few were already dead.

Illness lived in the organs. Heart, lungs, stomach, liver, kidneys—these were what made the women sick. He carefully removed those organs and dropped them into plastic garbage bags, since garbage was what they were. When that was done, the women were healed, cured, free of aches and pains and moral dilemmas, free of hard choices and vexing problems, free to join those who had gone before into the grace of eternal life.

And he, the Surgeon, the healer, would have taken one step closer to permanent divinity.

Stopping had been hard, but only a crazy person would have continued, knowing that society would never understand the service he provided his patients, knowing he could be locked away forever, or executed. Every day now he saw women suffering from the illness their own organs inflicted upon them, and he could do nothing to help.

When the operation was complete—and they were always successful, he had a one hundred percent cure rate—he cleaned up, eliminating any trace of himself from the patient's now-healthy, pristine form, and then took her back into the city. He would leave her somewhere not far from her own neighborhood, so that someone might recognize her. He didn't want her loved ones worrying about her, after all, especially now that she had no worries of her own.

As he watched the brunette jog around the lake and out of sight, a twinge of sadness stabbed at him, like a cramp in his heart. She needed help that he couldn't offer.

Finally, he looked away. It hurt too much to watch without acting. And acting was beyond his capabilities.

Anyway, it was time to go home—by the time he got across the river and back to the little house outside Tappan, it would be late, and he tired early these days.

After wrapping up the purse-snatchers, I foiled a liquor store holdup, caught a guy trying to muscle a diamond wholesaler, and slugged it out with a gang of six goons hauling stolen electronics out to a waiting truck. Not a bad night, but nothing that had made me break a sweat.

That was B.C.

Before Carrion.

I was airborne—that's the closest word I can find, other than webborne (which is not, according to Mr. Webster, a word at all) to describe that exhilarating feeling somewhere between free fall and flying—when he showed up. He actually slammed into me in mid-air, which is an unusual feat in itself, more so in this instance because my spider-senses didn't give me any warning at all. He wasn't there and then he *was* there, in a flash of light, and the collision was instantaneous. I caught a familiar whiff of sulfur and death.

Knocked off my trajectory, I plummeted like—well, just about anyone would if they were falling from two hundred feet above the city pavement. By the time I'd dropped a couple dozen feet, I was able to regain my balance and shoot webbing out to the buildings on either side, stopping my fall. Hanging over the streets, I caught a glimpse of my assailant in the ambient light from below. He hovered, suspended as if on strings, up above me where he had first appeared.

I recognized him right away.

But I couldn't admit that I was really seeing what I saw. It made no sense.

Because Carrion was dead. Or in S.H.I.E.L.D. custody, depending.

Only there he was, grimacing down at me with that ugly mug he had, the one he kept inheriting no matter who the virus had settled on. Maybe that was why he was so foul-tempered—looking at that face in the mirror would put anyone in a bad mood.

I swung over to the nearest rooftop. If I was going to fight a levitating, teleporting supervillain able to decay any organic material, I wanted to at least start the ruckus with something solid under my feet.

"Okay, Carrion," I said as I landed. "Let's get this over with. I was having a perfectly decent night until you showed up."

"You know my name?" he asked as he floated to the rooftop. "How do you know me, Parker?"

Great. I had almost forgotten that part—Dr. Miles Warren had followed me, one evening when my mind was on some other problem (there had been lots of problems in those days) and had watched me change into Spider-Man. Not only did he know who I was, but whenever a new Carrion was born, he had Dr. Warren's memories up to a certain point—so he always thought I didn't know him. It would have been comical if he hadn't been so ghoulish.

And so dangerous.

"Let's just stipulate that I know you and you know me, so we can get on with this."

"You're in a hurry to die, Parker?"

"I'm in a hurry to get past this part."

"Which part is that?"

"The part where you blame me—falsely, I have to add—for Gwen Stacy's death."

He charged me, hands outstretched. "You aren't fit to utter her name!" he snarled.

I dodged the attack. Letting Carrion get a hand on

you was a bad idea under almost any circumstances. "Funny, the way I remember it, I'm the one she liked. You were the obsessive freak who stalked her."

He hurtled a couple of steps past me, then spun around before I could clock him from behind. Just for jollies, I covered his face in webbing, blinding him.

For all of about five seconds. As soon as my webbing came into contact with what passed for flesh, where Carrion was concerned, it started decomposing. My powers are so organically derived Al Gore could pin a medal on me, but that put me at a definite disadvantage with Carrion.

"You killed her," Carrion said, wiping the last shreds of webbing from his brow, "and you're going to pay for that." Everything about him spoke of deadly determination—the set of his feeble jaw, the coiled tension of his stance, his steady advance across the roof toward me.

"Sorry, I'm flat broke," I said, backing up into an air-conditioning unit. "We'll have to go dutch." Not that I was afraid of him, necessarily (not that I wasn't), but he had to be dealt with just right. If he got his hands on me I'd wind up looking like one of those spiders you find at the back of the cupboard you rarely look in or inside a mug you never use, the kind that have been dead since last winter, all curled up and dry. Only it would take all of ten seconds.

Since there was duct-work right behind me, I spun and wrenched some of it from the rooftop. With any luck, the hot spell would break and it could be repaired before winter's cold set in. I hated doing property damage, but when Carrion came around, people died, and preventing that had to be my priority.

Eight feet separated us. With his teleportation ability, he could close that in a millisecond if he wanted to. I rushed him, holding four feet of inorganic sheet-metal ducting ahead of me like a lance. He dodged it nimbly at the last second. It took all my balance and coordination not to sprint right past him and off the edge of the roof.

He moved in while I was correcting course and swept one leg under mine, at the same time swinging an arm like a club into my shoulders. The combination sent me sprawling. His power ate through the fabric of my costume and the flesh of my ankles and shoulders burned where he had touched me. I'd have to keep away from him, because costumes cost money I could ill afford to waste.

Worse than that, it had been a pretty sophisticated move for him. Miles Warren had been a clever scientist, but no skilled street fighter. I rolled and regained my feet, putting some distance between us at the same time.

He wasted no time closing the gap again. This time he came at me like a boxer, arms up guarding his face, jabbing swiftly with his left, testing me. I could have caught his arm, if he had been anyone else. Instead I protected myself, blocking his probing punches (burning each time he landed one). He feinted with a right hook toward my gut, and when I dropped my left to stop it, he threw a left that glanced off my jaw, but would have flattened anyone without my enhanced reflexes.

Carrion didn't slow down. He moved inside my reach, grabbed my throat in one hand and aimed a snap-kick at my left knee. With my throat on fire from his touch, I couldn't get my leg out of the way again and his foot slammed into me hard, buckling me. I powered his hand off me and hurtled into the air, doing a backflip and landing on my feet, ten feet away. I had to finish this fast, before he finished me. And I had to do it without touching him, or even getting close.

I decided to make more use of the climate-control equipment on the roof. Standing behind an A/C unit, I shot webbing to a chimney about eight feet to my right and the same distance in front of me, stretched it to its limit, and then stuck another strand the same length to the lip of the rooftop on my left. Adhering the two ends together gave me a kind of slingshot, which I wrapped around the air conditioner, giving it a powerful kick at the same time to loosen it from its moorings. When I released the webbing, the big metal unit went flying. Carrion had watched the whole thing, apparently unsure of what I was up to or curious to see if I could pull it off.

To his surprise, I did. The A/C unit rocketed into him. He staggered under the impact, falling back one step, two, then with his arms windmilling in the air, he cartwheeled over the roof's edge.

I raced to the edge and snagged the A/C unit before it crashed to the street below. Carrion could take care of himself.

Which he did. As I stood there hauling the air conditioner back to the roof (I could secure it with webbing—it ain't duct tape, but it'd do the job for a while) he blinked out of sight, still forty feet from the ground. I had hoped he would land hard and I could find a way to secure him until S.H.I.E.L.D. or the Avengers or someone took him off my hands.

But Carrion was gone, vanished, leaving nothing behind except the stink that followed him around like a starving puppy.

And me? I was pretty much wiped.

8

"**THE THING IS,**" I said, "he never fought like that before. He knew what he was doing, as if he had been combat-trained. Before, he was always Mr. Grabby, all 'I'll suck the life out of you with my touch,' or throwing his nasty red organic-material-eating dust all over things. But tonight, he used all these sophisticated moves—he put me down a couple of times, or close to it."

Mary Jane considered for a moment before she spoke. I liked that she did that instead of just responding reflexively. We were sitting at our kitchen table. Outside, the city was as peaceful as it ever gets, the four in the morning hush. The bakery workers would be getting started on the morning's wares, but they would be quiet until the racks started rolling toward the vans. The garbage collectors were getting up, maybe thinking about how they could bang cans and Dumpsters against the sides of their trucks in new and atonal ways. "Maybe he's been training."

"He's been dead."

"Which often interferes with physical activity."

"Usually."

The first thing I had done when I got home, even before MJ got back from rehearsal, was to call a connection at S.H.I.E.L.D. (Yes, I have some—J. Jonah Jameson may have spent most of his newspaper career trying to convince the world that I was a menace to civilization as we know it, but with only partial success.) Julia Darst informed me that Dr. William Allen had been killed in a Hydra raid a few days earlier. Which meant the Carrion I had battled wasn't him. He'd had S.H.I.E.L.D. training, but had been primarily a scientist and never the most powerful physical specimen, and when I fought him as Carrion, he hadn't seemed to remember any of that training.

There were too many layers, too many possibilities and not enough data. Sometimes it helped to talk things through with MJ. Truth was, it always helped to talk to MJ, if only because I could look at her and listen to her voice while I did.

"I'm sure I've told you the whole story before," I said. "About how Miles Warren had this major crush on Gwen when we were at ESU, how he figured out my secret identity, and how he experimented with cloning, trying to turn his assistant into me and another student into Gwen in some crazy revenge scheme."

"I remember. I was tired and wanted to sleep. Much like now, in fact."

"There's more to it, MJ. Lots more."

"And it can't wait till morning?"

"No. He knows who I am. He could show up at any time. I have to figure out what's going on and how to find him."

She sighed. Just a little one. It was adorable. "Okay."

"Warren was a brilliant scientist. Absolutely nuts, but brilliant."

"Sounds like someone I know and love."

"I suspect he's better than me at pure research." I hated to show false modesty, and real modesty was even worse, but the facts couldn't be denied. "At the High Evolutionary's lab—"

"Nice name."

"—yeah, he's that kind of guy. Anyway, he has a lab in the Wundagore Mountains—"

"You're making this up."

"—they're in the Balkans. In the country of Transia. I can show you in the atlas, but I thought you were tired."

"Very."

It had taken me ages to puzzle out all the pieces to this, and talking to her about it—maybe with fewer interruptions—would help me keep it straight in my head. "Okay, then. So at his lab, Warren helped the High Evolutionary create the New Men—"

"He had something against old men?"

"Different kind of New Men. These were mutated, semi-humanoid animals."

"Why not 'New Animals,' then?"

"You're never getting to bed at this rate, MJ."

She batted those lashes at me. "I bet I could think of something, Tiger."

"Only if you want my divided attention. Until I can figure this out—"

She slapped her palms down on the tabletop. Even with spider-senses, it is possible to be startled. "Mr. Parker, I am shocked. Shocked!"

"At . . . ?"

"Your *divided* attention? Have I aged that terribly?"

She was joking. I ignored it. "Remember what I said about Warren's brilliance? Now that I think about it, maybe not so much. He tried to take the next step, to turn the New Men fully human. Instead he turned them into living corpses."

"Ewgh."

"Yeah. Not pretty. There's no way to make this long story short, exactly, but he had a falling out with the High Evolutionary, came back to teach at ESU, became obsessed with Gwen and Spider-Man. When Gwen died, he tried to clone her. His assistant objected and Warren killed him, which was when he snapped completely. Inspired by a jackal-man he had created as one of the New Men, he developed an alter ego as the Jackal. I'm skipping over some of the intermediate steps, like the Scrier who helped him—"

"Scrier?"

"Don't ask. Warren combined some of his own cells with a genetic virus he had developed, trying to create a clone that would destroy the human race by poisoning everyone who wasn't a clone."

"Ambitious, wasn't he?"

"It didn't work, obviously. But it became Carrion. The clone was trapped in a special casket Warren had designed, and it died in there, apparently of old age, but somehow Warren's cells gave it a kind of undying life. A student went into Warren's lab and opened the container that held Carrion, so he was—well, born, I guess—as a genetic hybrid of Warren and the virus. Carrion came after me, believing I was responsible for Gwen's death. We fought. By sheer chance, Warren had also created a kind of spider-amoeba that I was able to use to negate Carrion's powers. The building we were fighting in had caught fire, and it collapsed on top of him. I thought Carrion was done for good."

"But he wasn't."

"No such luck. Turns out the virus is extremely contagious, but can only infect one host at a time. After Miles Warren's death, it picked on the next person to come into contact with it, Malcolm McBride."

"Who already didn't like you, because you beat him out for that research grant."

"That's right. He became the next Carrion. He had Warren's memories, up to the point that Warren modified his virus—so like Warren, he wanted to punish Spider-Man for Gwen's death. I beat him the first time by showing him Warren's grave, but ultimately he was only defeated because he turned his killing touch on himself. Another psycho villain named Shriek, who was trying to manipulate the McBride Carrion, was able then to draw the virus into herself. I did mention this was complicated, right?" I had started out trying to explain it to her in order to understand it for myself. But the deeper into it I got, the more I realized what a very strange occupation I'd chosen for myself.

"You mentioned."

"Good. Because now the Jackal comes back into the picture."

"But he was Warren, who is dead. Except—"

"That's right. Except it turns out that Warren, the one who was first infected with the Carrion virus, was a clone himself. The real Warren was still alive. As Jackal, he reappeared, stole the virus out of Shriek's body, and created a new, deadly version that he used to poison almost the entire city of Springville, Pennsylvania."

"I remember that. I was there for some of that clone craziness. Ben Reilly, and the clone Gwen who died— that's when Miles Warren really died, right? Trying to save her?"

"You got it. At least, I always thought so. I suppose that could have been another clone—hard to tell with this guy. But I think he was dead, because another man, a S.H.I.E.L.D. researcher named William Allen, was infected while studying Warren's corpse. I beat him, and S.H.I.E.L.D. took custody of him. That should have been the end of it. As long as he was alive—and no one like Shriek or Miles Warren had access to him—the virus should have remained inert."

"But it didn't."

"It didn't. Because he's back. And he's deadly, MJ. One of the worst I've faced, really."

She touched the back of my hand. "That's pretty extreme, Peter, considering your usual playmates."

"I know. But Carrion can teleport. He levitates because the air itself doesn't want to be near him—not that you could blame it—and he can use that repulsion to lift himself up or to hurl other objects."

"Ick," she said. "But levitating? That's pretty cool. Haven't you ever wished you could fly? Like Thor or Johnny Storm or someone?"

"Flying would be okay, I guess. Might be overrated though. Those guys probably wish they could web-sling."

Her smile could have—by someone with less innate generosity than me—accurately have been termed a smirk. I ignored it and kept going. "He can turn himself immaterial at will, allowing bullets or other weapons— my fists, for instance—to pass right through him. He can decay or control organic material. His red dust is pretty much death on toast, unless you get a light dose, in which case it only incapacitates you and causes incredible pain. He has limited telepathic abilities. Somehow, he doesn't trigger my spider-senses. And this is the part that bothers me the most—the reason I want you to get out of the apartment and stay away until this is over—he knows that Spider-Man is Peter Parker. And in the past, he has threatened to go after everyone I've ever loved."

She bit her lower lip, but her gaze never left my

face. "That's not who I am, Peter. I mean, not that I haven't ever run away from trouble. But not anymore. Where you are, that's where I am."

"Unless you're rehearsing in Brooklyn," I said. "Look, Mary Jane, you're killing yourself going back and forth anyway." Poor word choice, but it was already out before I caught myself. "Just get a motel room somewhere close to the theater. It'll blow the budget, but only until the show is a raging success. I'll try to come out and see you, even stay there when I can. But you'll be safe from Carrion, and if I know you're safe, then I can focus on finding him and finishing him once and for all."

"Like you've done three times before."

"I know. There's got to be a way, though. I tried to get the High Evolutionary to help once, and he refused. Reed Richards couldn't do it. But I'm sure if I get enough of the best scientific minds working on it, we can come up with something."

"Not to minimize this, Tiger, but shouldn't they be working on cancer or AIDS or global warming or something?"

She had me there. Carrion posed an enormous threat, as the Springville incident showed. But that was the worst he had done so far. Cancer killed more people in a day than all the Carrions combined had ever done. And S.H.I.E.L.D. had been working day and night on the problem, but according to Julia Darst, without much success.

"It's not for long," I said, dodging her point as astutely as Spider-Man dodged bullets. "Just until I shut him down. And like I said, it'll help you get more sleep and be more rested for your play."

"You think I'd sleep, worrying about you back here fighting Carrion?"

"You usually manage."

"You just told me he's more dangerous than the run-of-the-mill super-creep."

"Man, you're good."

"The best."

"Don't I know it? Please, MJ. Think about it. I can't run all over creation looking for Carrion if I have to be afraid he'll show up here while I'm away." I would have given her my puppy-dog eyes if I thought they'd help. But MJ had demonstrated, many times, her ability to resist my charms when it suited her. This time, logic would have to win her over. Then it would have to win Aunt May over, because I'd have to persuade her to move out of her house in Forest Hills for the duration, too. I couldn't take the chance that Carrion might know her, too.

Logic would have to be my ally. Of course, if logic had been my strong suit, I'd never have put on the costume in the first place.

We finally made it to bed around five. Fortunately, Aunt May didn't show up until eight, so we got almost three whole hours of sleep. When she rang the bell, I stumbled toward the door, groggy, rubbing my eyes. I can function on little sleep when I have to, but the fight with Carrion, and then the extended conversation about him, had taken a lot out of me. And I hadn't even figured out the things that bothered me most—who had been bopped with that ugly stick this time, and where'd he learn to fight?

Aunt May came through the door with a lively stride, wearing a flowered dress that fell below her knees, a white sweater, and a worried expression. She carried a paper bag of groceries. "You look terrible, Peter," she said by way of a greeting. "Are you getting enough sleep?"

"Not right at the moment, no. Hello, Aunt May. How's my favorite supermodel?"

"I think you're confusing me with Mary Jane."

"I bet lots of guys do that. What's in the bag?"

"Since I doubt that you've had breakfast, I thought I'd make some for you."

"Breakfast? Oh, we had—"

Before I could get the rest of the bluff out of my mouth, MJ emerged from the bedroom, looking every bit as bedraggled as I felt. "Hiya, May," she said, stifling a yawn. "Is it really daytime?"

"Honestly, the hours you young people keep, it's a wonder you function at all." She carried her bag past us into the kitchen and took out a dozen eggs, some whole wheat flour, sugar, and other ingredients. It was almost as if she had never been here and seen that we do manage to keep staples in the pantry.

Most of the time, anyway.

"If you want to know the truth," she said.

"Always."

"All right, then. I'm not doing well at all this morning, Peter."

"What's the matter?" Aunt May had raised me and loved me all my life. If something troubled her, I wanted to know about it. All thoughts of Carrion flew from my head.

She started measuring ingredients into a mixing bowl—wheatcakes or waffles, I couldn't tell which yet, but either one sounded spectacular to me—and didn't look at me while she spoke. "You know Claudene Slown, right?"

It took me a couple of seconds to recall her. She was a longtime friend of Aunt May's, a heavier woman with a broad, friendly face and a beaming smile. "Yes, I know her. How is she?"

"She's just fine. I had dinner with her last night. The problem isn't with her; it's with her son, Vincent."

I didn't really want to ask. But this was Aunt May. I had to. "What about him?"

"You've met him, right?"

Husky, with a moon face resembling his mom's. He had worn funky rectangular black plastic glasses last time I'd seen him. They were a bad match for his face, not to mention his pink Polo shirt and pleated khaki pants, as if he had swiped them from someone far hipper than he. "Sure."

"He was laid off from his job at Globitek Worldwide last year. When he couldn't turn up something else in a reasonable period of time, he decided it was a chance to start his own business. Now he has a little design and printing shop going, but it takes up an awful lot of his time. He and his wife have two little ones, too—twins, just seventeen months old."

"Sounds like things are going well for him," I said, knowing the bad news had to be on the way.

"The sad thing is that he's just been diagnosed with stomach cancer."

I flashed back to the conversation MJ and I had had—what, four hours ago? "I'm sorry to hear that, Aunt May."

"That's not all of it. He lost the insurance he had through Globitek. He bought new health insurance, of course. But now they're refusing to cover the cost of his treatments, because they say the cancer was a preexisting condition. Which is true, as far as it goes, but he didn't know about it until after he had changed to New York Health & Life."

"That totally stinks, May," MJ said. She had started making coffee and had taken some melon out of the refrigerator; Aunt May had wheatcakes on the griddle, and the kitchen was beginning to smell like a very happy place.

"Yes, it does. And here's the . . . what do they call it? The kicker." She picked up the bowl, containing batter she had already mixed, and started stirring it again, just for something to do with her furious energy. "New York Health & Life, it so happens, was bought this past spring by Globitek. So it's the company that fired him that's refusing to pay for his cancer treatment. Without that treatment, his business will fail, he'll probably die, and those two infants will be left without a father."

"Wow. Like MJ said, that does stink. Big-time."

"I know it does, Peter. That's why you have to do something about it."

"Me?" She had discovered my secret when she found me half-dead after Morlun beat the tar out of me. So when she said something like that, I suspected she meant Spider-Man had to do something, not Peter Parker, science teacher. "Aunt May, Globitek is a giant multinational corporation, it's not someone I can beat up."

"Why do you think beating someone up is the answer to every problem, Peter?" She put the bowl down, picked up a spatula, and turned the wheatcakes already on the griddle. "Weren't you raised better than that?"

I put my arms around her and kissed her on the forehead. "You know I was. I have no one but myself to blame for that one. What'd you have in mind? You and me put on a benefit kickboxing exhibition?"

"You still have friends at the *Daily Bugle*, right?"

"Sure."

"Maybe they can do a story about Vincent and his problems with the insurance company. Shine a light on what they're doing. Some sort of exposé."

I thought about it for a few moments. She had surprised me. My tendency was to think that Spider-Man was the problem solver, but sometimes Peter Parker could do more without the mask. "That's genius, Aunt May. Get public opinion behind Vincent. That might budge them in the right direction."

"That's what I was thinking."

"Well, it's no wonder they always call you the smartest woman in America."

She scraped wheatcakes off the griddle and dropped them onto a plate. "And they call you the silliest man, right?"

"Something like that, Aunt May. I think you're right on the money."

9

ROBBIE ROBERTSON'S HAIR had gone gray during the time I had known him, and he might have put on a few pounds. He carried the weight well, though, and the gray hairs just reinforced the impression that he had earned the position of editor-in-chief at the *Daily Bugle*. I could have called a reporter, or even called Robbie, but I was still laboring under the belief that puppy-dog eyes might be called for. Anyway, people always have a harder time refusing favors in person. The operative word, "people," not including folks like the newspaper's owner, J. Jonah Jameson.

I had always liked Robbie, though, and the reverse was usually true as well. Which was why, when I showed up without an appointment, he didn't have me thrown out onto the sidewalk. Instead, I was sitting in a comfortable visitor's chair in front of Robbie's desk. He leaned against the side of the desk, legs crossed at the ankles, casual and comfortable, listening intently as I explained my mission.

"It's for a good cause," I said after summing up. "It's because Aunt May asked me to."

"And better causes are few and far between," Robbie said.

"You got that right."

"Pete, I'm happy to stick it to big corporations when we can. You know how I feel about that, about this paper's obligation to stand up for the little guy. The thing is, the *Bugle* is still a newspaper, emphasis on news. An insurance company screwing a customer is hardly news—it's an everyday thing for insurance execs, I'm pretty sure. You know, get up in the morning, take a shower, get dressed, deny somebody in need, cash their premium check, have breakfast."

"You're probably right," I said. It was disheartening to hear, though. I didn't want to have to explain to Aunt May that I had failed, that Peter Parker really wasn't as useful to have around as Spider-Man was. "I just figured it was worth a try."

"No harm, no foul," Robbie said. "There was a time that would have worked as a story. We're up against the Internet and cable news now, though, and you've got to have something a little sexier. Some sort of hook."

"A hook?"

"Pete, you've spent enough time within these hallowed halls to know what a news hook is."

Of course I knew. Something visual and exciting, something that would make this particular evil insurance company stand out. "Sure," I said. "If I can come up with a hook, you'll run a story?"

"If it's a good enough hook," Robbie said, "I'll consider it. Best I can promise."

"Okay then. A hook you want, a hook you shall have. Thanks, Robbie."

"Don't mention it," he said. "Especially if you bump into Jonah."

I needed a hook. But I also needed to find Carrion, before he found MJ. She had agreed to take a motel room in Brooklyn for a week, which wouldn't take her all the way to opening night, but which we could just barely afford and would allow me to concentrate on Carrion without feeling like I had to guard our apartment at all times. Still, if Carrion went looking for Peter Parker, it wouldn't be hard to find out that I was married to Mary Jane Watson, and there had been plenty of publicity about her appearance in the play. So even in Brooklyn she wasn't totally safe, a fact that heightened my sense of urgency.

Mixed with that urgency, however, was my desire to see the previous incarnations of Carrion for myself. I could find out a lot with a phone call, but I couldn't always trust what I learned. Although I knew it would eat up valuable time, I rented an old beater and drove out to Westchester County, to the Ravencroft Institute for the Criminally Insane, twenty-five miles north of the city. I intended to go inside as Spider-Man though, not Peter Parker, since unmasked I had no more pull here than anybody else off the street. Spider-Man, though, was responsible for filling ten or twenty percent of the beds in the place; and since they were funded by the government proportionate to how many patients they confined, he was an honored guest.

The institute was housed in a castlelike redbrick structure, with a communications dome on top of one of the towers its designers would never have imagined there. The front walls were heavily windowed, but I knew that on the interior, and the rear façade facing only the grounds and then empty forest, there were few windows, only solid walls to keep the patients inside and out of sight. I parked half a mile away and walked up to the front gate, in costume. When I pushed a button on a communications panel at the gate, I was buzzed in immediately.

The massive oak front door opened as I approached, and a woman in a conservative dark suit met me. She was maybe thirty, pretty, with blond hair clipped back behind her head, no-nonsense glasses in front of pale gray eyes, and a trim figure. The only clues that she was not all business, all the time, were multiple piercings on her ears and a pair of shiny black boots with four-inch heels, partially covered by the black pants. I hoped she didn't go for guys in costumes, because I had hoped to make it through the day without some attractive woman falling in love with me. "Welcome to Ravencroft, Spider-Man," she said, gesturing me into a large reception area. This space was more modern than the exterior; the hardwood floors were carpeted, contemporary chairs and sofas were scattered about for visitors to use, and a uniformed nurse sat behind a check-in desk with a uniformed guard standing nearby. "I'm Melissa Bullock," she said. "Doctor Samson is out of town today, but I'd be happy to be of any assistance I can. I'm the new assistant director of operations."

"That would be great," I said, offering my hand. She took it and gave it a firm shake. I paid attention, but she didn't seem to have any difficulty letting it go. Maybe she would be able to resist me after all. "I won't take up much of your time," I said. "I just wanted to check on Malcolm McBride."

"Of course," she said. "The former Carrion."

I was impressed. She must have had a couple hundred patients to keep track of, at least. "That's right."

"He's here. Doing as well as can be expected, I suppose."

"Can I see him? I don't need to talk to him, I'd just like to verify that he's still here."

She gave me a sidelong glance, like I had a lot of nerve doubting what she had just finished telling me. I did, in fact, have a lot of nerve. I also had an overwhelming desire to make sure the new Carrion wasn't really an old Carrion. "Of course," she said again. Dr. Leonard Samson probably loved having a pretty young assistant director of operations who answered every request in such a definitive, positive fashion. "I'll take you to him myself."

"Thank you."

She led me to an elevator, an old one with wooden

walls and glowing round buttons, and pressed the one
for the seventh floor. The elevator lurched and labored,
but eventually the door opened again. We stepped out
into a long hallway lined with heavy doors, each of
which had multiple locks on it. Each also had a panel
that could be opened from the outside for viewing purposes, and a slot near the floor, also accessible from the
outside, through which trays could be slid if necessary.

"It's kind of sad, really," Melissa Bullock said.

"What is?"

"Cases like Malcolm McBride's. Apparently he had
some anger issues, maybe some antisocial tendencies,
but nothing that should have interfered with his life to
any great degree. He might have wanted psychoanalysis,
maybe anger management courses. If he hadn't become
infected with the Carrion virus, though, he never would
have ended up here."

"That's very true."

Her boot heels clicked on the hardwood floor.
This wing was as antiquated as the reception area was
modernized. Visible conduits, tacked to the ceiling
and painted white, connected each of the overhead
lights. The doors were new, but the walls and jambs
looked original to the building's construction. The
place smelled of floor polish and disinfectant, but not
Melissa—walking beside her was like strolling through
a flower garden during a soft springtime rain. "And
since the virus was extracted from his body, and my
understanding is that it has since infected someone else,
who is in S.H.I.E.L.D. custody, there would seem to be

very little reason to keep him here. It's only the aftereffects of the virus that continue to make him a danger to anyone, right?"

"I think so."

"Don't you find that sad? A life utterly ruined by something entirely beyond his control? Chances are he'll spend the rest of his life at Ravencroft."

"You'd better not let Doc Samson hear you talking like that," I said. "Or the people who fund this place. They'll think you're soft on crime."

"Now you're making fun of me."

"No. Well, yes, a little. But I find it very refreshing. It's nice to talk to someone who isn't all about locking them all away and throwing away the keys."

She might have blushed a little. I might have too, but she would never know.

She stopped in front of one of the doors. A little plaque on the wall beside it said, 7249: MCBRIDE, MALCOLM. Below that a piece of paper was affixed listing Malcolm's prescriptions. Penciled initials showed who had delivered the prescriptions, and when, for the past five days. In two more days the paper would be changed.

"Here he is. You don't want to talk to him, right?"

That would make things much more complicated, I knew. I would have to go to a waiting area, and he would have to be manacled and brought in. All I needed to do was look, and I said so.

"Very well." She slid back the panel in the door. I peered inside. Malcolm sat in a chair reading a book. His blond hair had faded toward white, his skin was sallow and pasty, and he had developed a paunch. Otherwise, it was the same guy. He looked perfectly normal. At the sound of the panel, he lowered the book to his lap and turned his head, staring at me over his shoulder.

I was glad I had the mask on. Seeing him there, a prisoner because of something Miles Warren's virus had done to him, made me unspeakably sad.

After a few seconds he got tired of looking at the white one-way lenses in my mask and returned to his book. I closed the panel. He wasn't the new Carrion.

"That's it?" Melissa asked.

"That's fine," I said. "Thank you for your time."

She made a business card appear from somewhere and held it out to me. "If there's ever anything else . . ."

I took her card and held on to it, back down the elevator and out the front door. The drive out had taken far longer than my short visit, and the drive back would take just as long. But I had seen Malcolm, and I knew enough about the Carrion virus to know he hadn't simply teleported out of Ravencroft and come into the city looking for me. When someone became Carrion, that was it—they didn't go back and forth between looking like a yellow, rangy, half-dead lunatic and looking like themselves again.

When I got to the car, made sure no one could see me, and changed, I looked at myself in the mirror awhile. As Carrion, McBride could have done incalculable damage. Unchecked, he might have murdered thousands, even millions. He'd had to be stopped.

But really, wasn't I just as nuts? I put on a colorful costume and ran around the rooftops, beating up whomever I pleased. Sure, I picked on criminals, on those victimizing the innocent. But I did my thing to them before they had faced jury or judge. I was undeniably a danger to myself and others. How hard would it be to make the case that I belonged right there in Ravencroft, roomies with Malcolm McBride, maybe?

I shuddered, then started the car and drove back into the city.

My next stop was the cemetery where Miles Warren was buried. The granite headstone was new, since I had sort of smashed the original one with McBride/Carrion's skull. I wasn't sure what I hoped to learn here, but I was a little relieved to find that the earth over his coffin hadn't been churned up from below. Still, if both Warrens I had seen die had been clones—or if one was the real deal but there was still a clone out there—I wouldn't find that out by looking at an undisturbed plot of earth.

Since I was in the cemetery anyway, I dropped in on Gwendy.

She had been my first real love, the girl I thought would always be my everything. For a time, there, MJ had been new and exciting and had drawn my attention away from Gwen, but somehow Gwen always drew it back. She was smart and funny and had a streak of decency in her—quite possibly inherited from her father, police captain George Stacy—that I still believe inspired everything I tried to do as Spider-Man. Every bad guy I put in jail, every innocent life I saved, was one more example of me trying to live up to what I thought she would have wanted from me, to be deserving of the love she had offered. The fact that I had learned, long after her death, that she'd had a secret affair with my friend Norman Osborn, and had twins with him, colored my memory of her but didn't destroy my sense of her innate decency.

Then Osborn—as supervillain Green Goblin—abducted her, killed her, and threw her from the top of the George Washington Bridge. I snagged her foot with webbing and kept her out of the Hudson River, but too late to save her life. For the longest time I blamed myself, suspecting that she would have been fine if I had just let her hit the water, and that I broke her neck myself by stopping her fall so abruptly. I was wrong, of course—she was already dead, and even if she hadn't been she would have died as soon as she slammed into the river. Still, if she hadn't known me, hadn't been my girlfriend, Osborn would never have had a reason to go after her. One more life on my conscience, one more death in a long line of them that began with my uncle Ben, whose life I could have saved had I been less self-involved.

I ran my fingers across Gwen's headstone, tracing her name. Stacy, Gwendolyne. Her parents, George and Martha, rested nearby beneath similar stones.

Every life is precious, I thought, *but some are more precious than others. At least to me.*

I headed home. I couldn't check on William Allen in person. I didn't know precisely where S.H.I.E.L.D. had kept him, and Julia Darst was almost as trustworthy as Aunt May, so I took her at her word when she said he was dead.

So whoever this new Carrion was, the probability was that he was someone newly exposed to the virus. He had Dr. Warren's memories, but he had also been trained in hand-to-hand combat, and that training remained locked in his muscle memory, which was why fighting him had been so different from before.

It was a piece of the puzzle. But it was an awfully small piece in a puzzle the size of the world.

Most of the day was already gone, and I was no closer to figuring it out.

10

SINCE MARY JANE was going to spend a week exiled to Brooklyn, I had promised to take her out for one last dinner in Manhattan first. We went to Ristorante Sorrentino on West Sixty-seventh, near Columbus, because it was a favorite of both of ours, it was cheap enough not to bust a schoolteacher's bank, and because I was pretty sure we could get in without a reservation. Gina Sorrentino greeted us at the door and took us to a quiet table in the corner, lighting a candle on our table and leaving us with menus we wouldn't need.

". . . so Janice Sheldon cracked up when I missed my mark," MJ said, continuing a story she had begun on the way to the restaurant.

"Nice."

"Seriously, she was doubled over laughing. I looked at her, like, *what the hell*? And when she could speak again, she said, 'I thought hitting marks on the floor was all supermodels had to do. Pout, look waiflike, and stand where you're told.' 'It's a little more complicated than that,' I told her. 'You also have to suck in your stomach and swell out your chest and remember not to fall down.' "

"You make it sound so hard," I said. I flipped open the menu, remembered why I wasn't bothering with it—the manicotti here was what all other manicotti in the world aspired to being—and closed it again. A house salad, Italian bread, and that manicotti would be perfect. The servings here were generous but not so big that I'd feel like I was webslinging with a bowling ball in my gut later on.

"I was ticked," she said. "I mean, we all know Janice is a serious actress. She won't mention the name Macbeth, even miles from the theater, which by the way she spells with a final *re* instead of *er,* and she doesn't own a TV, and she makes herself cry real tears on command every morning just to prove to herself that she hasn't lost the knack, but give me a break. Just because I've been a model doesn't mean I can't act. Does it?"

"Of course not. MJ, you're the best. You're like whichever Redgrave is the good one mixed in with Meryl Streep and Helen Mirren. Only way prettier than whatever mess that would look like."

"Aw, Tiger, you say the . . . erm, sweetest . . . things."

"I know, I'm a goof. But you're as talented an actress as anybody else."

"I think so, too. On Broadway I can even believe it. But in this crowd of *artistes,* with all their off-off-off

Broadway sensibilities, it's like I'm constantly being challenged to show that I'm not just a pretty face."

"And a great body, don't forget that."

"As if you'd let me. Anyway, part of it is that I don't fit in with them because I'm not the kind of person who would judge someone the way they do. I like to think I'm not, anyway."

"If you were you wouldn't be here. Or you might be, but not with me."

She paid me no attention at all, which is often for the best. "It's just a little weird. If I was down on myself for having been a model, they'd probably accept me. But because I'm not, they don't. Seems kind of backward."

"Maybe they get kickbacks from a self-esteem coach somewhere," I said. "When you're at your lowest, they'll give you a referral."

The waitress—Delia, Gina's sister—came to deliver a basket of bread, still steaming from the oven, and to take our orders. We gave them to her. When she was gone, I offered MJ the bread, which she declined, which made me happy because hey, more for me. I broke off a piece and was pondering whether to butter or not to butter when a man came into the restaurant holding a device about the size of a cell phone. He paused for just a fraction of a second, then walked straight toward me. He was white, average in every way, wearing a lightweight dress shirt, pants, leather shoes. He looked like he had just passed by on his way home from work. I had never seen him in my life.

"Can I help you?" I asked.

He eyed me for a few moments more, then checked whatever it was he held as if to confirm a suspicion. "He's touched you," he said.

"Who has? Who are you?"

The strange man spun on his heel and hurried out of the place. Everyone in the restaurant was looking at me now; if I bolted after him it would attract all kinds of attention. Instead, I shrugged, smiled, and said, "Only in New York," loudly enough for everyone to hear. Everyone did, many of them laughed, and I turned back to MJ.

"Friend of yours?" she asked.

"Not that I know of. I'm pretty popular, though."

"That was exceedingly odd."

"It was, at that. Did you get a good look at whatever he was holding?"

"No," she said. "Looked like a phone or a PDA, maybe."

"Not a spider-tracking device?"

"Is there such a thing?"

"I hope not." Delia brought our dinners and placed them on the table. The aroma made me think I had passed out of Manhattan and into heaven. "Maybe he really was just one of those New York crazies."

"The city's full of them," MJ agreed. "But when they focus on you I just assume it's because it's you."

"There is that." I didn't want to talk about it anymore, because I wanted to engage my mouth in a far more enjoyable activity. I broke off some still-warm bread and put it into my mouth.

Next to kissing Mary Jane, it was the most fun my mouth could have in a restaurant.

"It worked!" Scrier Greenwald had burst into the old church, his enthusiasm carrying him past all the usual ritual greetings. Sanden Sturtevant only knew who it was because he recognized Greenwald's voice—Sanden had run into the man outside the Scrier meetings, and he spoke with high-pitched tones that edged into squeakiness when he was excited. As he was now. At least he had remembered to don his robes and mask. In his left hand he waved the detection device certain members of the Cabal had been issued.

"You found Carrion?" Scrier Everett asked.

"No," Scrier Greenwald said. The simple question had dampened his excitement somewhat. "But this thing detected traces of him. It led me to a man in a restaurant. The reading was unmistakable. This man had touched Carrion."

"Who is this man?" Sanden asked.

"I . . . I don't know," Scrier Greenwald said. "I didn't find out."

"Then your information does us exactly what good?" Scrier Everett asked.

"I figured you'd want to know. That the devices really work. That they can track an individual's energy signature."

"We knew that before we invested eleven million dollars in them," Scrier Everett pointed out. The research had been begun in Azerbaijan when it was part of the old Soviet Union, and after the disintegration of that body, Cabal funds had kept it going. Theoretically, the device could detect the individual energy signature that every human being emitted, up to fifteen minutes after the subject has left its presence, and then would function as a kind of homing device. If it came within a few miles of the subject, it would link up with a global positioning satellite and display the subject's location. Minutes after Carrion had teleported away from the Delany building's basement, Scrier Everett had used one to record his signature, then beamed it to the hundred other units they had on hand.

"But, I mean—you know, Carrion isn't your standard guy. The fact that it could find him—traces of him, anyway—that's important, right?"

"It could be," Sanden answered. "But it would be more helpful if we knew who the person was you claim has touched him. What if they know each other? What if he could lead us to Carrion?"

"I thought about that, but I couldn't think of any way to find out," Scrier Greenwald said. "I didn't want to hang around and try to follow him, because I let him see me. I know that was a mistake."

"It was indeed," Scrier Everett said.

"I was just excited. I got carried away."

"It's understandable, Scrier," Scrier Everett said. "And yes, in fact it's good to know that the device was able to detect Carrion's energy signature. Next time, you might want to think through your response a little better—it would have been more efficient to call someone while you waited nearby and watched, for instance. But if we go back to the same vicinity in which you found this person, maybe we'll get another reading."

"That's what I was thinking," Scrier Greenwald said.

Frankly, Sanden wasn't sure Scrier Greenwald had been thinking at all. Still, his finding seemed to indicate that Carrion might not have left New York, and that, at least, was progress. Some of the Scriers had been put to work trying to find another way to acquire the *Darkhold* from the S.H.I.E.L.D. vault, but most of them had fanned out across the city with the handheld devices, looking for any sign of Carrion.

When they found him, they would still have to negotiate a deal. Maybe after some time on his own, he would be willing to come to terms.

Remembering who he was, that was the hardest part. He was Stanley Carter, and he sat on the edge of a bed in a spare room of his uncle Emory's house. The room was crowded with cardboard boxes, overflowing shelves holding books, magazines in cardboard binders, DVDs, and more—Uncle Emory seemed never to have thrown away anything that touched his hands. The house was an older one, and the room had been wallpapered sometime in the early- to mid-twentieth century, apparently by vandals while its owners were asleep. The wallpaper had thick velvet bands running vertically, with silvery-white stripes between them. Now the velvet simply looked like fast-growing mold or lichen on white walls, and the paper was peeling at the corners.

He was Stanley Carter. He wondered if he should write that down, because there were moments when he was Miles Warren and others when he was someone named Malcolm McBride or William Allen. In between moments of lucidity like this he lost himself completely, and those other people crowded into his brain and left him spinning in circles, confused, enraged, violent. Looking at his hands—yellow, with long, gnarled fingers, the skin rough, he knew something else—he had become Carrion, and that, he would stay.

It was a wonder his uncle had let him in the door. He hadn't looked like Stanley Carter, after all. He'd been lucid then, and he suspected Uncle Emory's mind was slipping more than the old man cared to admit, and he had talked his way inside by reminding him of things only his nephew Stan should know. He hadn't known where else to go—Stanley Carter was dead, that much he understood, although somehow those robed freaks had brought him back, and they'd infected him with the Carrion virus in order to keep him alive and . . . he couldn't remember what, if they had even told him, but they wanted something from him, that much was certain. They could keep on wanting as far as he was concerned.

Since he no longer had a home of his own, and he couldn't exactly check into a hotel looking like he did (not to mention the lack of money, credit cards, or identification), he had settled on visiting his only living relative, his father's brother, Emory Carter. And to his good fortune, Emory was far enough gone that he let the freakish-looking being inside and given him a bed.

From his S.H.I.E.L.D. days, Stanley knew a bit about Carrion, and by delving into the memories of Miles Warren—and to a lesser extent, McBride and Allen—he was able to piece together the rest. Some of it, anyway.

He knew enough to know that there was no cure. He would be Carrion until he died, unless someone with sufficient scientific knowledge

Parker

or magical ability could be found to extract the virus from him,

Stacy

but if that

Spider

happened he would die again, because whatever power or technology had brought him back was not enough to

Spider-Man

keep him going indefinitely. He was dead, and he was being preserved, kept alive by

Spider-Man killed Gwen Stacy

the virus, and nothing else. If he lost it, he would descend back into that darkness from which he had emerged, darkness he could barely recall now, and

and he must die.

if there had been anything else, there, on what was so optimistically referred to as "the other side," the heaven or hell that his religious upbringing had taught him to expect, he couldn't remember it at all.

Carrion had slept awhile—even this body needed rest. He looked out the window (curtains so faded and moth-eaten they looked like lace, although they hadn't originally been) and saw that it was dark outside. The house was quiet, so Uncle Emory was probably out. For an old man, he didn't spend much time

Spider-Man must die.

Not die. Not yet. First he must pay.

He must suffer.

Yes, suffer.

sitting around the house in robe and slippers, watching TV.

Carrion held his head between his hands—the unfamiliar shape of it still felt odd, because it was Carrion's head and not Carter's. He felt the other personalities crowding in, the other urges tugging at him. He of all people should hate Spider-Man—the hero had destroyed him, sent him into an institution, crippled and broken in every other way, too, but he recognized that he had been doing wrong, and needed to be stopped.

He had tried to devote his life to good, to service, combining his faith and his scientific acumen to help humanity,

Red blood flowing down the gutters, rushing into the sewers, rising

but all his efforts had come to

back into the streets, choking the life from the cities full of human

naught, when weighed against the evil he had
filth that wallowed there and needed to be cleansed away.
done, the lives he had taken.

Stanley Carter wanted to scream, wanted to drive the encroaching madness from him before it consumed him again, but even as he thought that, his vision filled with a crimson wash through which he saw body parts draped over the boxes, fingers and feet on the shelves, part of a face over there, here a scalp glued to the velvety wallpaper, and he knew it was upon him and there was nothing he could do but give in to it.

11

AFTER DINNER I put Mary Jane into a cab with a couple of suitcases and sent her to the budget motel in Brooklyn. I resisted the impulse to jump on the taxi's roof and ride along—for one thing, I was still in Peter Parker guise, and that wouldn't exactly have been the height of discretion. But more importantly, MJ would have hated it.

So I stood there on the sidewalk and watched the cab drive away, watched it join the yellow river of cabs clogging Manhattan's streets, watched until I couldn't tell anymore which one was hers. Then I went home, put MJ's leftover pasta *pomodoro* in the fridge, and changed clothes. Ten minutes later, anyone looking up at the right moment would have seen only a red-and-blue blur passing by. I already missed her, and I intended to direct my anxiety and frustration into bruising my knuckles on the jaws of the city's lowlifes.

I was moving fast, switching from one web to the

next to the next, racing along rooftops when there weren't enough tall buildings to swing from. There was a certain exuberant joy in sprinting all out, not bothering to slow down when I reached the edge of a roof but launching myself blindly into space, knowing that the strength of my legs was enough to carry me across the gap between most buildings. Sometimes it wasn't, but then I'd do a tuck-and-roll, aiming for a sturdy awning, or I'd latch onto a flagpole or some bit of architectural ornamentation, or I'd just let loose with another strand of webbing. Plenty of options, and the moments of free fall while I picked one were uniquely thrilling on their own.

As usual, I didn't see Carrion coming. I was between two six-story buildings, when suddenly that telltale glow appeared and he was floating in the air directly ahead of me. If I continued on my path I would smash right into him. But he didn't let that happen—instead he raised his hands toward me and blasted me with his organic material-repulsing power. The impact of his blast knocked me out of my arc, and I rolled over backward through the air. I shot webbing through my open legs and snagged the building opposite, halting my rearward motion, and started swinging forward again. "You used the same basic stunt last time, Carrion!" I called, although he had vanished from sight. "You running out of ideas already?"

His usual brimstone stink lingered in the air. I wondered if I could use that to track him. I hadn't tried it before, but I didn't think he could teleport for great distances, and since that smell showed up anyplace he went and lasted a while, maybe if I covered territory fast, I could sniff him down like a hound dog. Not my usual animal totem, but hey—whatever works, right?

I was astonished by how many different odors filled the air above the city streets, generally ignored—at least by me—except when I was trying to locate one specific scent in the stew. Exhaust, diesel, the smells of cooking on large scales and small, restaurant grease, garbage, urine in alleyways, the waste of cats, dogs, and the ammonia-laced stink of pigeon droppings, candles, incense, the sweaty, unwashed odor of homeless people, men in cologne, women in perfume, hopeful teenage boys drowned in body spray all assailed my nose.

Four blocks away, headed toward Midtown, I caught another whiff of Carrion's sulfurous stench. I came to a stop on a window ledge and scanned all around, looking for him. There were people on the sidewalk, people in shops, people inside their apartments, visible through the windows. None of them were pale yellow, gangly, and looked like they'd had facial reconstruction surgery performed by being dragged facedown under a truck. Carrion had been here, I was sure, but then he'd moved on.

I moved on, too. Rather than circling the blocks, I stayed on a straight-line path, following the direction Carrion had taken from point A to point B. That strategy seemed to pay off. Three blocks away I came across a more pungent pocket of his brimstone. No sign of Carrion, but I was gaining on him. I kept to the same course, picking up his scent once more. Strong this time. Then a sudden breeze, the kind that funnels between Manhattan's tall buildings like a subway rocketing through a tunnel, blasted me and wiped the smell away.

I moved. Same path, right into the heart of Midtown. Seventh and Forty-ninth. Was he headed for Times Square? There was nothing special going on there tonight, but it was another warm evening and there would probably be a few thousand people around. If he was going to try releasing yet another killer virus, I had to stop him.

One more block and the smell was stronger than it had been since the moment he had run into me in midair. He was here, somewhere. I scoped out the sidewalks, the shop windows, then started scanning higher.

Then I heard a scream, male, full-throated, a cry of gut-wrenching terror. It came from a cab stopped at the intersection. I aimed for it, dropping toward it like a missile. One midair somersault to fix my landing, and I came down on its hood, hard, and stuck there.

Inside, the driver had both of his hands on the wheel. But his flesh was desiccated, bone showing through on some of the fingers. His head was tipped back against the headrest, mouth open, skin drawn and tight. He looked like a mummy, dead a thousand years. More patches of bone were exposed by gaps in his cheek and brow. The work of Carrion's red death, no doubt, the organic matter-eating stuff he carried in a pouch at his hip.

Behind the rear seat, directing a ghastly grin at me, sat Carrion.

I leaped to the sidewalk and grabbed the door handle. Too late, though. Carrion blinked away. When I yanked the door open, the brimstone stink enveloped me like a horrible fog.

People started rushing toward us, shouting. I didn't expect to be accused of the driver's murder—I hadn't opened his door, and there were plenty of witnesses to say I never had. But I was the only one near the car. When the first spectator reached me, I tried to sound commanding. "The driver's dead," I said. "Call the cops. I'm going after the killer."

I shot webbing high into the air, stuck it to a building, and got out of there. A hundred feet above the ground, my frustration caught up to me. "Carrion!" I shouted, as loud as I could manage. "Come and face me! If it's me you're after, don't pick on innocents!"

If he was close enough to hear me, he didn't respond. Still furious, I slammed my fist into the corner of the building. The stone crumbled under my punch. I could have stood there pretending it was Carrion's face, but the building's structural integrity might have suffered if I took out the whole façade. Instead, I took to the heights again, trying to sniff out Carrion once more.

It didn't work. I tried Times Square first, but over the smells of booze, burger wrappers, traffic, and teeming humanity, I couldn't detect any brimstone. I widened my search area again, covering blocks in an ever-expanding pattern. Nothing. The more I searched, the more I thought my nose was going to fall off—only the snug mask held it to my face, I was sure.

Whatever hole he had crawled into, I couldn't find.

The evening had started out beautifully, as they generally did when they included fine food and MJ. Even that had been strange, though—that freaky guy with the funny PDA or whatever it was, and before that, Mary Jane's story of her fellow actors not respecting her had bothered me. That had been driven from my mind by the odd encounter, then the food, then the good-bye and the visit from Carrion.

Now it all came back to me, slamming into my consciousness like one of Rhino's fists. Suddenly I might as well have been back in high school, a walking bundle of neurosis and insecurity, wrapped up in a nerd's body. I couldn't catch the bad guy, and he was killing people. I couldn't protect MJ from the cruelty of others. I had let someone walk away from me who might have meant me or my family harm. *And you call yourself a super hero?* I thought. *Pretty poor excuse for one, you ask me.*

Fortunately—funny how someone else's pain can just make a guy's day, isn't it?—I overhead a ruckus that dragged me out of my pool of self-pity. The unmistakable sounds of a scuffle reached my ears—a cry for help, cut off abruptly. Thumping sounds, as of kicking feet. A male voice cursing, then saying, "Keep your piehole shut if you know what's good for you!"

Action was required. Anyone who would use the

word "piehole" on a public street needed to be disciplined. The sounds weren't coming from far away, so I went up and over a building and saw two guys dragging a woman toward a waiting van. One of the guys had his hand clamped over the woman's mouth and his other arm around her waist. The other was getting into the driver's door. Okay, that was bad, too.

The woman was young, maybe MJ's age. I felt bad all over again about making her go to Brooklyn, letting her out of my sight when there was a powerful and largely insane killer after me.

I shook that off—time to focus on the immediate problem, not to return to my own. This looked like a garden-variety snatching, nothing too sophisticated. The guy holding the woman got into the back of the van with her, and the other one started to drive away.

I dropped lightly to the ground and fired some webbing at the escaping van—keeping it low, connecting to the rear wheels. I held on, spread my legs, bracing myself, and sticking to the street like I do to a building.

The force of the van almost pulled me off my feet, but I managed to hold steady. The van stopped, however. The driver tried to give it more gas. In the rearview mirror, I saw his eyes go wide when he spotted me. He stomped on the accelerator and the van pulled apart, leaving the rear wheels behind. The back end hit the ground and scraped, kicking up sparks and smoke.

I was laughing so hard as I dealt with their pathetic attempts to fight me I could barely remain upright. The young woman thanked me profusely, and I brought my-self under control well enough to assure her that I had, indeed, taken her plight seriously.

But when I was back on the rooftops, thinking about the way that guy looked when he saw me behind him, I cracked up all over again. My night hadn't particularly improved, but my mood had. Or else I had slipped into hysteria, which was possible, too.

I got a grip on myself and continued on my way. The night turned into another standard one, in which I foiled a half-dozen other crimes, large and small, and rescued a toddler who had wandered away from his window-shopping parents and toward traffic. I swung down and snatched him up, Tarzan style, right before a DHL van mowed him down. His parents were just turning away from the window when I deposited him. He was grinning like a fool, the whole thing having been a grand adventure for him.

On my best days, I felt the same way. This had not been one of my best days.

And it was about to get a lot worse.

Quitting while I was ahead seemed like a plan. The city seemed to have quieted. I started for home. It would be a good idea, after the relatively sleepless night before, to get some shut-eye before I had to teach again.

And that's when I heard his voice, like the devil's claws scraping the world's biggest blackboard. "Spider-Man!"

I spun around. The sickening scent of brimstone wafted to me. I couldn't see Carrion, but I saw a slender blond woman drop toward the street from a nearby rooftop. *Gwendy?*

I had seconds. Less. I crisscrossed webbing between myself and the building she had fallen from, making a wide net, almost a hammock. She dropped into it, bounced a few times, then was still. She had on a vivid blue jacket, exactly the same color as Marge Simpson's hair, and blue jeans faded to the color of the sky in winter when you can glimpse it between pewter clouds.

I crawled across the webbing, feeling as much like a real spider as I had since that time I had six arms. It wasn't Gwen—I had known that from the first, but that one instant when I saw a blond ponytail flopping as she fell had made my heart jump into my throat. Just the same, the way she was just lying there on the web-net rather than trying to scramble off worried me.

She had fallen facedown. When I reached her, I touched her shoulder gently. She didn't budge, except for a shudder from the webbing swaying beneath us. I turned her over.

She was dead. Had been dead, since before he had thrown her over the side. Her throat and jaw were decayed, eaten away, bone and gristle open to the night air. She might have been older than Gwen was when she died, but it was impossible to tell for sure. I checked her for ID. Her pockets were empty. I lowered her carefully to the ground, called the police and told them where to find her.

I darted up the side of the building to see if Carrion had left any clues on the rooftop he had thrown her from. He had not, of course—he was too smart for that—but he had left a message. Scrawled in what looked like red dust were the words *Many more to come, Spider-Man*. He had used the same stuff to leave a note on my apartment wall the first time he had been unkind enough to force himself into my life. That one had said *The dead walk, Parker,* and it remained disturbingly true. I rolled up the bottom third of my face mask, sucked in a huge breath, and blew the words into nothingness, wishing I could eliminate Carrion as easily.

Then I spent the next two hours searching for any sign of him.

Searching in vain.

He was gone again.

He was a madman, a killer.

He needed to be stopped.

All I had to do was figure out how.

12

I WAS TEACHING when I had the brainstorm. To be perfectly fair, it was suggested—albeit unknowingly—by Amber Collier, who asked if there was a safe way to demonstrate the way magnesium powder flared when ignited in the air. "It's just so cool," she said, "I'd like to show some of my friends."

"I'll work out a simple and safe demonstration and show you how to do it," I said. "Just give me a couple of days." When I said the word "demonstration," it hit me.

As soon as class was over, I went to the office I shared and grabbed the phone. Unfortunately, my inspiration had nothing to do with how to find Carrion. It was about Vincent Slown's troubles with New York Health & Life. So while it wouldn't do much to save humanity, it would help ease Aunt May's worries, and that was worthwhile, too.

My first call was to Robbie at the *Bugle*. It took a few minutes for him to pick up, but he finally did. "Pete?"

"Hi, Robbie. Listen, if we held a demonstration outside New York Health & Life, would that be enough of a news hook to make the paper?"

He thought it over briefly. "I think so. It would depend on how big it is, of course. Bigger the crowd, closer to the front page of the Metro section."

"I'll do what I can," I promised. "I'll let you know when the details are firm."

I ended that call and looked up Vincent's number. It was entirely likely—probable, even—that he'd think I was some sort of crank, since I had only met him once or twice and would be calling out of the blue. But after a minute and a couple of reminders, he caught on. Aunt May's name opens a lot of doors. Once that was out of the way, I steered the conversation to business. "So I have friends at the *Daily Bugle,* and they'd like to do a story on your battle with New York Health & Life, but they need some sort of newsworthy angle on it. I was thinking if we held a demonstration outside their Manhattan office building, that might do the trick. It'd bring some heavy-duty attention to the issue."

"A demonstration? Like with picket signs and all?" he asked. His voice sounded weaker than I remembered, kind of faint, and I realized he was sicker than I had been imagining.

"That's what I had in mind. Really play it up. 'NYH&L UNFAIR TO SICK PEOPLE,' and all that. Enough attention might just humiliate the company into acting decently."

"I'm not sure they're capable of that," he said. He laughed, but it degenerated into a coughing fit. I waited until he had finished. "Sorry," he said.

"Don't be. So what do you think? If you're up for it, I'll talk to Aunt May. She can get a crowd out there."

"When were you thinking about doing it?"

"Tomorrow's Saturday," I said. "Their offices might not be open, but the building will be. The good thing is, it tends to be a slow news day. We should be able to make the Sunday papers, and that's the *Bugle*'s biggest circulation day by far."

"I'm game if you really think it's a good idea."

"I don't know if it's good, but it's an idea," I admitted. "And I've been a little short on those lately."

He chuckled, but this time managed not to cough. "Let's do it."

"We'll say nine o'clock tomorrow morning. We'll plan to stay until one in the afternoon or so, give the *Bugle* plenty of time to get photographers out there. Maybe we'll be on the evening news as well."

"What about the police? Do we need a permit or something?"

"Leave them to me," I said. I hoped I sounded confident. The permit hadn't even occurred to me, but Vincent was right. The last thing we needed was for he and his family to be hauled off to jail before the demonstration even made the news.

The next step was trickier. Spider-Man had more friends at City Hall and the NYPD than Peter Parker did, but more enemies, too. I racked my feeble brain and finally came up with Harold Dunagan, who worked for the mayor as a legislative aide. He wouldn't know Parker from Betty Brant, so I left the office and changed in a men's room on campus, webbing my clothes to my back.

A few blocks from City Hall, I called him and asked him to meet me in five minutes in City Hall Park, near Chambers Street. The day was bright and beautiful, with clear blue skies, and I didn't want to cause a stir by walking into City Hall. The park was bad enough, but I found an unoccupied bench and waited there. A few minutes later Harold showed up.

"Hi," he said.

"You don't look happy to see me."

"Should I be?"

Three years ago Harold Dunagan had found himself jammed up, owing gambling debts to a mobster called Snake Mondello, whose office was a booth in the back of Moreno's Little Italy, a restaurant on Mulberry between Kenmare and Broome. I had found out about it because I interrupted two goons about the size of VW busses taking Harold—who was tall but skinny, a guy whose idea of physical exertion was watching TV without a remote—into an alley to work him over because he had been unable to come up with Snake's vig for the week. He made his payment, mind you, he just didn't cover the interest Snake demanded, which was about a million percent a day. Once the thugs were unconscious, I told Harold that my best advice was never to place bets with a guy named Snake in the first place. He assured me that life lesson had already dawned on him.

Then he told me he never would have done it if he hadn't been desperate—his elderly mother had been taken in by a con man, lost all her savings, and was about to lose her home. She needed to pay off the loan before the house was foreclosed, and Harold didn't have anywhere near enough money to make the payment. Thinking he had a pretty good handle on some upcoming college football games, he made some bets. He lost, and then he was told that Snake Mondello had covered the action that day. So he didn't owe the guy he thought he did, whom he had met in a sports bar—he owed Snake.

"Were any of the bets on ESU?" I asked him.

"Yes, I was sure they'd win on Friday night."

I just nodded, convinced now that Harold Dunagan was a two-time loser. And counting.

But I felt bad for him—the Aunt May syndrome again, I think—and went to Snake's office. We had a chat. I'm sure the restaurant was able to reopen after a month or so, and a lot of contracting work, but I was also pretty sure that Snake knew some construction guys who were drawing paychecks without showing up to work, and no doubt they'd appreciate a chance to actually ply their trade.

What I didn't do was report Harold Dunagan. Snake generously offered to pay off his bets as if he had won. I took only the amount Harold's mother had lost to the flim-flam artist and gave it to Harold, who paid off her house loan and banked the rest for her. Then, much as Snake Mondello would have done, I stored Harold away in my memory for a time when I needed a favor at City Hall.

"I'm always thrilled to see me coming," I said. "I need a favor. At City Hall."

"Why am I not surprised?" He sat his lanky self down next to me on the bench. He was so tall and thin, he seemed to have more joints, bends, and folds than most people.

"Unless you'd rather I left you alone," I said. I didn't have to add the unspoken threat of telling his boss, or the police, what had happened. I wouldn't really, of course—I like to think I'm a better person than Snake, all things considered.

"No, that's okay. I owe you. I always figured you'd collect some day."

"It's not for me." I felt like I had to say that. The fact that it was true didn't make it sound any more convincing.

"Okay."

"I need a permit for a demonstration. Tomorrow, outside the New York Health & Life Building."

"That's in Midtown?"

"Sixth and Thirty-seventh," I said. Like most natives, I had never learned to use the name "Avenue of the Americas" for Sixth. And I never intended to.

"Right. And you want this for tomorrow?"

"Nine a.m. until maybe two. And if it can be open-ended, that would be good."

"What do you mean?"

"Tomorrow's Saturday. The demonstrators might want to go back on Monday, when the company's offices are actually open. It all depends on the results."

"Do I want to know what the results might be?" he asked. He had taken off his glasses and wiped the lenses on his white dress shirt.

"Ideally, justice for sick people the company refuses to cover."

"That's not a bad thing." Harold had made some bad choices, but he was fundamentally a decent person.

"Not at all. Is that doable? A demonstration permit that allows for activity there every day for a week, let's say?"

He sighed. I could tell he didn't want to get involved in my scheme. But he didn't feel like he had a choice. I hated putting him in that position, but I didn't have a choice either. "We'll have to set up a free speech zone for them."

"America is a free speech zone, Harold. Or have you forgotten about the First Amendment?"

"But . . . they can't block the sidewalk. Or the street."

"If they're not in anybody's way, there's really not much point to it. That's what a demonstration is about—inconveniencing a few people in order to make a larger point." I stared him down, silently reminding him about Snake Mondello. "You can do this, Harold."

He sighed once again. It was overly dramatic this time. "I can do that," he said.

"Okay. The permit should be in the name of Vincent Slown." I spelled it for him, and gave him Vincent's address. "He's a friend of a friend, and he's the sick guy. If you can courier it to him as soon as it's done, that would be great."

"Anything else? Mayoral proclamation? Key to the city?"

The fact that he was getting sarcastic meant it was time to go. "Just the permit. He'll be waiting for it. And Harold?"

He stood up. It took a long time to unfold all those kinks. "What?"

"Thank you. We're even now."

"We'll never be even, Spider-Man. But thanks for saying so."

I webslung home—forget "truthiness" and "subprime," *that's* a word that should really be in the dictionary—and let Peter take over again. I called Aunt May and told her what was up. She had already heard about it from Vincent's mother, and said that Claudene and Vincent's wife Yselda were already calling everyone they could think of. Aunt May had just sat down to do the same.

"You know what I love about you, Aunt May?"

"What?"

"Everything. But especially the fact that you'll bend over backward to help a friend."

"Bending over isn't as easy as it used to be," she said. "Even forward."

"But you do it anyway. You're the greatest."

"Well, thank you for saying so. Unless I'm mistaken, you've already done the hard part."

"What's that?" She had friends everywhere, but surely she hadn't heard about my little talk with Harold Dunagan.

"Coming up with the idea, of course. And arranging for the press coverage. That's a lot of work."

"I'm just glad I could help. If it is a help."

"I'm sure it'll be just the thing." May Parker, eternal optimist. "Will you be there tomorrow?"

"I wouldn't miss it," I said. I was a little surprised to find that I actually meant it.

13

His mind was a churning, fevered soup of blood and body bits, winding in on itself like a closed nightmare loop he desperately wanted to wake up from but couldn't, a swirling cesspool of sickness and sadism, and although there was a ladder out, he was unable to scale it; it was too short and the rungs were slick with filth. Always, always a pair of white teardrop eyes stared at him from behind a scarlet scrim.

The moments of clarity were fewer than before, and they came and went swiftly, with no warning. One minute he was all holy wrath and righteous vengeance, then he was a simpering student worried about his grades and who would win the grant money, then he was a S.H.I.E.L.D. scientist (and that part, at least, was familiar to the Stan Carter who surfaced now and again), then they all melted together like the wax from a dozen different candles all tipped toward the same vessel and he lost every part of himself again.

He must have killed four or five people last night, but he didn't know if Spider-Man had found them all, and that was the important thing—their deaths meant nothing to him if Spider-Man wasn't tormented by them. He wanted Spider-Man to feel absolutely ineffectual, hopeless, like he—*not me! Warren!*—had felt when he—*him, not me!*—had failed to reach Gwen Stacy in time. When Spider-Man had killed her.

He would kill more tonight. He would let Spider-Man get close and then he would kill, while the wall-crawler was watching him. When Spider-Man was near enough to taste victory, he would deny it. When Spider-Man knew an instant of hope, he would snatch it away. When Spider-Man had purpose, he would crush it like a . . . like a spider in the corner.

Still, he wanted more. He wanted to drag Spider-Man down to the depths he himself had experienced. He wanted the man's every waking moment to fester in misery. He wanted Spider-Man to consider suicide, and then to give up on the idea because hell would just extend his suffering.

He couldn't do it all alone. He had a moment of startling lucidity, when he remembered that he was Stanley Carter and he had become Carrion. He remembered the Scriers who had resurrected him, and he could pick his way through the memories of those who had been Carrion before, even Shriek, who had held the virus so briefly. During this time he realized that the virus was not affecting him as it had the others—he shouldn't have had his own memories, his own consciousness, only Miles Warren's. It must have been the experimental S.H.I.E.L.D. drugs he had ingested that had made him react differently, the drugs that were supposedly flushed from his body years ago. Either that, or the fact that he had died and come back, or both factors in combination. He would probably never know for sure.

But he remembered why he had been brought back and infected with the virus. That Scrier, Scrier Everett, his name had been, had mentioned a vault he had worked on during its design stages, when Stanley Carter had been a S.H.I.E.L.D. operative. He hadn't been paying much attention, since he was just getting used to Carrion's body and powers—but one of Carrion's powers was telepathy, and he had drawn the man's thoughts into his memory. He accessed those thoughts now, saw the book—the *Darkhold*—and understood the power its possessor could wield.

Carter had only worked on one vault, at a S.H.I.E.L.D. facility in the hills of rural Pennsylvania. With his team, they had made the vault virtually impregnable. Besides the *Darkhold*, it held a number of other potentially dangerous texts from over the centuries. He remembered that it contained an original printing of the *Necronomicon*, bound in the flesh of an executed murderer. There were also copies of *De Vermis Mysteriis*, de Rochemort's *Grimoire of the Dark Brotherhood*, and *Unaussprechlichen Kulten* by Friedrich Wilhelm von Junzt, among many others. The occult wisdom protected within its steel walls could give anyone incredible power, which was why S.H.I.E.L.D. kept those tomes locked away.

But no vault was completely secure. Especially from Carrion.

If he acquired the *Darkhold*, the Scriers would do anything for him. Anything at all. And there were enough of them to harass Spider-Man, and Peter Parker, day and night.

He believed he could do it. But only if he could keep his wits about him and stay tapped into Carter's mind.

He left immediately, knowing that even with his limited teleportation abilities it would take a while to get all the way to Pennsylvania. He couldn't bridge long distances in a single "leap," but would have to make many of them. It would tire him, but he obviously couldn't drive or take public transportation.

To leap he simply closed his eyes and willed himself to another place. He didn't have to know it, or picture it. Midleap he opened his eyes again. The world rushed past him at an incredible blur, but he could make out enough detail to pick a "landing" spot. As often as not, these were in midair, where there were fewer obstacles and hazards than at ground level.

In less than two hours he was outside the S.H.I.E.L.D. facility, situated on two hundred acres in a rolling green valley of western Pennsylvania. It featured what looked like miles of razor-wire fencing coiled on the ground outside a twenty-foot-tall electrified chain-link fence with strips of razor wire across its top edge. Towers, positioned every fifty yards along the perimeter, were each staffed by three armed guards and also contained machine guns. Antiaircraft weaponry was stationed on the roofs of several of the taller buildings, along with laser-pulse cannons. After a stretch of twenty-five yards, a patch of carefully mowed grass kept clear of even the smallest weeds, stood a second fence, shorter but also razor-topped.

Guards on foot constantly patrolled the perimeter. A series of cameras fed constant video to a security bunker inside the complex. Other precautions, including a team of resident mages, had been taken against super-powered attackers. The base was vulnerable to a well-planned raid utilizing nonmainstream weapons, but although such a raid could do some damage, it wouldn't last long.

And attackers wouldn't get near the vault, which was thirty feet underground beneath multiple layers of adamantium-reinforced concrete slabs.

Carrion remembered William Allen's last minutes, the terror he had felt at the Hydra raid, the running feet and the screaming, klaxons blaring, sirens wailing, gunfire and explosions. It had been deafening, and billowing smoke cut visibility to almost nothing. He was in a lab, strapped to a gurney, a power inhibitor bracelet on his left wrist like some futuristic watch, and at the first hint of trouble the lab had emptied but they'd left him inside, alone. Smoke scorched his nostrils and he tasted flame and he kept trying to tell someone, *This is a mistake! I don't belong here!* But there was no one left to listen to him. Delving too deeply into Allen's memory risked making Carrion lose the control he was trying so desperately to hang on to, so he forced himself to put that in a box and close it away. All the teleportation had taken much of his strength, and he needed to focus on the task ahead.

He caught a vivid, brilliant image of Spider-Man's broken body, and he knew that was Miles Warren's consciousness trying to regain control. The voices had been still for a while, possibly understanding that he was doing this in order to make Spider-Man's life a living hell, but if they came back now all his efforts would be for nothing. He could waste no more time.

To get to the vault, one had to pass through multiple layers of security that included armed guards, retinal scans, and several massive steel doors. Anyone trying to get in without undergoing the proper procedures would be subject to assault by poisonous gases, power inhibitors, .50-caliber armor-piercing bullets, and more, depending on whom they were and what abilities they had.

Unless, of course, one could teleport.

There had been, Carrion remembered, one defense against teleportation built in when the vault was designed and constructed. A surge of highly charged electromagnetism would fill the vault in response to the unauthorized presence of any living being. Someone could teleport in, but that would activate the defense, and anyone attempting to teleport out would find his or her molecules hopelessly scrambled and some of them fried, the only bright side being that she or he wouldn't live long enough to regret it.

Anyone, that was, except someone who was already dead. Stanley Carter had died, and although he had been brought back by the Scriers, he didn't think his body contained enough living tissue to set off the surge.

When he got into the vault, however, living or not, he would show up on surveillance cameras. He could hope that the humans watching monitors were dozing or scratching themselves or chatting or otherwise not paying attention, but in a S.H.I.E.L.D. facility that was a dangerous thing to count on.

He had to count on being quick enough to find the right book and get out before other defensive weapons were put into play. There was nothing to be gained by more waiting, and everything to be lost if he was observed. He focused on where he knew the vault to be, closed his eyes, and willed himself there.

When he opened them again, dirt and rocks, roots and insects paraded past at the periphery of his vision. When he sensed he was moving through the multiple layers of concrete and steel, he slowed his progress. Another few seconds brought him into the vault itself, where he levitated a few inches above the floor so he didn't set off the pressure alarms underneath it.

The vault contained thousands of books, manuscripts, even scrolls and new media, CDs and DVDs. Made sense, he supposed—the quest for mystical knowledge and power never ended, and technology had to keep up with it. He had always been more interested in science than in magic—every one of him, Warren and McBride and Allen and Carter had all been men of science. He couldn't deny, however, that the way he looked now, and the nature of his abilities, would make most people suspect that occult forces had been responsible for him, not biological experimentation.

Now, of course, he was the product of both, because the Scriers had employed magic in his resurrection. As a result, he had greater respect for the mystical texts surrounding him than he would once have, back in his pure science days. Instead of dismissing them out of hand, he accepted that unexpected truth might be found within their pages.

With so many books, the air inside should have been musty and stale. But the most advanced air filtration and climate control systems on Earth were at work in here, and the vault was essentially odorless.

He only had to find one book, and he knew what it should look like, or at least what Scrier Everett had believed it looked like. However, it would have a black cover and spine, and black appeared to be the default cover for occult books. *Didn't their makers have any imagination?* he wondered. A mystical text bound in canary yellow or pastel blue would stand out from the crowd so much, it would probably get far greater use than the others.

Trying to be absolutely still, Carrion listened for the book to speak to him. When it didn't, he didn't want to waste any more time. He turned in a slow but steady circle, floating above the floor, scanning the many shelves as he did so. He didn't see it, and he knew time was growing short. S.H.I.E.L.D. agents would be racing for the vault soon, if they weren't already.

He made one more revolution. This time, instead of looking at the volumes themselves, he tried to look at the patterns they formed on the shelves, on the negative space around them.

This time, he found it.

One book sat by itself, its neighbors pushed aside to give it space. This particular book had several inches of clearance on each side. It looked like it had been brought in recently, and handled with care so that it wouldn't infect the books near it. It fairly tingled with energy, which Carrion put down to the fact that humans had touched it far more recently than anything else in the place.

Carrion floated closer to the book and saw the green lowercase "d" inscribed on its cover. That was the one, then. He put his hands on it.

And that's when the door flew open.

S.H.I.E.L.D. agents armed with guns and more sophisticated armaments burst into the room. "Freeze, pal!" one of them shouted in a voice that demanded obedience.

Instead of obeying, Carrion released the book with one hand and reached into the pouch hanging at his side. He cupped the hand, filling it with the red death, and hurled some toward the agents crowding the door-way.

Its effect was instantaneous. Burning, painful boils appeared on the agents' flesh wherever the dust landed. A couple of them got off shots, but Carrion dematerialized, allowing the bullets to pass harmlessly through him. Once the agents had fallen to the floor, writhing and screaming in agony (Carrion heard the thunder of more boots out in the corridor, running toward the vault), he materialized again, long enough to grab the *Darkhold* and teleport away.

He stuffed the book in the bag he wore against his hip, in with the red dust he carried there. He wasn't afraid of whatever power the book might hold, but he could feel it, tingling in his hands, willing him to do things he didn't think were entirely in his own interests. He fought off an impulse to show himself on Interstate 280, with the intention of causing a huge multivehicle crash. While the idea of multiple fatalities had a certain undeniable appeal, he couldn't see that it would serve his agenda in any way, and he put it down to the book planting ideas in his head.

He hadn't bothered to ask why the Scriers wanted it. They had talked about it as something that would bring them power, and he supposed it might—the vault had been constructed, after all, to house texts that could accomplish just that. But their goals were not his own, and his only interest in the *Darkhold* was that it would help secure the cult's cooperation in harassing Spider-

Man. Spending time with the book convinced him that the Scriers didn't know what they were in for—he could withstand the book's unspoken urges, but he was something far more than human. He would be curious to see what happened when he delivered it. Would they immediately be taken over by it? Or would they manage to hold it off for a while, thinking they controlled it while it insinuated itself into their very pores?

By the time he got back to Uncle Emory's home, he was exhausted. He dropped the book onto the foot of the bed, stretched out on it, put his hands behind his head, and was asleep within seconds.

And in his dreams, Miles Warren, Malcolm McBride, William Allen, and Stanley Carter all vied for command over Carrion. By the time Carrion woke up, he had once again forgotten whom he had been in the past, and remembered only one urgent need: to destroy Spider-Man.

From what he had heard and read, criminals in general weren't the sharpest nails in the hardware store. They went into banks bearing holdup notes written on their own deposit slips or job applications. They held up liquor stores but left their own wallets lying on the counter. They called the police to report other, less dangerously stupid, criminals stealing their stashes. He had heard about one who, when informed that only a store manager could open the safe, left his own cell phone number with the staff, along with instructions to call him when the manager came in. Then when someone called him, he returned to the store, still not realizing that he would be arrested the second he walked in.

The Surgeon had avoided those mistakes, and more. He had taken great pains not to leave his own fingerprints or DNA on any of the women he helped. He never took one when there were witnesses around who could identify his van. He applied the same rule when dropping them off, after his treatment was finished.

Criminals were caught when they made stupid mistakes or when they couldn't keep their mouths shut. He had made no such errors. Even now, all these years after he had retired, he had never told another living soul about the women he had helped. And he never intended to.

So when he looked in his van's rearview mirror and saw a New Jersey state trooper behind him on the Garden State Parkway, light bar flashing, a sudden panic gripped him. What had he done? Had someone reported his van, all those years ago? Had they been looking for it ever since? He had driven to a home improvement superstore because he had to buy a toilet seat to replace one that had cracked. He had looked at a few women—recognizing the need in them, urgent, almost desperate—but he hadn't approached any of them.

He pulled over to the side of the road, gripping the wheel tight to control the shaking of his hands. When the trooper came to the passenger door, he had to make an effort to release the wheel and thumb the power window button. "S-something the matter, Officer?" he mumbled.

"License and registration please," the trooper said. It was a woman, he realized, with ash-blond hair and a spray of freckles across her nose. Her face was broad and flat, not the type that appealed to him. He didn't know what he would have done if she had been. He had a couple of scalpels in the glove compartment, just in case, although he hadn't used them in years and years.

"Yes, of course," he managed. "Just a moment." Now he had to let go of the wheel entirely, and it was like releasing a lifeline that held him fast in the midst of a furious tornado. The van seemed to tilt and spin away from him. He swallowed and opened the glove compartment, shifting his whole body over to try to block the policewoman's view. "Just one minute," he said.

"Yes, sir," she said. She sounded impatient. He rifled through the various papers he had shoved in there, found the car registration. His license was in his wallet, and for a second he was afraid he might have more than one in there, or one that didn't match the name on the registration. But that was one of those stupid mistakes he had never allowed himself.

She inspected both documents for a few seconds. "I'll be right back, sir," she said. She carried the driver's license and registration to her car. He grabbed the wheel again, watching her in his mirror, trying to imagine what she would look like with her throat cut and the eyes plucked from that flat face. If she tried to take him in, he would palm one of the scalpels, use it on her before she could handcuff him. He was an old man, she wouldn't expect something like that from him, and he would use her expectations against her. He would leave her body by the side of the highway, switch license plates with some other vehicle before twenty minutes had passed, and be on his way. The Surgeon wouldn't be brought down by a lady cop. That just couldn't be allowed.

A couple of minutes later she came back to the open window and handed back his papers. "Here you are," she said. "Are you aware that one of your taillights isn't working?"

He almost burst out laughing. "No, ma'am," he said, holding his mirth back.

"You need to get that taken care of."

"I will. Thanks for telling me. I guess a person doesn't often stand behind his own van while it's in operation."

"Happens all the time," she said. "Just deal with it, okay? Soon. It's dangerous to drive this way."

"I will. Right away, I promise."

"See that you do," she said.

When she was back in her patrol car, the Surgeon drove away, pulling carefully out onto the Parkway when there was a big enough break in traffic. The last time he glimpsed the cop, she was still sitting in her car beside the road, writing something down.

She would never know how close she had been—either to solving more than a dozen open cases, or to having her throat cut and bleeding to death beside the Parkway. Her life would go on as it had, her shot at fame having come and gone.

And so would his. But the urge was getting strong in him, stronger than it had been in decades. He didn't know why it had gripped him so suddenly, but it was almost impossible to ignore. His hand ached to wield the scalpel.

He didn't know how much longer his retirement could last.

14

IN NEW YORK City, nightclubs come and go daily—okay, nightly—often with no one even noticing their presence, or lack thereof. Sometimes they're legitimate places with business licenses, liquor permits, and the like. Other times they're gypsy clubs, raves or gigantic parties held in empty stores, warehouses, even people's homes. These can be illegal but hard to pin down. The right people can text a few other right people, and before anybody knows it, two thousand New Yorkers will descend on a location for a night of loud music, drugs, dancing, sweat, and sex. In about that order.

Other clubs, legit ones, can spend hundreds of thousands on décor, sound systems, permits, and marketing. Some of them pay celebrities to show up, in hopes that they'll attract the paying customers. These are the ones that usually have long lines waiting to get in, velvet ropes, and bouncers the size of Buicks deciding who is rich enough, powerful enough, or just plain hot enough to be allowed inside.

One of the newer of these legitimate nightclubs was called Blitz. It occupied a former warehouse in a less-than-trendy neighborhood, the stretch of Eleventh Avenue south of the Javitz Center. Still, people flocked to it every night, because famous people had been spotted there and one had even shown up on the Internet coming out of the club with various body parts on open display. That had been the magic ingredient—ever since then, Blitz had been swamped every night. Some people were even speculating that it was already on the way out of fashion—that it had become too popular, so the celebrities didn't go there anymore, and without them the regular clientele would drop off. It had been open for three months and if it lasted two more, it would be a miracle.

The reason Blitz was on my mind was that gunshots had been fired outside the club. I was less than a block away and moving fast. The buildings here weren't tall, so I ran across the rooftops, vaulting the gaps, trying to avoid the traffic on the street. Already I heard sirens descending on the scene, competing with the shrill shrieks and screams coming from up ahead.

When I reached the edge of the last rooftop, I saw the reason for the commotion. The line to get in must have been a hundred people long, or more. I counted five would-be clubgoers sprawled out on the ground, bleeding, and there might have been more behind knots of onlookers. Flashes from cameras strobed the night;

other people had their phones out, taking digital shots that would mostly be meaningless dark blurs when they looked at what they had shot. Leave it to a former pro to criticize the amateurs.

I dropped down next to a uniformed security guard who looked like he had just awakened in a foreign country with no money and without knowing the language. And also naked. He was waiting for the cops to get there, because he had no clue how to handle a situation like this. "What happened?" I asked.

"Everybody has a different story. But it sounds like someone showed up and killed one or two of the people in line. Someone had a piece—we don't let 'em through the doors, we got metal detectors, but that don't mean they don't try—and pulled it, shot at the perp. Only—here's where it gets really weird—some people say he missed, and others say his shots went right through the perp and hit the people on the other side of him. Someone else drew down and before you know it, there's five or six people wounded or killed, not counting the first two."

"How did the first two die?"

"Looked like old age or something," he said. "Their skin's all dried out and rotted, like. Just all of a sudden."

Which was pretty much what I was afraid he'd say. And here I'd been hoping Carrion had decided to retire to New Zealand and hang out with the Hobbits. "Anybody get a description of him?"

"Not one that makes any sense. But a crowd like this, half the people already got a buzz going, people see what they want to see. Somebody said he had yellow skin, was almost naked except for a hood and shorts, and looked like something out of a video game."

"Or a horror movie," I added. "That sounds about right."

"You know him?"

"I'm afraid so. Thanks for the help. Try to keep these people calm; the cops will be here any second now."

I pushed my way through the crowd, taking in the scents of blood, tobacco, and clove cigarettes, dope, perfume, and cologne splashed on in swimming pool quantities, and vomit from the unfortunate ones who got too close to the victims. I found one of the original victims, someone Carrion had killed directly instead of indirectly. His trademark red dust of death had eaten through clothing and skin. I didn't see any messages, but that didn't necessarily mean anything. The victim had been female, young, and shapely, dressed in reveal-ing club wear, with straight black hair. I doubted she was out of her early twenties.

I went up the wall to the warehouse roof. It looked like I expected, mostly flat, with heating and air-conditioning duct-work, and the sorts of things people might take from their pockets and hurl onto roofs just before being patted down by a bouncer—needles, broken bottles, a couple of small, cheap handguns. Somebody would have to be pretty desperate to get into a nightclub to throw away their gun, I thought. But then again, the cops might be able to link those guns to crimes, so better to toss them than to be caught with them.

I looked again for a message. He hadn't left any.

Turned out he hadn't needed to, because he had hung around.

"L-looking for me?" he asked from behind me.

I spun around. The sight of the bodies below had filled me with rage, like gunpowder in a barrel, and the sight of him ignited it. "If you're killing these people to get my attention, you can stop now. You've got it."

"I-it isn't that," he said. "I'm not c-concerned with your attention. It's your s-suffering that interests m-m-me."

Suffering interested me, too, but mostly the suffering I was about to inflict on Carrion. I blasted a thick glob of webbing right into his eyes. It wouldn't last long, but I wanted him blinded while I got close enough to pound on him.

To my surprise, it worked.

In the half second it took him to decay the webbing, I wrenched up a four-foot length of angle iron used to bolt down some duct-work and exploded at him. I swung it like Mark McGwire trying to knock the stuffing out of a ball and nailed Carrion in the side of the head.

When I fought regular people, I pulled my punches. I usually delivered openhanded slaps, using less than a quarter of my full strength. Even going up against someone who could take it, Rhino or Kraven, maybe, it took me a little while to remember that I could go all out.

Against Carrion, I put my back and shoulders into the swing, giving it everything I could.

Carrion staggered a couple of steps to his left.

I drew it back and jabbed it at him, catching him in the gut. He folded around it and rank, sour breath blew out of his mouth. But as soon as I lowered the angle iron he came at me, hooking his left leg around my right. I tried to pull away but he was too fast, even for me, and he caught my shoulders and did—something, I couldn't say exactly what, and then I was flipping through the air and coming down hard on my back, the angle iron bouncing away from my hand. I scrambled for it and his instep landed on my wrist. I thought it was broken, but I rolled away from him, jumped into the air, and landed a kick in the center of his chest.

That knocked him back a few feet. "Who are you?" I asked. The Carrion I had known would never have been able to pull off a move like that.

"Miles W-Warren."

"Miles Warren didn't have a stammer. Or fight like that."

"Malcolm McB-McBride."

"Wrong."

"William Allen."

"Try again, Einstein."

"P-P-Peter Parker."

A shudder went through me. Warren had created a Parker clone once. Was I fighting a version of myself?

No, I didn't think so. He didn't move like me, and his fighting techniques, though vaguely familiar, weren't mine. He was lying, trying to throw me off guard. And reminding me that he knew my secret.

I thought maybe contact with him would eat through my costume, so I grabbed the angle iron. By the time I swung it again, he was moving fast toward me, no doubt to throw one of his fancy new moves. I shifted the angle of my swing and just managed to clip his left shoulder.

"Y-you've lost your t-temper, Sp-Spider-Man," he said, rubbing it like someone who's just been given a charley horse.

"That's right. You wonder why?"

"I just think you're st-starting to feel like I d-do whenever I think about you."

"Think? You don't think. Your skull is full of old dirty rags and red dust, just like the rest of you."

"Doesn't it make you f-feel better about yourself to believe that I'm the same as you? A k-killer?"

I started to respond with a snappy comeback, but I couldn't spit it out. I was seeing Carrion through a red screen, and hovering around him were all the people who had died because of him just in the last few days. All because he blamed me for something that I not only hadn't done, but that had hurt me far more than him. My feelings for Gwen Stacy had been real, and returned, while his were only a delusional obsession.

Instead I swung away with the angle iron again. I expected him to teleport away from it, or to dematerialize himself, but he did neither. The iron slammed into his left arm, bending a little. He fell to one knee, glaring at me with his ghastly face fixed in a mask of surprise.

I was surprised, too. That one seemed to have actually

hurt him. Instead of standing there wondering about it, I took another swing at him, this time bringing the iron down on his skull. It hit with a resounding crack.

That blow drove him to his knees.

His clawlike hands scrabbled at the roof's pebbled surface. He tried to say something but the words caught in his throat. I wasn't interested anyway. I was lost, someplace deep and dark that most of the time I tried to pretend didn't exist. I covered it up with the one-liners and the idea that I was doing good things for a world that was often bad, but if I really faced it I had to accept that I spent most of my nights beating people up. Even if the darkness hadn't always been buried inside me, years of violence had to have planted a seed, germinated it, and brought it to the surface.

At that moment, I wasn't really into self-reflection, though. I was a machine, my arms swinging that iron bar, pounding Carrion again and again. He whimpered and writhed under the blows I rained down on him. When it started to cross my mind that I might be killing him, I hesitated—just for an instant, catching myself mid-swing.

Carrion used that moment to teleport away.

I didn't chase after him—not that I could have found him anyway, if he didn't want me to. I was beat. The adrenaline-and-anger cocktail that had fueled my attack drained out of me in seconds, leaving me limp and sweating under my costume.

Below, emergency vehicles had rolled in. Cops were bringing order to the scene, detectives questioned witnesses, and the victims were rolled into ambulances. Carrion and I had made plenty of noise, even over the commotion beneath, and I could hear footsteps on the interior staircase leading up to the roof.

That was my cue. I dragged my sorry self off the roof and hit the air, nailing a webline to the next building. The rush of near-flight revived me a little, but I knew I would have a long, hard night ahead.

All I really wanted was to keep busy, so I didn't have to think.

15

SATURDAY MORNING I dragged myself out of a bed that felt cold and empty without MJ in it. I could have slept in—I could have slept for a month—but it was the day of Vincent's demonstration outside the New York Health & Life building, and I had promised I'd be there. MJ was going to show up, too, and we had made a lunch date. After the night I'd had, I looked forward to a sympathetic ear.

I took a long shower, dressed, ate some breakfast, and then headed for Midtown. As usual, I wore my Spidey costume under my clothes, because you never knew when trouble might turn up. When I turned the corner onto Sixth, I was astonished by the size of the crowd. I had expected the Slowns, maybe some extended family, a few neighbors and friends. But somehow they had reached out far beyond that. There must have been a hundred people thronging the sidewalk. Most looked respectable, middle class—less like the sort of people you would expect to be demonstrating outside a corporation, and more like those who would line up for its IPO. A pretzel vendor worked the corner, the aroma of his wares wafting over the demonstrators, and seemed to be doing big business.

The protest signs ranged from straightforward ones, like, NYHL UNFAIR! to more creative ones. I saw a middle-aged woman holding one aloft that asked, HEALTH INSURANCE OR PROFIT INSURANCE? An African-American guy in a pastel golf sweater and khakis had a sign saying, DOCTORS SHOULD MAKE HEALTH DECISIONS, NOT CORPS!! And a woman about Aunt May's age waved her sign to the honking cars passing down Sixth. Hers said simply RX OR $$???

I moved through the crowd until I found Vincent. He had a wide smile pasted to his face, and although his color was pale, he looked infused with energy. "Peter!" he shouted when he saw me. He shoved toward me, stuck his hand out, and when I gripped it he squeezed tight. "Look at all these people! Isn't it great?"

"It's quite a turnout," I said. "Any sign of the press yet?"

"Not yet," Vincent started to say. But he didn't have the words completely out when a woman I recognized only belatedly as Yselda, his wife, grabbed his arm.

"Vinny, look!" she shouted, pointing up the street. A TV truck was rolling up with satellite dishes on its roof.

"I take it back," he said.

"They'll want to interview you," I told him. "You

should go greet them so they don't get sidetracked."

"Right, yeah." He hurried off through the demonstrators toward the truck.

Yselda grabbed my arm. She was a few years younger than Vincent, petite, with short dark hair, olive skin, and brown eyes that glistened with excitement. "Thank you so much, Peter. Vinny told me this was all your idea, and I just wanted you to know how great it is."

"I just hope it has some impact, Yselda. I'm sure it's been rough for you both."

"Nothing else we tried seemed to get through to them, so this can't make things any worse. And the public attention seems like it'll have to help. I think you were just brilliant."

I was sure I had turned as red as my costume. "Aunt May is really the one who started it all."

"She's been great, too," Yselda said. "Have you seen her yet?"

"Aunt May's here already?"

She pointed toward the far edge of the group. "She was over there, last time I saw her. Looked like she was having a ball."

I thanked her and headed that way. Yselda was right, Aunt May did look like she was having fun. She was on the fringes with Vincent's mother, Claudene, so she could be seen by pedestrians and motorists. She waved and smiled and hoisted a sign that said, NYH&L: IF YOU TAKE HIS MONEY, PAY HIS CLAIM!

"I didn't know Angelina Jolie was going to be here," I said to Claudene as I approached.

"Peter!" Aunt May spotted me, lowered her sign, and gave me a kiss on the cheek. "You look tired," she said.

"I'm fine, Aunt May. This turned out better than I expected."

"This is wonderful," Claudene said. She enveloped me in a crushing, rose-scented hug. I might have resisted, but she was putting Aunt May up at her place until I had Carrion dealt with—not that she knew that part of it—so I felt like I owed her. "I think you could have a future in politics if you wanted, Peter. Putting this together so quickly—"

I cut her off. "I didn't do anything."

"That's not what Vincent says. You had the idea, the plan, you got the permit somehow. You contacted the media. Without you, none of this would have happened."

"Well, I'm just glad it all seems to be working out." A career in politics was the furthest thing from my mind. Talk about skeletons in my closet—I didn't think even New Yorkers would vote for a guy who wore spider-webbed long johns under his street clothes.

Then I saw Claire Urrea and Derek Tyler of the *Daily Bugle* working their way through the mob. Derek had a camera in his hands, another strapped around his neck, and an equipment bag slung over his shoulder. Robbie had come through. I started toward them, to steer them to Vincent, and felt pretty good about what I had helped accomplish.

• • •

Carrion couldn't have said why he had let Spider-Man pummel him so hard. He wasn't sure Spider-Man could actually kill him. But the blasted wall-crawler had come close. He had been tired to begin with—seemed to almost always be tired, these days—and when Spider-Man had gotten in that first lucky shot, he just felt dispirited. He tried to fight back a couple of times, but Spider-Man shrugged off his efforts and just kept coming. For a few moments, Carrion honestly believed he had lost the motivation to go on, and he let Spider-Man do whatever he wanted. He had known Spider-Man's fury with him—you didn't hide things from a telepath, especially when every fiber of your being screamed your intentions at full volume, dial turned up to ten— and he had, for a time, been willing to let himself go. At least, that part of him that still had Stanley Carter's consciousness did. Finally, the other voices in his head had insisted on retreat, and he had teleported away.

At his uncle's house later, he was thankful. Giving in to his hated enemy would have been the worst thing he could have done. He needed to have his revenge, and to drive Spider-Man as mad as he hoped, he still needed the cooperation of the Scriers. Now that he had the book they wanted, he didn't think that would be hard to enlist.

He didn't know how to get in touch with them. But he knew where to find them, and that should work just as well. When they had brought him back, he had teleported away from them, but he knew where they had been, in a mostly empty office building in Hunter's Point.

That would just have to do.

There were exceptions, but for the most part, crime was a cash business. Sanden Sturtevant spent the greater part of every morning accepting deliveries, organizing and counting, checking bills to make sure they weren't marked, and if they were sequential, rearranging them into bundles with other, nonsequential bills, then making deposits or arranging for them to be made in a series of banks around the greater New York area. Cash deposits of ten thousand dollars or more raised red flags, so he had to make multiple smaller deposits each day, and never in the same bank more than once a week.

Afternoons he spent online, moving money around. Much of it was transferred into offshore accounts in the Cayman Islands or Switzerland. Some was used to purchase foreign currencies, which could later be unloaded (sometimes at a loss, but ideally at a gain), effectively laundering that money. Some of those profits were churned into buying stock in legitimate companies the Cabal owned, helping keep their stock prices inflated.

Sanden had become fairly expert at various laundering techniques. This afternoon he was making some online "investments" in foreign stocks, which he would cash out in a day or two. Anything he lost would be considered a cost of doing business, but if he made money at it, so much the better. He was switching from one online brokerage account to another when he heard a frightened bellow from outside his heavy office door.

Sanden hid the browser window and hurried to the door, pausing only long enough to pull a SIG Sauer 9mm automatic from his desk drawer. He had never shot anybody. But he was willing to try.

On the other side of the door were five bruisers whose job was to keep intruders out of the room where Sanden dealt with the money. When he opened the door, he saw three of them on the floor. The fourth sat in a rolling desk chair, arms slack at his sides, his head tilted back. Blood covered almost every surface in the room, dripping from the ceiling, smeared down the walls, coating the black, white, and yellow tile floor.

Carrion had backed the fifth Scrier up to a wall. The Scrier's hands trembled uncontrollably, pattering against the wall like he was finger-drumming along to a rock and roll song, and he was making a kind of "uhhh . . . uhhh . . ." noise. When he saw Sanden appear in the doorway, a look of relief washed over his face so clearly that Sanden could read it through his chalky mask.

"Carrion," Sanden blurted out.

Carrion glanced back over his shoulder without turning around. "You were one of them," he said.

Sanden fought to keep his voice steady. "One of who?"

"Those who b-brought me back."

"Yes."

"I seek the one called Sc-Scrier Everett. You know where he is."

Sanden wondered for a fraction of a second how Carrion would know that, but then he remembered. Telepathy. No point in arguing, then. "I can reach him."

"Then do so," Carrion said. "I have something he wants."

The Darkhold? Sanden thought. That was the only thing Carrion could know Scrier Everett was trying to acquire.

"Don't trouble yourself t-t-trying to g-guess. Just b-bring him here."

"Don't hurt this Scrier, or anyone else," Sanden said. Ordering Carrion around, as if he could enforce it. "I'll call him. He'll be here in fifteen minutes." He went back into his office and closed the door. Not that it would keep Carrion out. But if Carrion decided to finish off the fifth guard, at least Sanden wouldn't have to listen.

In the office, he called Scrier Everett, who was just over at the nearby church, then opened the browser again and completed the interrupted transaction. When that was done, he shut down the computer and waited, wishing he knew if a closed door could shield his thoughts from the murderer outside. At least Carrion stayed put instead of following him inside.

Sanden had been torn between telling Scrier Everett why he was being summoned, half afraid that the man would skip the country instead of driving the few blocks over. Finally he went ahead and told him, figuring Scrier Everett wouldn't want him to disobey Carrion's command. Anyway, Everett wanted the book, and if Carrion really had it, or had decided to cooperate, he would want to know.

The longest twelve minutes of Sanden Sturtevant's life passed. Finally he heard Scrier Everett's car screech to a stop on the street outside. A glance out the window confirmed that the Scrier had arrived, having driven himself over from the church in robe and mask. Risky, but Sanden was glad the man had hurried.

Scrier Everett came into the building, and Sanden dared to venture from his office again. He waited until he heard Scrier Everett enter the outer office—the one that more closely resembled a slaughterhouse now—before he stepped into it himself. Carrion was still there, although, maybe out of sheer boredom, he had killed the fifth guard and set about peeling the man's decayed flesh from his body. Sanden's stomach did a little flip and he swallowed back bile.

Scrier Everett, on the other hand, seemed delighted to see Carrion. "Thank you for coming," he said, walking right through the gore without apparent dismay, except when his shoe stuck in a pool of tacky blood. He looked like he wanted to offer a hand, but wasn't sure if Carrion would shake it or bite it off. He ended up holding it close to his side. "Have you reconsidered our offer of assistance?"

"I don't n-need your help," Carrion said. "I do, however, have the book you are looking for. And I would like a f-f-favor."

"You have the *Darkhold*?"

"I just s-said that, d-didn't I?"

"Where is it?"

"It's safe."

"May we have it?"

"If you d-do something for m-m-me."

"Name it."

"There's a man named Peter Parker. He teaches at Midtown High School. For r-reasons of my own, I want him to have no r-rest, no peace. I want him harassed, disturbed, p-p-prevented from having any kind of no-normal life. I don't want you to hurt him—I'll t-t-t—I'll do that myself. But I want him to suffer, every min-minute of every day."

"For how long? A week? A year?"

"For as long as I let him live. Which pr-probably won't be very long."

"Done," Scrier Everett pledged. "When do we get the book?"

"I want to see how it's handled," Carrion said. "When I see your pe-people in action, then you can have it."

Scrier Everett's head bobbed enthusiastically. Even standing amid the carnage that Carrion's brief visit had caused, he looked like he wanted to rub his hands together and dance with glee. "That," he said happily, "we can do."

16

OUR LUNCH DATE ended up being at home, because it was cheaper than going to yet another restaurant, and also because we had spent the night apart and after a certain amount of smooching, some restaurant patrons tend to get a little put out. I can understand that—I wouldn't want to watch someone who wasn't me kissing Mary Jane, either.

The spirit of frugality won out over the spirit of romance, though. MJ had her leftover Italian, and I went with PB&J. While we ate, we watched the midday TV news coverage of the demonstration. The on-scene reporter talked briefly to Vincent, showed lots of generally cheerful demonstrators, and gave a quick rundown of why the insurance company's actions had led to such a drastic step. When it was over, I clicked off the TV and caught MJ's gaze.

"You rock, dude," she said. "I mean, that was a great

piece. And there'll be something similar in tomorrow's *Bugle,* right?"

"More in-depth, I hope, but yeah."

"That's great, Peter. That's got to be just what the Slowns were hoping for."

"I think they were hoping the head of the company would come downstairs and hand Vincent a suitcase full of cash," I said. "But failing that, I guess this is the next best thing."

"Peter Parker, community organizer."

"Or outside agitator. Depends on your point of view."

"I'm serious, Peter. You did something good today. Not that you don't every day—fighting crime is good, and so is teaching kids who need an education. But you know what I mean."

"I guess, yeah."

She leaned toward me, putting one hand on my leg. "Have you ever thought about getting involved in politics? Trying to make a difference to people in a different way? One that wouldn't necessarily involve your wife having to leave her own apartment because some crazed killer might attack it?"

I'd been on edge ever since MJ suggested we have lunch in the apartment. I hadn't seen Carrion since we had tangled on the roof of the nightclub, but that didn't mean he wasn't around, watching our place and waiting for the right moment to show up. I was willing to let her be at home for short periods, as long as I was there with her—but that didn't mean I could relax while she was. "That would be a good thing," I said. "The part about not being attacked. The whole kissing babies, knocking on doors, and raising money bit, though? Not so much me, I think."

Still, she was the second person to suggest it today. I knew it was just because the demonstration had come off reasonably well—although it was surely Aunt May and Claudene Slown who were responsible for that, having called everyone they had ever met, apparently—but still, hearing it twice made me feel like I had to give it some thought.

The way I had pounded on Carrion scared me. There was a reservoir of violence inside me that I didn't want to acknowledge. But if I pretended it didn't exist, I would remain a slave to it—I had to face up to it in order to control it.

If I did decide to try politics, it would be because I'd be able to help people in a different way. A way that didn't involve punching anyone. A way that could make a difference in many lives at once, rather than simply by taking on super villains one at a time. A mayor, a city council member—those people held a lot of power, especially in a city the size of New York, and they could do a lot with that power. With great power, my uncle Ben had always said, comes great responsibility. I had tried to live by that credo, as Spider-Man, using the power I'd been saddled with by the bite of a radioactive spider for good. Did I have another power I hadn't even considered? The power to influence people without the threat of bodily harm? The power to use my brain—a not inconsiderably powerful organ, I had always liked to believe—to come up with good ideas and ways to implement them?

Sitting in my comfortable apartment with my talented and beautiful wife, I thought I had things pretty good. Even if I had just dined on a third-grade lunch staple. At least I hadn't washed it down with milk out of a little carton that I drank through a miniature straw.

And to be perfectly fair, I didn't just battle the occasional super villain. I also took on muggers, thieves, murderers—any criminal who crossed my path. As a politician, though, what if I could address the root causes of crime: poverty, addiction, economic injustice, hopelessness? Wouldn't that have a greater overall impact? And one that could save lives, without endangering my wife and my beloved aunt?

I wasn't going to make any rash decisions about it today. But I also wasn't going to write it off out of hand, like I had thought I would that morning. If there was a chance that I could make a difference to society and at the same time quell the violence that lived in me, become a person of peace, I had to give it fair consideration.

Not right at the moment, however. I didn't want MJ hanging around the apartment too much longer. And now that our high-end lunches were done, we had a little more smooching to get out of the way.

Before I could run for president, or even dogcatcher (although for as many times as I had heard that cliché, I had never once seen "dogcatcher" appear on any ballot), I still had another job to do. That evening I was back in the upper elevations of Manhattan, trawling for bad guys and keeping an eye open for Carrion. So far, it had been a quiet night. That, however, was always subject to change.

When it did change, it was not at all what I expected.

Generally, I kept my attention directed downward. Most crime took place at street level, and even if it was higher than that, it was seldom all the way up where I was. Not much to steal on rooftops, after all.

But I heard a soft whirring sound, above me. And dropping fast, out of the clouds and toward Manhattan. My spider-senses didn't kick in, so I didn't necessarily see it as a threat—but then, Carrion didn't set them off either, so they weren't infallible. Since 2001, all New Yorkers' hearts quickened when they heard anything unusual in the sky. I was no different. I got on a rooftop, braced for anything, and waited for it to show itself.

A S.H.I.E.L.D. jump-jet buzzed toward me, making no more noise than a fan set on low, on one of those warm days in early spring when you don't dare turn it up higher because you know there are lots of hotter days to come and you don't want to spoil yourself too soon.

The thing landed on the flat roof, kicking up no more dust than a handful of pigeons and depositing far less waste. Its engines settled to a low whirr and a hatch opened up. From the illuminated interior, Julia Darst stepped out, wearing a tight black leather bodysuit. She could have graced the front page of a fetish magazine, except they might have had a hard time with the weaponry strapped and belted around her. Or not.

"Spider-Man," she said. She pulled off a flight helmet and shook out her short blond hair. "It's good to see you."

"And you. Is meeting like this a coincidence, or do you come to this roof often?"

"My first time," she said. "Thanks for finding one that had enough room for us to land."

"You were looking for me?" I realized that wasn't the truly interesting question. "You found me?" One tiny spider in the big, big city.

"You'd be surprised what we can find."

"I don't think I want to know. What's up?"

"Our Pennsylvania facility had an unexpected visitor earlier," she said, lowering her voice in case anyone in the upper floors of the building might be listening in. "I thought you should know."

"Who was it?"

"We have a special vault there," she said, not actually addressing my question. "We mostly keep books and other forms of texts there. Magical stuff. Dangerous stuff, in the wrong hands. And with some of these, there aren't any right hands."

I'd heard rumors about that collection in the past, although I hadn't known where it was. "Okay."

"Well, our security cameras caught Carrion inside it. He had apparently teleported in, and he hovered above the floor so he didn't set off pressure alarms, but we spotted him anyway. I know you're looking for him."

"I am indeed. Did he get away with anything?"

"One book. But it's a doozy. A little number called the *Darkhold*."

I had heard of that, too. You could never tell which stories about it were myth and which were true, but even the most mundane ones were pretty terrifying. "That's not good."

"You've always been a master of understatement. No, it's not good. But there's a twist."

"Beautiful. Like it wasn't bad enough already."

"Like I said, our cameras showed us that someone was in the vault. It looked like Carrion. Some of our agents rushed the vault, but he killed them with that red dust he carries."

"Sorry to hear that."

"Not half as sorry as I was." Her voice caught a little, and I had the sense that she had been friends with at least some of them. "Still all signs point to Carrion, because that's kind of a trademark of his."

"I don't get where this is going. We know Carrion's on the loose again—"

"Here's the thing. We don't just have cameras on that vault. It's too important. We have all kinds of detectors on it, all the time. Nobody goes in there without having all kinds of biometrics read. Gait, stance, facial recognition, body temperature, energy signature, stuff I'm not even authorized to tell you about."

"But you're going to tell me something. . . ."

"If you shut up and let me. From those biometrics, we got a surprising result—a match to someone who's in our system. Remember Stanley Carter?"

"Carter? Sin-Eater? Of course."

"The very same."

"He's dead. I saw him die."

"He *is* dead. No denying that. But he was in our vault."

"So he's in cahoots with Carrion."

"Spider-Man, there was only one . . . um, person . . . in that vault. Carter *is* Carrion."

Mary Jane will tell you it takes a lot to leave me speechless. Julia had accomplished it, however. I didn't doubt the engineering and scientific geniuses who made S.H.I.E.L.D.'s toys, but I was there when Stan Carter died. It wasn't some abstract thing to me—I had held his body in my arms. And as far as I knew, he was one of the few people in New York who had never been cloned.

Julia took advantage of my stunned silence to continue. "This isn't a guess, Spider-Man. I don't know how it happened, but that was Stan Carter in there. He helped design the vault, before that whole unfortunate incident with the experimental drug that backfired on him. The other people who worked on its design and construction are all still alive, and working for S.H.I.E.L.D. They've all been questioned, and none of them have given any of the vault's specs away—according to our best lie detector technology, anyway. Carter is the only one who's not accounted for—except for being dead, of course. He knew how to get past the vault's security. We have some pretty good tricks in there, and he avoided them all. That wasn't chance. It was Carter."

"I'm not arguing with you," I finally managed to say. "It's just . . . it's weird."

"I thought weird was your stock in trade. That get-up you wear . . . "

"Let's not get into a fashion debate, leather girl."

"Point taken."

"I don't suppose while you were buzzing around looking for me you happened to spot Carrion. Or Carter, whoever."

"Correct," Julia said. "Haven't seen him. We couldn't even follow him out of the vault, once he teleported away. He's just smoke."

"Yeah, I've had the same problem. Got any more anvils to drop on my head, Julia?"

"That seems like plenty for now."

"Yeah. Plenty. Thanks."

Julia wasn't much for small talk. We said good-bye, and she got back in the jump-jet and it took off, and I sat down on the edge of the roof with my feet dangling over the side.

Stan Carter was dead.

But Stan Carter had a stammer, in the last months of his life. And a limp. I was responsible for that. Carrion didn't have a visible limp, but he stammered, and none of the previous Carrions had. Carter had also been a S.H.I.E.L.D. agent, and every S.H.I.E.L.D. agent went through rigorous combat training, and this Carrion had thrown moves at me that none of the other Carrions had known. Those moves would have been second nature to Stan Carter.

Stan had ended up with the short end of the stick, throughout his last years. He had volunteered for an experimental S.H.I.E.L.D. program that, as Julia had said, backfired in a big way. The violent rages it caused had ended his S.H.I.E.L.D. career and launched him into a series of problems with alcohol and mental health. Those issues, along with a twisted religious background that played into them, led him to become Sin-Eater, and to kill people he considered sinners. Including my friend, police captain Jean DeWolff. I was there when Carter's life slipped away, taken by a rain of bullets from the guns of police officers. He had "threatened" them with a gun of his own—a gun he had never even loaded. Carter wanted to die, by the end. I'm not sure I ever knew a more haunted man.

Could he really be back?

On the other hand, why did I doubt it? I had seen some strange things in my time. Resurrection might have been near the top of the list, but it wasn't the absolute pinnacle. Maybe I just didn't want to believe it.

After all, Carrion was bad enough. Carrion with Stan Carter's training and background—and Carter's madness—was worse. *That* Carrion, in possession of the *Darkhold*?

That I didn't even want to contemplate.

17

HIS HOUSE WAS quiet, the way he liked it. When he turned on the TV, which was seldom, he kept the volume low. Same with the radio. He didn't like today's music anyway, and the voices of talk radio were always so strident, so angry. If there had been talk radio back in his glory days, it would have been interesting to hear what would have been said about the Surgeon. Just like the tabloids, he expected, they would have demanded more urgent police action, a resolution to the mystery.

Like the tabloids, they would have been disappointed. Or perhaps not—the tabloids always sold more papers when there was a Surgeon story on the front page. That would have been the same for radio, he guessed, only it would have been more listeners tuning in, and therefore more advertising sold, or else higher prices for the same ads. Alive and on the loose, he was better for them than captured or dead.

He didn't care about any of that now. The Surgeon had retired, and the impulse that had almost driven him to attack the state trooper on the Parkway had only been a temporary thing. He still noticed all the women out there with sickness growing inside them and wished he could help, but he knew he couldn't. He had grown old, and he liked his quiet life. He lived in his old house where the memories were strong, where he could still almost smell his patients, that aroma of living tissue and bodies in full function, so thick you could almost lean on it. Their essence hung around after so many years, aroma-ghosts, he supposed, that only he could detect.

He had kept a few souvenirs. He supposed most of them did, those people they called serial killers now. He knew they would apply that term to him, even though it wasn't completely accurate—his purpose had been to heal, not to kill, and it wasn't his fault that only death could defeat some forms of disease. But they would call him a serial killer and in the most basic, wrongheaded sense, they would be correct. He didn't try to deny that, and he knew there were things he had in common with others, with what he considered run-of-the-mill killers, and keeping his little reminders was one of them.

With the house empty and quiet, he felt safe taking them out. He had been thinking a lot about those days lately, and the souvenirs called to him from their wooden box at the back of his closet. Someday he would die, and his house would be emptied out, and whoever found the wooden box would open it and wonder at the contents. Perhaps the right conclusions would be drawn, and perhaps not. He would be beyond caring.

He unlocked the box and opened the lid. The items inside were contained in small glass bottles, corked tight. They had shrunk and shriveled over the years, turned black, and it was only from their mostly triangular shapes, and his own vivid memories, that he could still tell what they had been.

The Surgeon had never wanted his patients to tell anyone who had healed them. He didn't want sick people beating down his door looking for cures, and he knew the authorities wouldn't understand anyway. It may have been redundant, considering the condition of his patients when he left them, but there was something to be said for symbolism, wasn't there? So before he took the patients from his workspace, he cut off the tips of their tongues and corked them into glass bottles, and then he put those bottles in his wooden lockbox. Without tongues, his patients could not tell where they had been, or with whom.

He had written a few letters on each bottle. Not really code, but nothing that would be understood by the casual observer. He wrote the initials of the cross streets closest to where he had found the patient—like this one, Park Avenue and Fifty-ninth Street, which he had jotted down as PAFS. He knew what it meant, that was the important thing. And looking at the letters reminded him of that long-ago summer's evening. Music had come from every window, it seemed, cars and apartments alike, all open and spilling song into the air. Stars had glimmered in the slices of sky visible between the city canyons. The patient had worn a red dress, tight across the bodice and flaring at the hips, and when she walked those hips swung from side to side like the arm of a metronome, and her skin had been olive-tinted, as soft as skin could be, and her hair was dark brown and loose down her back.

The sickness had been strong in her. He remembered the pleasure he took in driving it out. Looking at the small triangle of black tongue, he felt it all over again. Wouldn't it be a joy to do it again, to help just one more needful, deserving person?

Just one . . .

Sunday morning the demonstration had ballooned to three or four times its original size. People had seen the reports on TV, or on the websites of the *Bugle* and other newspapers even before their print editions hit the streets, and they had responded. I knew Vincent's case wasn't unique, but I guess I didn't understand just how common it was. As I moved through the crowd, I heard story after story, people telling about how their insurance company had denied their claims, or refused to cover them at all, or paid out only a tiny portion of what had been promised. I heard about people who couldn't afford health insurance at all because the premiums had climbed into the stratosphere. Most of those in the crowd didn't appear poor, they just looked like regular folks. And they were fed up.

The mob spilled into the street. Police had surrounded it, and occasionally one of them would bark something into a bull horn about not blocking traffic. For the most part, they seemed resigned, knowing they'd have to stick around in case of trouble but not really expecting any. The demonstrators were passionate, but their ire was directed at New York Health & Life—at all insurance companies, really—and it being Sunday, the NYH&L offices were once again closed.

Mary Jane met me there. She looked weary, and I asked her about it. "Rehearsals are going okay," she said. "I mean, we're really solid. Everybody's got their lines, and the blocking—technically, we're there. We're starting to really act now, you know what I mean? Emotionally. And it's a difficult piece, so everybody's a little raw."

"So when you got back to your luxury hotel, you didn't sleep well? The maids forget to put the chocolates on your pillow at turn-down?"

"As long as they pick up the empty bottles from the parking lot, I'm happy," she said. "I don't know if it was that. Partly, I guess. The energy level from being onstage and going through that kind of emotional trauma—it's hard to just leave it behind. And there's still some of that nonsense I told you about before going on. I feel like I'm doing a good job, and I'm definitely tapping into some feelings from deep inside myself. But I'm still getting some of that 'you're so pretty, what could you know about real pain?' flack."

I had a quick mental flash of delivering some real pain to anyone who would say that to MJ. She was pretty, but she wasn't shallow, and she had been through more than many people could survive. MJ and Aunt May were my rocks, the forces that kept me as close to stable as I could be.

Because MJ was so solid, though, I had to let her handle the jerks in the cast on her own. Spider-Man could knock heads together, but MJ would resent it if he did.

"That just stinks," I said.

"I know. It's not just that, though. I was all alone and lonely when I finally did get back to the motel. And when I'm not with you, I worry about you that much more."

"It's only for a few more days, I'm sure," I said. "I've got some new information on you-know-who. I'll be able to track him down."

"Sooner the better. Now that I'm used to sleeping beside you, Tiger, it doesn't work so good without you there."

"I know what you mean, MJ."

Someone grabbed my arm as we weaved through the protesters. I had met the guy once, I think—he was the son of one of Aunt May and Claudene Slown's friends. "Peter," he said, "Awesome turnout today!"

"It is, isn't it?"

"Vinny said it's all because of you. You ever think about running for mayor?"

He had a broad smile on his narrow face, and I was pretty sure he was kidding. That's how I chose to take it, at any rate. "I think I'm a few million bucks short for that one. Or is it billion?"

"Maybe it's time a working Joe was mayor here. Bring a different perspective to City Hall."

I put an arm around Mary Jane's shoulders. "And a little spunk to Gracie Mansion," I said.

MJ snarled at me. On her, it looked good. Scary, but good. "You hate spunk."

"That's Lou Grant," I said. "You've been watching too much TV Land."

"You, Ed Asner—I always get you confused. Especially when you threaten to get all political on me."

"Hey, I didn't bring it up."

"I'm just saying," the guy whose name I couldn't remember said. "Nice job, Pete."

"Thanks." I let MJ lead me away from him. Gratefully.

MJ needed a new pillow. She didn't like the ones at the motel, and she had needed one at home for months anyway. Somehow the demands of work and webslinging kept getting in the way, though, and she had gone without. No longer. Today we were out and about and had no particular agenda after wearing out some shoe leather outside the insurance company. The day was a little cooler than the previous ones had been—far from cold, but with that hint of sharpness in the air that told you that autumn would show up after all, and probably soon. It was a glorious day for walking through the city with the woman I love.

Without really discussing it, we wound up outside the big Macy's on Herald Square. "Pillow?" I asked.

"Right now?"

"Pillow shopping," I clarified, although she had understood me perfectly well. "We're here. That's the world's largest store, or so I've heard. Surely they'll have a pillow."

"Surely they will."

"Shall we?"

"Oh, let's."

Hand in hand, we went into the store. As always, there was something a little thrilling and a little terrifying about it. The place was big enough to house ten restaurants, including two Au Bon Pains. It was a ten-story temple to commerce. Somehow I could always find at least one thing on every floor I couldn't live without—although, to be perfectly accurate, on some floors those were things I just wanted to see Mary Jane in—but to buy even that one thing on every level would set me back more than I made in a week. Or a month.

"Pillows would be where?" I asked.

"Ninth floor." MJ knew this Macy's like she knew our apartment. Not that she spent a lot more time there than I did, at least to my knowledge. She just seemed to *get* it in a way I never had. I was a slave to the directory, and could still get lost.

"Elevator?"

She scoffed. "Going up the escalators is half the fun! You miss too much on the elevators."

I wondered about her definition of fun, but went along with it anyway. Trying to resist the urge to possess all that I saw, I followed her up past menswear and sportswear and shoes, past furs and more sportswear and more shoes. In the higher elevations the escalators switched from modern steel and glass to wood, giving the store a certain Alpine charm. I wondered if we'd run into guys in *lederhosen* accompanied by St. Bernard dogs. I wondered if the altitude gave people nosebleeds. I realized I was asking these things out loud, and Mary Jane was pretending she didn't know me.

On the eighth floor, making the transfer from up escalator to up escalator, the first one came at me. I'd had the sensation of being watched since we had entered the store, but I figured it was just my natural paranoia combined with the fact that, without doubt, we had been watched since we entered the store. You didn't have that much merchandise packed into a single building without taking careful security measures. And my spider-sense hadn't kicked in, so whoever was watching me wasn't a threat.

Until he was.

He came out from behind a display of silverware, although I was sure Macy's had a classier name for it. I guessed that he had not worn the robe and white mask into the store, but he wore them now.

The uniform of the Cabal of Scrier. I knew it well. My onetime best friend, Harry Osborn, had managed to become the Cabal's head for a time. Those days were over, and my recent encounters with them had been infrequent.

But this guy came straight at us, arms out like he wanted to hug me. He didn't have a weapon in his hands. Which did not mean I trusted him. "Go downstairs, MJ," I whispered. "Get outside, and wait for me at Penn Station. If I'm not there thirty minutes after you, get out of town and wait for me at your hotel."

Her green eyes were wide and liquid. She wanted to argue with me. But she didn't. She went straight to the down escalator, at a fast walk.

I turned and ran toward women's coats.

The Scrier followed. And he had friends—three more of them emerged from hiding and came at me.

From the escalator, I heard MJ shriek. Like she was startled, not frightened. Still, I didn't like it.

I figured the store had cameras all over the sales floors. I couldn't just duck into a rack of coats and yank off my street clothes, because at some point, a security guard would look at the video and see it happen. But I thought there might be a way around it.

Against the far wall was an employee access door, leading to the storerooms and corridors that customers never saw. I dove through a rack of coats, came out the other side, and darted through the doors. A middle-aged woman carrying half a dozen winter coats saw me, yelped, and dropped them on the floor. "Sorry," I tossed over my shoulder as I ran past her. "Men's room emergency!"

Which was not remotely true, but I hoped it would keep her from asking questions. I hurried down a hallway until I saw a swinging door leading into a storeroom. I went through the door and crouched behind a shelving unit, tearing off Peter Parker's clothes and shoving them under the bottom shelf. Then I pulled my mask up over my face.

As Spider-Man, I went back out into the hallway

and ran in the other direction. The hallway angled around the building, and I came out through a door far away from the one I had entered. With any luck, whatever guard was watching the video wouldn't see the feed from both cameras and put it all together.

The eighth floor was crawling with Scriers wondering where Peter Parker had gone. They weren't harassing the employees or customers, which didn't mean those people weren't thoroughly freaked out by their presence. My concern was below, though—whatever had made MJ cry out.

"Hey, ghost-faces!" I cried as I ran for the down escalator. "Betcha can't catch someone who's really trying!"

"Ignore him!" one of the Scriers shouted. "He isn't the one we want!"

Ouch. I'm no huge fan of rejection at the best of times. Being dissed by a gang of criminals in funny clothes, though? Especially stinging.

I didn't want to play footsie with them, but I didn't want them to tear the eighth floor apart looking for Peter Parker and endangering innocents, especially when I knew they wouldn't find Parker, and they might put two and two together even if store security didn't.

So I did what I had to do to get their attention. I waded into the thick of them. "I'm talking to you, Bozo," I said to one. I smacked him, openhanded, knocking him sprawling into four others. "I'm talking to all of you."

"Hey!" one of them said, scrambling to keep his balance. "You can't do—"

"Funny, I thought sure I was." I tapped him on the

chin and he collapsed like a Macy's parade balloon the day after Thanksgiving. "Tag, you're it!" I said. I worked my way toward the escalator, tossing enough of them around to make them mad and forget what they had come for. At least, that was the goal.

The down escalator was full of frightened people, mostly staff and customers trying to escape the chaos on eight. I raced around to the up side, and it was jammed too, mostly with Scriers looking to join in on the action. I had no idea there were so many Scriers in New York, much less in the store. Maybe it was Krazy Kultists' Discount Daze at Macy's and I had just missed the signs downstairs.

MJ was somewhere down there, though, and since they had targeted Peter Parker, not Spider-Man, they might know who she was, too. Since I couldn't squeeze onto the escalator's treads, I jumped to its ceiling and climbed down that way, my hands and feet sticking to the slope. That gave me the opportunity to reach down and flip off the hoods of some of the Scriers going up, which was entertaining because they took their goofy getups so seriously.

I finally spotted MJ on the second floor. She was fine, still heading for the exit, along with what seemed like hundreds of customers. The store was approaching panic, and there were so many people inside that it could be dangerous. I dropped to the floor and tried out my most commanding voice. "Proceed in an orderly fashion to the exits!" I shouted, feeling more like a flight attendant than I ever had. "There's no danger, and nothing to be afraid of! These people are a nuisance, nothing more!"

Some people heard me and calmed a little. Others saw me and freaked out all the more, because after all, I'm a PUBLIC MENACE, if you believe the *Bugle*'s banner headlines.

But then store personnel with bull horns showed up, and they started to call out evacuation commands. The fleeing customers responded better to them than to me, and that was fine. All I wanted was for innocent people to get out of the way, because there appeared to be a hundred or so Scriers in the place, and if they wanted trouble, I was happy to oblige.

But not on the second floor. I wanted to be higher up, so most of the customers and staff would already be out of harm's way. Which meant taking to the ceiling again, reversing course. Once again, it was comical to watch the Scriers reacting to me, switching from going down to up against the motion of the escalators and the tide of their fellow cultists.

On the fourth floor, I staked out a position and held my ground. Scriers surrounded me. A few of them pulled guns from under their robes. But others spoke up, insisting that I wasn't part of their task and that engaging with me would be a distraction, possibly leading to disaster. They were after the man named Parker, and he had apparently slipped away in all the commotion.

I can't deny that a sinking sense of disappointment filled me as they filed out. Those guys bugged me, and I wouldn't have minded knocking a few of their heads together. But except for pulling guns in Macy's—and for all I knew, those might have been perfectly legal guns—they hadn't harmed anyone or broken any laws. They were obnoxious, and they had caused a panic, but I couldn't prove that was their intent. In fact, it didn't seem to have been—it looked like they really had just meant to throw a scare into Peter and the crowds had simply reacted to the presence of a large number of masked and hooded freaks in their midst.

Several of them shot me unfriendly glances, or so it looked, although with the masks it was hard to tell. I knew the cult was essentially a criminal organization, so it was no surprise that I didn't have a lot of fans among its membership.

When they were gone, I performed a reversal of my earlier maneuver, heading back into the storage room through one door and becoming Peter Parker again. Then I had to wait until the store began filling up with people before I went out, through a different door. While I waited, I called MJ on her cell phone to tell her I was fine, but would be delayed a little longer.

"I'll head back to the store," she said. "Penn Station has a peculiar reek to it today anyway."

"Call me when you get here, then."

"I will. And by the way . . ."

"Yes?"

"We still need to find me a pillow."

18

HE SUPPOSED HE shouldn't have been surprised.

Scrier Everett reported that when numerous Scriers tried to swarm Peter Parker, he eluded them, and then Spider-Man showed up so they aborted the attempt.

He could have told them Parker and Spider-Man were one and the same, but he wanted to hold that secret close for now. There might come a time when it would be to his advantage to reveal it, but that time hadn't come yet.

At this moment, a couple of Scriers were breaking into Parker's apartment. They weren't there to steal anything, just to upend some furniture, pull out some drawers, make a mess. The idea was to make Parker feel violated, off balance—to let him know that his life would never be smooth sailing again, for as long as Carrion let it continue. The idea was to cause Parker mental anguish, to make him suffer before he died. He didn't know if Parker kept spare Spider-Man gear in the apartment, but if he did and the Scriers found it, then he would lose that particular advantage. But it would certainly throw an additional scare into Parker.

It would be a delicate balance. Parker couldn't suffer so much that he welcomed death. He still had to cling to life, in order to make his death enjoyable to Carrion.

Not to me, the part of him that was Stanley Carter thought. He tried to wrench control of his mind back from the others. It was Miles Warren who wanted Parker dead. Stan Carter had never had anything against Peter Parker, and he had forgiven Spider-Man for the damage he'd done, understanding that as Sin-Eater he had gone too far, had been killing relative innocents, and had to be stopped.

You have always been the weakest of us, Carter.

Not physically, but you lack will, resolve.

You lack the courage to fulfill our destiny.

"No!" Carrion shouted. He was in Carter's uncle Emory's house, in his little room there. He had covered the mirror with a sheet so he wouldn't have to see himself, wouldn't have to look at the ghoulish body he inhabited now. When he became cogent enough to consider his plight, it made him sick. He had been brought back from death—a death he had sought out, at that—and made to exist inside the repulsive form of a murderous being, a not-quite-human *thing*. As if that wasn't bad enough, the thing's primary goal was the destruction of Spider-Man. Certainly there had been times in Carter's life that he had felt the same way, but in his later days he had learned better, had come to recognize Spider-Man as someone to be respected, even appreciated.

Spider-Man is the enemy.

Spider-Man killed our Gwen.

"No he didn't!" Carrion yelled. But what did he know about it, really? Spider-Man denied it. Didn't most killers deny their crimes, though? Especially someone like him, who claimed to fight for law and justice? Hadn't he done the same thing, when the demons inside him drove him to murder?

He's guilty!

Carrion knew—Carter knew—better than most, that any man could become a killer under the right circumstances. Spider-Man wasn't immune to that. To the contrary, with his incredible strength it would be hard *not* to kill on occasion.

Spider-Man is guilty!

Anyway, Warren and Allen and McBride were smart, he couldn't deny that. Carter had been an intelligent man, too, in life. All together, they could hardly be wrong.

He tried to push the others away again but he got confused, about who he was pushing and why. The confusion made him angry. He balled his fist and hit the bed he was sitting on, then hit his own thigh, hard. It hurt. That made him angrier. He stood up, paced around the room. It was small, confining, like a prison cell. Or a coffin.

Against one wall was an old dresser, covered with things that weren't his. At the back of it a sheet had been draped over something. He snatched it away. Behind it was a mirror, and in the mirror he saw his face, with yellow skin and lines so deep they looked like fissures in the earth, wrinkles around his mouth like used crepe paper, jagged, uneven teeth, and deep-set jaundiced eyes.

He was lovely.

He was strong.

He had a task to accomplish.

He was Carrion, and he had much to do.

The Scriers told Carrion where they had seen Spider-Man. The ones watching Parker's apartment reported that he had not returned there. He started outside the Macy's store and tried to locate his enemy. He tapped into the minds of people on the street (ugly things, people's minds, like sewers running with frustration, rage, jealousy, and hatred—sometimes he was not so different from them, after all) to find out if they had seen Spider-Man anywhere. He teleported around the city in short bursts. Every now and then he sprinkled red dust down on some unsuspecting fool, hoping to draw the wall-crawler out. Lights flickered on—streetlamps, bulbs in brownstones and high-rise condos and three-story brick row houses, floodlights on playgrounds, the neon of restaurants, bars, and nightclubs—summoning the night.

He would find Spider-Man. He would find him tonight.

And when he did, he would hurt him. Not kill him, not quite yet. But he thought the time had come to break some bones. Maybe the sight of Spider-Man confined to a wheelchair would amuse him.

Dash Garrett had known Stan Carter. Not well, but when you worked for S.H.I.E.L.D. for a long time, you met a lot of your brother and sister S.H.I.E.L.D. operatives. But it was a little strange to be riding in a jump-jet looking for a guy with whom he had broken bread—stranger still when that guy had been in the grave for a good long while now.

They covered the five boroughs, figuring that Carrion had business in New York and hadn't skipped town yet. He was a hard one to track because of his unique nature and abilities—even when their instruments caught a trace of his energy signature, by the time they reached the scene he had vanished again. He seemed to be moving around, mostly in Manhattan, as if he was searching for something just as elusive as he was.

He and Julia Darst had settled into their seats, which were surprisingly comfortable for such a compact, utilitarian vehicle, and silently watched the city lights pass by beneath their windows. He had known Julia since his first month with the agency, and the two had even dated briefly, before she decided they had no future together. He wouldn't have minded trying again. She was gorgeous and smart and damn near as strong as he was, which he found incredibly appealing. She seemed intent on keeping their relationship on a strictly professional footing, however.

"Agent Darst? Agent Garrett?" A young operative had

stepped into the passenger compartment. His name was Jenks, and his function on board wasn't much different from a flight attendant's on a commercial airliner—he fetched beverages, carried messages from the cockpit and technicians to the passengers, and presumably would help people fasten their seat belts if they didn't know how.

"Yes?" Julia said.

"We have a lock on the subject." The kid said it in slow, measured tones. Dash thought he could have shown a little more excitement.

"A lock?" Dash asked.

"Yes, sir."

That was different from a trace. A lock meant they *had* him.

"Move in as close as we can," Julia said, with a sharp look at Dash, her right eyebrow arched. This was her mission; he was backup and needed to remember his place. "Ready the plasma burst cannon."

"Roger that." He ducked back into the cockpit. Dash heard the murmur of voices, and then Jenks came back.

"We're closing on him. Plasma burst ready."

"On low," Julia said. The plasma burst cannon fired an energy projectile that could take out a building—a big one—on full power. Carrion might be a tough opponent, but even on the lowest power, one of those projectiles might not leave enough of him to scrape up with a spoon.

"Right," Jenks said.

Julia looked out the window. The city was much closer than it had been a minute ago, Dash noted. "How far out are we?"

"Two thousand feet and closing," Jenks said. He may have been dispassionate, but he was efficient.

"How solid is the lock?"

"Ninety-three percent."

"Any civilians present?"

"Not that we can detect."

At two thousand feet, the jump-jet's instruments were capable of detecting a stray rodent within twenty feet of Carrion. Maybe even a flea on the rat's back. Dash knew the kid was hedging. Carrion was staying put, and he was alone.

"Fire," Julia said.

Jenks relayed the command. The whisper-quiet operation of the jump-jet was interrupted by a soft thump. A moment later, the sound of an explosion reached them along with the flaring of white-hot light.

Everybody stared out the windows as the jump-jet sank toward the city. A concussion wave from the explosion rocked the jet, but it continued on course, dropping hard into a cloud of smoke and debris.

Dash saw a paved parking lot, cratered now. A couple of cars had been close to the target and were blown to pieces, with flames licking some of the bits.

In the middle of it all stood Carrion, staring at the ship with fury in his eyes.

"How the hell—?" Julia began.

"He should be dead," Dash said. "Nobody could survive that."

"Clearly *someone* could," Julia snapped. "Prepare to engage the subject! Bring this machine down!"

There were seven combat operatives on board. They had waited patiently in the back, knowing the chances of seeing any action were slim to none. No one wanted to mix it up hand-to-hand with Carrion, and everyone knew the plasma burst cannon would finish him off.

As happened so often in life, everyone was wrong.

The jump-jet nestled down on a cushion of air in the street about fifty yards from Carrion. The combat ops rushed out first, bristling with enough weapons to wage a small-scale war. Julia and Dash pulled down visors and went out behind them.

Carrion hadn't teleported away—he still looked like he wanted to dish out some hurt in exchange for having been bombed—but he had moved closer to an occupied building. There was a fish market downstairs that looked closed at the moment, but that didn't mean it was empty. Upstairs were apartments, and people had gone to the windows (some shattered by the plasma burst) and watched the action from there. Dash tried to wave them away, but few of them paid him any attention. He was just a guy in a helmet and a dark bodysuit. The real action was the yellow man wearing rags.

The last thing Julia had said before the jump-jet landed was an instruction to deal with Carrion using "decisive measures." In other words, don't mess around— take the freak out.

The combat ops stopped about twenty yards from Carrion, forming up into two ranks, three men down on one knee in front, two more men and two women behind them. They all aimed assault rifles at him and opened fire.

Dash watched as the bullets slammed into Carrion—or should have. But he shimmered and suddenly the slugs pocked the brick wall behind him, sending little clouds of dust and cinders into the air.

Dash aimed his own assault weapon and fired a round at Carrion's head. A round containing drugs developed in S.H.I.E.L.D. labs that could neutralize the powers of many superpowered beings. His shot achieved the same result as the others—nothing at all. The loaded round smashed into the bricks, which would be without superpowers for the next thirty minutes.

Carrion grinned, a sight Dash knew would haunt him for the rest of his life.

Then the ghastly being took a couple steps backward and disappeared.

"Do you have a read on him?" Julia barked into her helmet-mounted comm unit.

"He's still close by." Jenks's voice, from on board the jump jet. "He's inside the building."

Inside. No more plasma bursts, then—too many innocents in there. Dash wondered if he had planned this whole encounter—drawing them in by making himself a target in an open area, then switching gears on them by moving inside the nearest occupied structure.

He wanted to shout out commands, but he held his tongue and let Julia do it. He didn't have to wait long.

"Inside, people! Door-to-door! He'll kill anyone who gets in his way, so we don't have much time!"

The combat ops rushed the building's front door and went inside, using a tactical entry formation drilled into them in S.H.I.E.L.D. training. Dash and Julia brought up the rear. The back of Dash's neck tingled. He wanted to scratch it under his helmet, but couldn't. Somewhere in this building, Carrion was waiting for them. He couldn't imagine a scenario where that wasn't bad news.

"Location?" Julia asked.

"Can't pinpoint it," Jenks said. "He's moving around."

"Door-to-door!" Julia repeated.

Two of the operatives crashed through the glass door of the fish market, releasing the pent-up seafood odor onto the sidewalk. The rest streamed into the tiny lobby of the apartment building—cheap tile on the floor, streaked walls, mailboxes that had been broken into so many times the doors didn't close anymore. A dark staircase led up from there. The sound of boots on the wooden stairs was like rippling thunder.

Dash followed the team and Julia up, chambering another power-inhibitor round. No way to know if it would work on Carrion, but if he could manage to hit the guy while he was solid, he could at least find out. On the landing was a light fixture, but the bulb had been smashed out, probably sometime around the Second World War, from the looks of it, and never replaced.

Dash's brief pause while he glanced at the light fixture might have saved his life.

19

CARRION APPEARED AT the head of the stairs with red dust trailing through the clenched fingers of both hands. "Welcome to my world," he said, drawing back his arms. The combat operatives opened fire, but even as they did (Dash, hearing the staccato bursts of automatic weapons, cringed at the idea of the people hiding behind flimsy wooden doors and walls that had been thrown together on the cheap decades before), Carrion hurled the double handful of dust down the stairs at the ops.

A couple of heavily armored men on the lower steps lurched backward, trying to dodge the dust. One of them collided with Dash, who hadn't left the landing yet, knocking him down the first short half flight of stairs toward the lobby. His legs flew out from under him and he cartwheeled backward, catching the action in quick bursts through the dim glow of a bulb somewhere higher up in the staircase—Julia, just above the

landing, ducking away from the dust and taking the
weight of one of the female ops on her back, a couple of
the others throwing their hands to their faces or necks
as dust billowed beneath their helmets' visors. Dash
landed hard, head facing down, and skidded the rest of
the way in unchecked free fall.

By the time he got to his feet, some of the operatives were already down, on hands and knees choking
or even, in one case, sprawled on the landing, one hand
slapping the floor at an ever-slowing pace. Julia was
pushing the other woman off her back, trying to squirm
out from beneath dead weight. Three of the operatives
seemed to have survived, while the others were dying
quick but painful deaths.

"Is he . . . ?"

"He's gone," Julia said.

"Get down from there," Dash said. "There might be
some of that dust floating around."

Julia glanced back up the stairs, as if she could will
Carrion into reappearing. But she nodded wearily and
helped one of the remaining ops down the stairs. The
other two had joined Dash at the bottom under their
own power.

"We're coming out," Julia said into her comm unit.
"Take this building out as soon as we're clear."

"Julia, it's full of innocent people," Dash said.

"Acceptable losses." Her voice could have refrozen
the polar ice caps. She started toward the door. "Jenks,
confirm my command. I want this place vaporized."

Jenks didn't answer. "Now what?" Julia asked. She

pushed out into the night. The two ops who had gone into the fish market were just emerging, shaking their heads.

"Jenks?" Julia demanded. The anxiety in her voice matched the way Dash felt. He broke into a run, Julia and the combat troops right behind him.

The jump-jet sat where they left it—but it was no longer alone. Instead, people wearing dark hooded cloaks over milk-white face masks swarmed it. Some of them were dead or bleeding on the pavement— Jenks, the pilot and copilot had fought back, but they weren't as battle-hardened as the others. Dash thought at least a couple of the combat ops should have been left behind—but that was a tough call to make, given the quarry they'd been chasing. He liked to think he would have been smart enough to make that choice, on the grounds that Carrion might as easily have teleported onto the jump-jet instead of staying in the building.

He hadn't challenged Julia's decision, though, and good people had paid the price. He couldn't wash that away with soap and water.

The freaks in the hoods were standing their ground. There were thirty or thirty-five of them, and most carried guns. A couple had heavy armament they must have taken from inside the jump-jet.

Dash figured the S.H.I.E.L.D. agents could take them under ordinary circumstances. But Carrion was still a factor in play, and he could show up at any moment, anywhere he chose.

"Take 'em down!" Julia shouted. She snapped her own

tactical assault rifle into position and squeezed the trigger. Hooded heads exploded. The other ops opened fire, too—but so did the hooded people. The parking lot became a free-fire zone, with no cover except the wreckage of the few cars the plasma burst projectile had destroyed. Dash flattened himself on the pavement and started firing, trying to present as small a target as possible.

He had an idea this whole mess would get worse before it was over.

And he didn't like that idea at all.

Manhattan is rarely a quiet place. To function there, you pretty much have to get used to the bleating of horns, the wail of sirens, the clatter of delivery trucks, the crunching of fenders, even the occasional crack of gunshots and screams of people in trouble.

But when a full-fledged shooting war breaks out, it's hard not to notice. Even for an airborne arachnid with other things on his mind.

I was mostly looking for Carrion, but leaving one eye and one ear open for other varieties of trouble. When I heard what sounded like a bomb going off on the Lower East Side, I started heading that way. When that was followed by the unmistakable bursts of automatic weapons fire, I sped up.

It didn't matter. By the time I arrived, the brief battle was over. Bodies littered a parking lot, S.H.I.E.L.D. agents on one side, Scriers on the other. Just like in high school, I was the last one picked. The confusing part was that the Scriers seemed to have taken control of a

S.H.I.E.L.D. jump-jet, while the S.H.I.E.L.D. agents had been defending a run-down tenement building with a fish market downstairs.

I dropped to the broken pavement, an unpleasant feeling sinking into my bones. Sirens closed in, but I wanted a look around before the police arrived. I ignored the dead Scriers and checked on the bodies of the S.H.I.E.L.D. agents, lifting visors, rolling them over on a couple of occasions.

My hunch was right. Some of the dead had bullet wounds, but others had the decayed flesh common to Carrion's victims. The Scriers hadn't been alone in this massacre.

The next body I checked made me feel like I'd swallowed a bowling ball-size chunk of ice. I had just talked to Julia Darst. She was one of my best friends at S.H.I.E.L.D. I didn't know her that well, but she had always treated me squarely, and I liked her.

She had three holes in her armored bodysuit. Blood seeped from two of them. Ordinary street ammo wouldn't have done that, but if—as it appeared—the Scriers had taken over the S.H.I.E.L.D. jet, there had probably been weapons inside that would.

The ice chunk in my belly would take a long time to melt. The only saving grace was that I was starting to be aware of a burning sensation below it. I recognized that as the fire of vengeance, and it burned hot.

It was past time to remind Carrion of why he should have stayed gone.

I went into the S.H.I.E.L.D. jet and tried to figure

out how to phone home. The control panel defeated me, though—chemistry had always been my strong suit, not avionics. And the sirens were getting closer.

I really didn't want to be found hanging around a couple dozen dead bodies. Time to make myself scarce. I started out of the jet.

And then I heard that now-familiar whirring noise from overhead and saw another one dropping toward me.

By the time the NYPD cruisers screeched onto the scene, S.H.I.E.L.D. was there, establishing a perimeter and examining the scene. A tall African-American agent named Shields—no really, Clarence Shields, he showed me his ID badge—had taken me aside. Some of his compatriots argued jurisdiction with the first cops on the scene, an argument that would no doubt be repeated, possibly with different results, when detectives, a crime scene unit, and police brass showed up. But for now, S.H.I.E.L.D. was winning the turf war, and the cops stayed out of their way.

I told Shields what I had seen. He nodded and listened intently, his expression grim. I explained that I had known Julia, and told him what she had told me about Carrion.

"So you're convinced it was Carrion," he said when I was done.

"Had to be, at least in part. Those agents who weren't shot, but whose bodies are already decayed? They haven't been dead for months or years and still running around in S.H.I.E.L.D. getups. Carrion killed them. That's kind of his trademark."

"Sounds like a real charmer."

"He's a beaut," I said. "And like Julia told me, he used to be with S.H.I.E.L.D."

"I've heard of Stanley Carter. Never met him."

"There was a time when meeting him might not have been so bad. But I mostly knew him as Sin-Eater, when he was a murderer. Now he's even worse."

"I thought you protected New York from creeps like him," Shields said.

"I'm trying. He's just a little hard to get a line on." An idea occurred to me. It had about as much chance of flying as the giant pig MJ and I had seen at the state fair, but I had to give it a shot. "S.H.I.E.L.D. could maybe help, though."

"I believe that's what this crew was doing," Shields said. He sounded a little perturbed.

Not that I blamed him. "Yeah," I said, "they were. But that's not what I mean. I'll take care of Carrion, I just need to know more about him. Or more about Stan Carter, really."

"What do you mean?"

"S.H.I.E.L.D. must have files on the guy. He was a S.H.I.E.L.D. researcher, he volunteered for an experiment that went bad, he turned rogue. S.H.I.E.L.D. must have whole filing cabinets full of information on him. Maybe there's something in there that will help me get a handle on him. Carrion's a strange case—he's never just any one guy, but now he's Miles Warren, Malcolm McBride, and two ex-S.H.I.E.L.D. people, William Allen and Carter. I know them all to some extent, but there might be some aspect of Carter's life I'm not familiar with, something that can help me find Carrion."

"So what, you're asking for access to our personnel files? Not gonna happen."

"There must be something I can see. It's important, Shields." In spite of the circumstances, I almost had to smile when I said his name.

"I'll see what I can do."

"I'd appreciate it."

Three hours later I was sitting at home in front of the computer. During those three hours, while I was waiting for S.H.I.E.L.D., I cleaned up the apartment that someone had trashed. They hadn't left any message that I could find—nothing like the time Carrion had painted on my wall with his red dust. I was convinced he was behind it, and once again, it showed a failure of imagination—how many times could one guy vandalize my home?

I was lucky that's all that had been done. Nine of the people living in the apartment building next to the battleground had been found dead in their homes. Carrion seemed to be getting more murderous by the hour.

Agent Shields had delivered four CDs to a rooftop I had specified. They contained everything from Carter's files that wasn't classified Top Secret or higher. I was privy to his salary, his behavior records (a fellow scientist had complained that he called her "sweetie" once, instead of using her name, which was Hildegard Ungraats. I would have gone to court and changed my name to "Sweetie" if I'd been saddled with that, but apparently she preferred Dr. Ungraats).

I also learned the places Stan Carter had frequented when he had been alive. Bars and restaurants he hung out at, where he bought his groceries, where he lived, where he sent his dry cleaning. Once he had gone rogue, S.H.I.E.L.D. had put a lot of resources into getting to know his habits and patterns. Which was just what I'd been hoping for. If Carrion was comprised of four different guys, maybe the most recent member of the club would have some control over his whereabouts.

I found out that his parents had died when he was nineteen. He'd had a brother who was killed in what looked like a drug deal gone bad, stabbed to death in an alley between West Ninety-fourth and Ninety-fifth. He had only one remaining relative in the area, a bachelor uncle who lived all the way out in Tappan, New Jersey. The uncle, Emory Carter, was a retired school bus driver.

I read on the monitor until I thought my eyeballs would bubble out of my head and down my cheeks. Nowhere did it tell me where Stan Carter might hide out if he was ever brought back to life inside the body of a supervillain. I found that a disappointing lapse on S.H.I.E.L.D.'s part.

Still, I knew more about him than I had before, and I had some places to try. Better than sitting on my tail reading about him. I shut the computer down and hit the rooftops again.

20

I WOULDN'T SAY my plan didn't pan out, but that's just because I hate to admit when I've been wasting time. The fact was, I might as well have been pumping dollars into an arcade video game, for all the good it did at locating Carrion. I skulked around some of Stan Carter's old neighborhoods. I watched people going about their business and felt like a voyeur, especially when they were couples having more fun than Mary Jane and I had for the past few days because they hadn't been threatened by inhuman maniacs.

Stan's favorite eatery had been a diner called Kenny's Hash House on Broadway in Noho. When I went there I found an empty storefront that had most recently been a Japanese import shop, but with the KENNY's sign still painted on the wall above the door. Carter had been dead too long—even if he had been tempted back to Kenny's Hash House (and I had no idea if Carrion needed to eat) he wouldn't have found it there.

He wasn't at his favorite bookstore (the Strand, closed at this hour) or his regular barbershop (also dark—not that Carrion had a lot of hair to cut). He hadn't moved back into any of his former apartments. If Carrion had picked up any of Stan Carter's old habits, I couldn't discover which ones.

Before, Carrion had been finding me regularly. Now that I really burned to put an end to him (I hadn't figured out how yet—I'd have to play that one by ear) I couldn't find him anywhere.

I crouched on a window ledge, eighty stories off the ground, and tried to make my brain function. Where would he hide? Who would know?

That was the right question. The Cabal of Scrier would know. I hadn't been sure at Macy's, but I was after the battle that had claimed Julia Darst's life— somehow, the Scriers were in league with Carrion.

All I had to do was find me some Scriers, and lean on them until they gave him up.

I didn't know precisely how to find any Scriers, either. But they couldn't hide as well as Carrion could.

And then I had one of those brainstorms that remind me that I was considered, once upon a time, a pretty smart guy.

Maybe I could find Scriers, and maybe not.

But they didn't seem to have had much problem finding me. The Peter Parker aspect of me, anyway. It had gradually dawned on me that the nut in the restaurant, with what looked like a little GPS unit, had been using some sort of device to track me. Maybe that's what had brought them to Macy's as well.

If so, they could just use it one more time. Spider-Man moved too fast, and probably at too great an elevation, for them. But if they could find Peter again, then I could follow them home.

I went home long enough to make sure no one had broken in again and to pull some Parker threads over the old red-and-blue. Then I went downstairs the usual way and out onto the street. They had found me uptown once, and down at Macy's the second time. I decided that heading toward downtown was my best bet. I walked at a deliberate pace, as if I had somewhere to be, but not like I was in a big hurry to get there.

By the time I had covered more blocks than most New Yorkers ever do—except when a sudden rainstorm breaks out at rush hour, the subways are too full to breathe, and all of the taxis are suddenly occupied—I realized I had company.

The guy was a lousy tail. Every time I glanced in a store window, there he was behind me. When I bent over to tie my shoe, he literally ducked into a nearby doorway so fast he bumped into a shopkeeper standing outside having a smoke. He wasn't wearing the traditional Cabal hood and mask, but he was so obvious he might as well have been.

I kept walking. Soon there were three of them around me, then six. They weren't trying for subtlety anymore. They knew I had made them and they didn't care. Once again, they didn't attack me, didn't seem intent on hurting me. They were just there. A nuisance.

Except this time I wanted them there.

I made a sudden right turn. There was an alley ahead of me. I sprinted for it and cleared it before the Scriers even reached the corner. Ducking inside, I stripped off the street clothes and webbed them to the bottom of a Dumpster.

By the time the six of them started combing the block looking for Peter Parker, Spider-Man was four stories up, watching them.

They searched for about twenty minutes. A couple of them had handheld gadgets like the guy in the restaurant, and they kept acting like they were getting some message from those gadgets and pointing them into the sky. I'm pretty good at not being seen when I don't want to be, though, and they eventually gave up, deciding that their little Parker-trackers had gone haywire.

They had a minivan—hard-core criminal cultists in a minivan made me laugh so hard I was afraid they'd hear me—parked a few blocks away. They tumbled in, a clown car in reverse.

They hit Bleecker and took it to Fourth, then followed that to Delancey, made the jog at Clinton and headed for the Williamsburg Bridge. I beat them to the bridge once it seemed clear that's where they were going, and kept pace all the way across it, racing along the girders of the upper chord as it made its graceful arc across the East River. On the other side they headed north up Bedford Ave. to McGuinness and stayed on that into Hunter's Point, in Queens. I hitched rides on top of cabs and buses and kept them in sight.

They parked around the corner from an old church. There was a signboard outside it, the kind of thing on which clever phrases would have been posted describing the contents of Sunday's sermon. But this one was blank and looked like it had been for a long time. Even the raised letters spelling out the name of the church had been torn off.

In their hoods and masks, they hurried into the church. The neighborhood was quiet, sparsely inhabited, and most of those who did live there probably stayed inside at night if they could, in hopes of surviving till morning, so the Scriers weren't likely to be observed, but they didn't take any chances. Maybe they were just embarrassed by their sartorial choices.

Once they were inside, I ran to the church wall and scooted up it. A big Gothic structure like this one should have multiple ways in, I figured.

I figured wrong.

The place was locked up tighter than a tycoon's soul. Some of the cultists might have been on the lame side, but the Cabal itself took few chances.

I waited among the battlements and crockets and chimney pots and other seemingly random bits of Gothic ornamentation for about ten minutes. I was starting to think I'd have to just go down and knock on the door when I heard another car approaching. Hanging back, I waited until it parked around the corner from the door, behind the minivan. Two guys got out, dressed in civilian clothes, but then the driver opened the trunk and pulled out some of those flashy Scrier duds.

I moved fast. Off the roof, across the churchyard. I hit them while they were tugging their hoods over their heads. They never saw me coming.

Instead of tossing them in the open trunk, I shoved their unconscious bodies into the backseat of the car and webbed them down. Anyone happening upon them before they came to would probably decide they were involved in something extremely private and leave them alone, especially since I had to borrow one's street clothes. I closed the car up, put my Spider-Man mask into a pocket and tugged on one of their hood and mask ensembles, then strode confidently up to the church door.

It opened as I approached it. I hoped the getup would be my entry card and I wouldn't be expected to know a password. A couple of Scriers gave me the once-over and greeted me. "Welcome, Scrier," they both said.

"Thank you, Scriers," I answered. Seemed to have been the right thing to say. They let me pass and closed the big wooden doors behind me.

The inside of the church smelled like incense and sweat. The weather was still cooling down day by day, but the Scriers all had hooded robes on over their clothing, and the church wasn't cool enough inside to make that comfortable. There were about forty people in the nave, milling around where the pews had once been. Except that no one was holding drinks, it would have looked like a cocktail party for fans of the villain from *Scream*.

I joined them, nodding and saying things like, "Hello, Scrier," when it seemed called for. Mostly I listened. The guys who had just come in after losing me must have given a report—a fairly humiliating one, at that—because I kept hearing the names Parker and Carrion tossed around like Frisbees at a rock concert.

I didn't like hearing them talk about Parker. If even one of these jokers figured out that I was Peter Parker— or if Carrion told them—my secret identity would be blown, and Aunt May and MJ would both become targets for every crank who had ever held a grudge against me.

Someone went to the front of the room and announced that the meeting would start in five minutes. I didn't necessarily want to hang around for the reading of the minutes, treasurer's report, and old and new business, if I could help it. The longer I was there, the greater the risk that someone would realize they had never heard my voice before, or find the guys out in the car, or there would be some sort of secret handshake or slogan I wouldn't know. Not that I didn't think I could beat up forty Scriers. But I was starting to sweat a little, and it smelled bad enough inside already.

So I simply walked up to a Scrier standing by himself and said, "I've been out of town for a few weeks. San Francisco—I don't know if you heard about that business out there?"

The Scrier hesitated. He might have looked confused, but I couldn't tell. He gave the slightest of shrugs. "I think so, yeah."

"Obviously I've missed something. What's this whole deal with Carrion and Parker?"

"Oh, that," the Scrier said. "We want this book that Carrion has."

Which had to be the *Darkhold*, I guessed. "Yeah?"

"He says he'll give it to us if we harass this guy Parker for a while. Just make his life miserable, right? And then we get the book."

"Easy as cake."

"I thought it was pie."

"I like cake better," I said. "So are we supposed to tell Carrion when we've made Parker sorry he was ever born? Or will he just know?"

He shrugged again. "Who knows? I guess that's why we're just the little fish—we don't get all those details."

I decided to play a long shot. "It's strange to hear all this talk about Carrion around here."

"What do you mean?"

"Out in California they're talking about him, too."

"Really?"

"Yeah," I said, "there's this rumor going around that Spider-Man's going to kick his tail into next year. They said he's laying a trap for him at the North Meadow tomorrow night, just before midnight, and when Carrion shows up Spider-Man will feed him his lunch." I tried not to get carried away with loving descriptions of how

Spider-Man would destroy Carrion, because I wanted to remain believable.

"That a fact?"

"That's what they're saying."

"How would they know about that, out in California?"

"That's why we're the little fish," I said. "They hear things we don't."

"Yeah."

"Listen, I'll catch you later," I said. I turned away before he could reply, and started toward the door.

Before I made it there, I looked back. He was talking to someone else, and from his body language, I was guessing he was passing on the rumor about Spider-Man at the North Meadow.

Start a rumor in a room full of criminal cultists, and it doesn't take long to spread. I could only hope the details would be kept somewhat consistent, so it wouldn't get back to Carrion as Sheep Meadow at noon. He wouldn't find me there.

I made it out of there before the sergeant-at-arms, if they had one, called the meeting to order, if they did that. Outside, I dumped the two webbed-together men onto the sidewalk, peeled off the hood and mask (one thing about Scriers I knew now—if anyone ever needed a DNA sample from one, it could be easily procured from the dried sweat on the inside of that mask), pulled my own mask back on, and got in behind the wheel. The keys were in my borrowed pants pocket. I started the car and drove it back the way I had come. In Noho I parked illegally, so it would be towed and impounded, and found the alley. My own clothes were still under the Dumpster, although the webbing had evaporated and dropped them onto the greasy pavement. I left the borrowed clothes in the alley, secured my own to my back in a web-pack, and headed for home.

Trying not to think about the dry-cleaning bill, I focused instead on trying to figure out how to beat Carrion. Assuming he made it to the North Meadow tomorrow night.

I would be there, and I would be ready.

21

HE HAD MADE a point of taking all of his patients from Manhattan, specifically because he didn't live in Manhattan. The cops and the press had always assumed he did, counted on him being too stupid to know he shouldn't hunt in his own backyard.

Maybe that was why they had never caught him.

The urge to operate had been filling him from the inside out lately. He could barely sleep for thinking about it. His appetite was shot. He spent most of his time in the city, prowling for women who were sick inside and needed the Surgeon's deft touch.

He was an old man now, not as strong as he had once been. But did that mean he couldn't operate? For the longest time, he had simply accepted that it did.

No more. The need was too consuming. He had to try. He still had a van, white, no windows in the back. He drove it into Manhattan and parked it and started looking for the right one. He had to take her from someplace where foot traffic was limited. If she struggled (they almost always did) he wanted to be able to get her secured inside the van before anyone could respond.

He settled on Madison Square Park. He had found one of his favorites there, back during his prime years. He still remembered her name. Anita Riddle. He remembered that her flesh had been unexpectedly freckled, and when he first started cutting, he tried to avoid the freckles, as if slicing through them would bring bad luck. But they were so numerous he gave up on that and just drew his scalpel right down the middle, freckles be damned.

He parked on East Twenty-sixth, in an illegal parking spot. But the license plates were fakes, stolen decades ago, and couldn't be traced back to him, so if he got a ticket he would just ignore it. He wouldn't be there for long.

This time of night, after eight, there weren't a lot of people in the park. He found the one he wanted sitting on a bench by the reflecting pool. She probably worked nearby, swing shift or night shift, maybe in the Flatiron Building, and she had come outside for a break. She held a bottle of green tea between her legs and ate yogurt from a cup with a plastic spoon. She wore a pink blouse and dark pants with black flats, and her brown hair had been styled within the past few days. She looked like a lower-middle-class girl trying to make it in the big city, probably living with roommates in some rent-controlled apartment.

He could smell the sickness in her when he passed by. Perfect. He stopped. "Excuse me," he said. He had used many lines, many approaches over the years, but now that he was an old man he thought he should just go with that. He tried to sound pathetic, and was unpleasantly surprised at how convincing he was. "I think I dropped my keys, but I'm not sure if they're in the gutter or inside my van or where, and I'm afraid my eyes and my knees are both too feeble to go hunting for them. Could you do me a favor and see if you can spot them?"

She studied him for several long moments. She would have seen a white man in his seventies, with white hair and pale blue eyes that had almost disappeared behind folds of skin. His teeth were uneven, his shoulders sloping, his back stooped. He played it up, of course—when he wanted to he could straighten his back just as he had in his younger days and add a good four inches to his height. Right now he wanted her to think she could knock him down with that plastic spoon.

Apparently he passed muster. After what seemed like an uncomfortably long time, she broke into a smile. "Sure, I can help you look," she said. "Where are you parked?"

He indicated the illegally parked van. "I really just stopped to look at the Seward statue. I proposed to my wife in front of it, you see, back in 1957. On one knee. She passed on in '83, rest her soul, but I still miss her like the dickens."

The girl bought it. She stood up, her figure lithe and

slim, just the way he liked them. She was still smiling, but there was sadness in her eyes that wasn't just from hearing his imaginary story. He put that down to the sickness that she needed him to cut out of her. All these years later and he could still pick them at a glance. "I'm so sorry for your loss," she said.

"Thank you." He started leading her toward the van, then pretended to stumble. She took him by the arm, helping him the rest of the way, chattering as they went about her mundane job monitoring international stock markets. She talked about it as if it would someday lead to riches of her own, but in less than a minute he could tell that her efforts would only ever make other people wealthy. She had reached a dead end and she was just smart enough to begin to understand that, although not honest enough to admit it to herself.

He was beginning to think it would be easy. At the van, she opened the front door and started pawing around the footwell. He said, "I'll turn on this light back here for you," and opened the side door. Just inside that door were an aluminum bat, a roll of duct tape, some strips of cloth, and scissors.

"I don't see any keys in here," she said.

"Maybe they fell in the gutter," he said. "I hope I didn't drop them by the statue."

"I'll check." She moved to do just that, and he brought the bat out from the back. But she glanced back at his motion and saw the bat. "What are you—"

He was going to lose her. He swung but she put

up a defensive arm, blocking the bat. It slid off her and slammed into the side of the van hard enough to send a shock vibrating up his arms and shoulders. The bat flew from his hands. The prospective patient jumped to her feet, screaming, clawed at his face with fingernails like scimitars (burning as they sliced grooves in his flesh), and ran away, back toward the Flatiron.

At least he'd been right about that.

He hurried into the van (his keys in his right front pocket, as they always were) and started it up. He barely made it to Park Avenue before he started hearing sirens.

Maybe he really was too old for this. Maybe the Surgeon was retired for keeps.

The thought of that made him even sadder than he had expected.

The day after my visit to the old church in Hunter's Point, during a midmorning break between classes, I went to the teacher's lounge and checked my cell phone for messages. There was one from MJ, telling me that she had had a great night, maybe a breakthrough—rehearsal had gone staggeringly well, and her fellow actors had been more than civil. That much I knew because she had left me a message last night recounting pretty much the same thing. Afterward they had all gone out for drinks and closed down the bar, and then she had slept in until ten, when I was already in class. That was the new part. Also she loved me. That wasn't new, but I never got tired of hearing it.

A second message was from Vincent Slown. "Pete!" he said. He sounded healthier than he had on Saturday, or at least more energetic. "I don't know if you've heard or not, but we're continuing the demonstration today, and it's bigger than ever! Sixth Avenue was closed for almost an hour, and then they made us move off it so they could open two lanes up. Not only that, but Globitek Worldwide stock has been falling steadily all day. The story about the demonstration has hit the wire services, and the cable news networks have all been here already today. I spent most of the morning doing interviews. It's all thanks to you, man. I owe you big-time."

I turned the phone off again and headed back to class. I was glad the demonstrations had gone over well for Vincent. Nothing had convinced me yet that New York Health & Life would reverse its decision, but tumbling stock prices would be more likely to tilt them in that direction than traffic jams in the streets.

But I had a problem of my own. In a few hours, I would have to be at the North Meadow of Central Park with a plan to defeat Carrion, and thus far I didn't have one. No matter what I threw at him, he had a defense ready. I had even thought about calling in some Avengers, or maybe the Fantastic Four, but I couldn't imagine how their powers could hurt him, either.

I needed some inspiration, and it just wasn't happening.

After dinner that evening, Vincent Slown was sitting down to watch news footage of the demonstrations he had TiVoed during the day. Yselda was bathing the twins before putting them in bed. He usually helped with that, since two wet squirming seventeen-month-olds could be more than a handful, but tonight he was anxious to see how the cable networks had edited the interviews he had done.

He was watching MSNBC's coverage when he heard a sharp rapping at the front door. He paused the image and heaved himself from the sofa, then stopped himself. It was getting more difficult to stand up quickly, and the fact that he had spent much of the day on his feet (although in the afternoon Yselda had insisted he use a wheelchair, and he had gratefully complied). The knocking came again, even more forcefully. He hoped it wasn't another bill collector.

"I'm coming," he said. He coughed, and tried to bite it back, not wanting to launch into one of his coughing fits while someone was at the door. Maybe it was a reporter—he'd had plenty of calls from them over the last couple of days. When he reached the door, he was still coughing gently and clearing his throat. He looked out the peephole and saw two clean-cut men in dark suits. He'd never seen either one of them before. One was white and the other black, and they looked like police detectives to him.

Vincent opened the door. The white man was standing in front. "Are you Vincent Slown?" he asked.

"Yes. What—?"

The man didn't say anything, but his eyes narrowed slightly and his fist lashed out. There was something in it, Vincent believed, or on it, brass knuckles maybe, because when it slammed into his gut it was like being hit by a guided missile. He folded around the fist, felt it sinking deep, probably into a kidney or something like that.

Powerful hands grabbed him and yanked him out into the hallway. Theirs was the only occupied apartment on the floor, so no one was going to look to see what was going on. Vincent tried to call for Yselda but the blows were coming too fast—mostly to his torso, but he also took punches to the head and face. He wanted to fight back, but he had never been a violent guy, didn't even really know how to fight, and all he did was claw at the two men. He heard fabric tear and a tiny thrill of triumph coursed through him—*at least I tore one of those expensive suits!*—and then he was being thrown down the stairs to the landing below.

He heard the big men coming down the stairs as if they were all underwater, their footsteps loud and resonant. He knew he was moaning, trying to get his knees underneath him, but he couldn't do it. He had never known such extreme physical pain, even in the worst stages of his illness. One of the men stopped beside him (he thought it was the black man, but the guy kept swimming in and out of focus, and his voice sounded like it was coming from far away), grabbed his shoulder with fingers like steel rods, and said, "Sick is one thing, dead is another. You don't stop playing games, you'll be dead. So back off."

Vincent wanted to throw some kind of tough-guy

response at him. But he couldn't think of one, and his mouth was full of liquid and when he opened it blood splashed out onto the floor and all he could make was a gurgling noise. That didn't sound very tough at all. By the time he had worked through that, the world had started spinning around him and his eyes closed and then everything went away.

22

AUTUMN HAD COME into the city overnight, almost as suddenly as if there had been a big electric blanket keeping us warm and it was snatched away without warning. I didn't mind, since the sudden cold snap meant the park was more deserted than it otherwise would have been, even at ten o'clock. Dew was thick on the grass and the air had a crisp tang I could feel in my lungs with every deep breath.

I got to the North Meadow early. I still was shy one good idea, and hoped the landscape might inspire something. I also didn't know if Carrion had actually heard about the rumor I had started. If he hadn't, this would be yet another giant waste of time. Carrion's victims weighed heavily on me, and that load wouldn't get any lighter if I couldn't put a stop to him.

The North Meadow, north of the park's big reservoir, encompassed twenty-three acres, so it was entirely possible that Carrion and I could both be there and be completely unaware of each other's presence. During the summer, its ball fields were used daily for baseball, but over the past few weeks they'd been converted to soccer and football. There was a Recreation Center with fitness machines, basketball and handball courts, and climbing walls. I walked around it all, trying to keep to the shadows. If anyone saw Spider-Man there, a crowd might gather—or worse yet, someone might call the cops. I doubted Carrion would show at all if there was a large police presence.

So feeling slightly creepy, I skulked around the North Meadow area, looking at the sports fields, at how the night stars glittered in the reservoir until the occasional chill breezes chopped the water and smudged them away. Inspiration was too grand a word for the germ of an idea that had come to me. It was more of a possibility than a plan, but it was all I had to work with.

When I had blinded Carrion with webbing, I'd been able to land a couple of blows. He had been thrown off-balance by that and hadn't maintained the presence of mind to teleport away or make himself immaterial. It hadn't lasted long, of course, because he had simply decayed the webbing. But if there was a way to repeat that, and maybe improve upon it, I had to try to find it.

By eleven, I had covered pretty much the entire area. It was essentially vacant, except for a few cars passing by on East Drive and the very occasional late-night jogger on one of the paths. There were no Scriers hiding anywhere, which had been one of my chief concerns. I had an hour to kill before my rendezvous, and was just starting to wonder if I should take a cruise around the city instead of waiting around.

Which was when Carrion appeared, in that now-familiar golden glow and stink of sulfur.

He shimmered into sight about fifteen yards away from me, out in the middle of a soccer field. Nothing around to hit him with except grass. Guy was smart.

"You're a little early," I said. "What if I'd been tussling with some other super villain? Wouldn't you have been embarrassed?"

"Don't m-m-mock me, Spider-Man," Carrion said. That voice gave me goose bumps, as it always did. They may have been a little goosier now that I knew his stuttering came from the dead Stanley Carter. "I d-didn't come here to have m-my intelligence insulted."

"What makes you think I'm insulting it? Maybe you really are that dumb."

"Wh-whatever I am, P-P-Parker, I am no fool." I knew that, but would never give him the satisfaction of saying so. Not that he gave me time. "If I were, would I h-have known this to be a tr-trap? I came early because I d-d-did."

He had a point. I had come early to set the trap but his early arrival wiped out some of that advantage. On the other hand, it had saved me from having to stand around for an hour worrying about the fact that the only part of the trap I had successfully planned was the bait. I was back to square one—angrier than ever, but with no clear idea of how to defeat him. "Okay, you're wise to me," I said. "Now that we've settled that, you might as well surrender, because if you're that astute you know I'm not going to just let you go."

The only thing worse than looking at his face was looking at him when he was smiling. "I was going to sug-sug-sug—recommend you d-do the same. Just give yourself over to m-me, Sp-Spider-Man, so this can all be over."

I liked the sound of it being over. I wasn't fond of his preferred conclusion, though. "Not going to happen that way, Carrion."

"I thought you might feel that way. T-tell me, have you enjoyed getting to know my f-f-friends?"

"The Scriers? Oh, they're a treat, really. I'll be sending you a bill for damage to my apartment."

"If you can find my address, feel f-free."

"I thought you might send them instead of coming here tonight."

"I c-c-c—I gave that some consideration. B-but I decided it was t-time to deal with you in a more final way."

Knowing that he had been toying with me instead of taking me seriously didn't improve my mood any. Or my confidence.

At least I knew where we stood. He was ready to kill me. As he had killed so many others.

Including Julia Darst. I held the image of her dead body in my head and let the rage fill me, fuel me. My gloved fists clenched. I knew what I had to do.

I would take some punishment—almost unbearable punishment—but I had to bear it because there was no way around putting my hands on him.

He just stood there waiting for me. Like he knew he could take whatever I might throw at him.

So I threw it.

I started by charging him, covering the space between us, but as I ran toward him I shot a thick glob of webbing into his eyes. As before, he threw his hands up to his face, and the webbing began to decay from both sides—from the contact with his face and his hands.

I stopped short just before reaching him and released more webbing, this time keeping it close and forming it into a short, heavy club. Hey, it's good enough for Daredevil, right? I held it in my right hand, and as soon as Carrion's eyes cleared from the first blinding, I blasted him again with my left. Again, he staggered under the assault, making a hissing noise like a snake trapped in a sack. This time, I was close enough, and I swung the webbing club with everything I had.

Carrion was twisting and writhing, so the blow landed on his shoulder. It had an impact, though, driving him down to one knee. I drew back and swung again. This time he threw up an arm to block the club, still pawing at his eyes with the other hand. The club hit his forearm. Carrion screamed, his mouth wide open, a repulsive odor spewing from it. I hit him again, this time in the upper arm. I thought I felt the bones there turn to dust.

The club was deteriorating and wouldn't last much longer. I could always make more, though, as long as he stayed put and let me keep beating on him.

I was pulling the club away for one more swat before I stopped to make a new one when he vanished. I halted, midswing. "Carrion! I know you're still here! Come out and fight me!"

He came out. The night air twinkled and he was there with his hands full of that toxic red dust. He threw it at me. I jumped away from him, hit a slope, rolled. When I came up the dust was settling into grass that was already turning brown, but he was gone again.

And then back again. He appeared behind me, grabbing my head in both hands before I even knew he was there. My mask started to decay and the heat of his hands burned through. I bent at the waist and lurched forward, hard, drawing him up onto my back. Then I tensed my legs and sprang backward. I wanted to land on top of him, but he teleported away en route and I came down flat on my back.

Carrion winked back in, standing on my chest. He smiled down at me as he tipped his pouch. Red dust spilled from its opening, cascading toward me.

I twisted and swept with my arm at the same time, knocking his legs out from under him. He started to fall, then blinked away. I could only hope he landed on his head, wherever he ended up. I kept twisting until I was on hands and knees, and then I scrambled away. Some of the dust hit me and started eating through my costume. I hurtled across the meadow, past the Rec

Center, over the fence and into the reservoir. I didn't know if water could wash the stuff off, or if it had made it to my skin. But at the moment I couldn't think of any other way to neutralize it.

I was climbing the fence again, dripping down onto the rocks—the water had at least slowed the decay—when Carrion appeared again. This time he was levitating before me. He kicked at my head. I dodged the kick and reached for his leg, caught it, and released the fence, determined to bring him down and finish this.

He vanished again, and I fell like a duck that had been shot out of the sky. I'm an agile sort and I caught myself, but by the time I found my feet again he was back. One of his gloved hands came out of nowhere, literally, and caught me in the jaw. I tasted blood. He was gone. He was back, his booted foot driving into my gut. Gone and back, gone and back. Every move I made, he was ready for. Telepathy, I remembered. By the time I knew what I was going to do, he knew it, too.

Gone and back. A fist, a foot. Back and gone. I was weakening. I hadn't landed one on him in what seemed like forever, while he was using me as a punching bag. I tried to hang onto my fury, remembering his victims, remembering Julia Darst. He appeared, slugged me in the temple, and I caught his hand. Held on. Maybe if I didn't let go, he couldn't get away. I knew that wasn't true, but I was grasping, hoping.

He didn't teleport or dematerialize. Instead, he levitated, wafting us across the park. I hung onto him, my costume peeling away, my hands burning, and punched at him as well as I could without any way to brace myself, any momentum.

About thirty feet off the ground, he vanished.

I fell, but despite my weariness I came down safely.

Then I saw that he had deposited me close to a boulder that must have weighed at least a ton.

Maybe I could trick him into smashing into it, as I had once made him knock himself out by breaking his own gravestone with his head.

I was still trying to figure out how (unsteady on my feet, the world seeming to tip first in one direction and then the other) when he appeared behind the stone.

He had the ability to repel organic material. But a rock, even a big rock, seemed like the very definition of inorganic material. So I didn't think he'd be able to move it.

I was wrong.

By the time I realized what he was doing and tried to dodge, it was too late. I saw the boulder coming, could almost feel the impact, and there was nothing I could do about it.

Carrion was glad that Spider-Man had fallen before he had. He was more easily worn out each day, and although he had successfully prevented the wall-crawler from doing any serious damage, the effort of battle had nearly exhausted him. When he saw the boulder smash into Spider-Man and land on top of him, he gave a chuckle of relief and teleported away, this time for good. Time to give the Scriers their book, let them do what they would with it. He wanted only rest, only peace, now that he'd had his revenge.

They had helped him and earned their reward. He didn't care what came next. When he had recovered, he would think about his next steps, a new goal. For now, his one overriding goal had been achieved, and he didn't even have the energy to celebrate.

The important thing? Spider-Man was dead. Carrion had done what so many others had tried to do, and failed at. He supposed New York's underworld would want to worship him as some kind of god.

He supposed he would let them.

After he slept.

23

HE THOUGHT HIS urges would consume him, as if someone had crossbred a tapeworm and a wolverine and fed it to him. He wanted to heal, to kill, to cut. Holding a scalpel felt like coming home after a long absence. But he had no patient and couldn't seem to acquire one.

The Surgeon looked in his bathroom mirror. The hand holding the scalpel was steady, but webbed with deep lines and spotted here and there with brown that looked like he had spilled cocoa on himself. If he cut those spots out, would the strength come back into his hand?

He thought not.

Somehow he had turned into an old man. Older than his father, who had died at forty-one. Older than his brother, also dead. As a boy, his grandfather had always looked ancient to him, but now, inspecting himself in the mirror with a clear eye, he remembered that his grandfather had never made it out of his sixties, and had never looked as old as he did right this minute. His jowls sagged with loose flesh, his neck was a mass of wrinkles, his eyes had virtually disappeared from view. He was old. Old! No one would ever fear him again. If he had managed to take that patient from the park, she probably would have broken him in half. If the police had caught him, they would have laughed.

He tore his gaze away from the awful visage in the mirror, the mask of age through which a much younger man peered. Thinking about his brother had reminded him of his brother's son, his nephew, who was staying in his spare room. The boy—well, he was a grown man now, for sure—was a strange one, not saying much, away most of the time. He said he had been abroad for a long time and had no home in the city anymore, so he had let him move in while he got himself resettled.

He found himself drawn to that spare room. It was small and crowded, packed with junk that had no place else to go. His nephew had asked if he could stay in the carriage house out back, but no one went in the carriage house. That was his operating theater, and he kept it locked up tight.

His nephew hadn't arrived with many possessions. Looking around the room now, only one thing looked new. On a shelf jammed with boxes the contents of which he couldn't even remember, there was a book he was sure he had never seen before. It was thick and black, probably bound in leather. A bible? His brother had been the religious one in their family, and he supposed that might have been passed down to his nephew as well.

He was reaching for it when his nephew showed up. He hadn't heard the usual squeak and bang of the front door, just a scuff on the floor and the words, "Don't touch that, Emory."

He turned around and saw his nephew standing in the doorway. But as the blinders had fallen away from his eyes in the bathroom, they did here, too. What he saw before him wasn't his brother's boy Stan, all grown up (and Stan had died, he remembered that now—why had he forgotten before? He had brought honor to a family sadly lacking in it, but then blood did tell, as it had a habit of doing, and he proved to be a Carter after all, and then he died) but some sort of monster. His skin looked like yellow sidewalk chalk and his face was gaunt and horrible, something out of a nightmare full of gnashing fangs, the kind he had sometimes that pinned him to his mattress and wouldn't let go. He wore rags, not clothes. He was lanky and tall, but his shoulders were slumped, his arm and shoulder bruised and broken, and he looked even wearier than Emory Carter felt.

"You . . . Stan?"

The unlovely thing smiled. The Surgeon's guts turned to liquid. "My name is Legion," he said, waving the arm that wasn't twisted and pulped. "Now leave me be. I need sleep."

I can see that, Emory almost said. But he decided he didn't really want to have any more conversation than was absolutely necessary with this . . . this being that had convinced him that it was his nephew, Stanley.

He left the room quickly, closing the door behind him, wanting to put some distance between himself and whatever Stanley had become. Some sort of supervillain he guessed, wasn't that what they called them? His injuries should have put him in the hospital. But no doctor would treat such a creature. Study him, maybe. All it took was a glance to know that, while he was basically human-shaped, he was not human, not in any real way.

They tried to keep it hidden, even from each other, but he knew the Carter family had suffered more than its share of madness. Police bullets had claimed Stan's life. Stan never knew that the same fate had befallen his father—he was told it was an accident in a car, but it was really a gunfight that tore more than a hundred holes through the walls of the Florida bungalow he was using as a hideout after being accused of the murders of four New York waitresses. He had killed them, and more— he had confessed it to Emory on a long-distance phone call from Fort Lauderdale. Emory hadn't bothered to tell him about his activities as the Surgeon. Both brothers knew their father had been a murderer, too, with bodies buried all around his Hackensack property.

So Stan never knew the truth about the Carter blood running in his veins. Scientists argued about nature versus nurture, but Emory had always believed that a person was like a book written long ago, and the story put down there couldn't really be changed. Pages could be cut out (using a sharp scalpel and precise surgical technique) and the tale might be altered that way, but when it came to the fundamental questions about who you were, the ink was already on the paper.

Stan had died, and yet there he was, in a different body, presumably sleeping off some terrible battle in the next room. He was seemingly a different person, but with the same tendencies toward madness and murder.

Like father, like son. Like uncle, like nephew.

The family that slays together, stays together.

But just in case, the Surgeon put one of his best knives—a straight razor, not a scalpel, safer because he could close it—in his pocket.

It didn't do to take chances where the Carters were concerned.

You know how sometimes you can swat or step on a spider over and over again without killing it? Spiders have tough exoskeletons that make them hard to squish, relative to their size.

My skeleton remained inside me where it belonged, radioactive spider bite notwithstanding. But I'm strong and agile and I know when to go limp. Which I did when it became clear that I couldn't dodge the oversized pebble that Carrion heaved at me.

Not to say it didn't hurt. I've been bounced around by some of the toughest opponents on the planet (and some visitors here, to boot). The Rhino has fists like a speeding semitruck. Sandman can knock a concrete building off its foundation with a single punch. The Lizard's tail packs a wallop like nobody's business, as

Aunt May often said. I never quite understood what that meant, and guessed that I would go to my grave not understanding it.

But not that night.

When I woke up, I realized a few things. The boulder was heavy. The ground was cold and wet. In fact, the dew might well have saved my life, making the grass spongy and the ground soft enough to cushion me instead of squashing me. And Carrion had weakened me and worn me out so much that moving the rock off me was going to be a slow, painful process. But it had to be done, because in time, spider strength or no, its weight would simply turn my internal organs to soup and my bones to powder.

Trouble was, I couldn't budge the thing. My arms were splayed out to my sides. My legs were out straight too, and I couldn't bend my knees. I couldn't get any leverage on it. When daylight came someone might happen along, notice that the boulder that had been sitting in the same place for decades had moved, and find shredded bits of red and blue spider-webbed arms and legs sticking out from beneath it. And my head; that hadn't landed under the boulder, which was good because it might well have fractured my skull. As it was, the headache throbbing in there made it feel like my head had taken the worst of it.

All I could see was boulder and dark sky. I could feel my limbs, so I knew they hadn't been severed or completely destroyed. But I could hardly move them.

The thing was, I had to move them. Since I couldn't

move the boulder on top of them, I realized, I had to move them out from under the boulder.

Well, why not? I asked myself. Trapdoor spiders dug holes all the time. Of course, they dug with mouthparts called *chelicerae* that came equipped with little rakes to loosen the earth and roll it into a ball that they could shove out of the way with their hind legs. I didn't have that particular advantage. But I didn't intend to stick around the hole and trap other insects, reptiles, and small mammals—I just needed to shift enough earth to give me some range of motion.

I started digging with my hands using a similar principle, clawing at the ground, getting handfuls of dirt and tossing it aside. Once I had cleared some space below my hands, it got more difficult. I had to shove earth with my forearms into the holes under my hands, then scoop the loose earth and remove it. I kept going in the same way, upper arms, shoulders, clearing away the ground underneath me little by little. It seemed like it would take forever. But once my arms had some wiggle room, I was able to begin clearing in toward my torso.

Then I had another idea. Once I had some freedom of movement for my left arm, enough to bend the elbow a little, I stopped digging that way and concentrated on my right side. I was lying on a slight left to right slope anyway. So I dug deeper on that side, increasing the angle of the slope, and then tucked my right arm close to my body.

I pushed with my left hand, palm flat against the boulder. I still didn't have much leverage, but I could bend my arm and flex it and I didn't want to die there.

I thought about Carrion, still loose, possibly still murdering people. If he thought I was dead, would his grudge against me end? Or would he go after MJ and Aunt May?

That was the impetus I still needed. I rocked the boulder between my right arm and left hand, then pushed hard with my left. It started to roll to my right— then stopped and settled again.

"*Nooo!*" I screamed. People in the apartments flanking the park must have thought there was a crazy man in there. They wouldn't have been far wrong.

I rocked it again, right arm, left hand. When it was definitely jiggling to and fro, I pushed.

Pushed.

And the boulder tipped.

Not all the way. But far enough to free my left leg. Ignoring the electric agony rippling through me when I moved it, I bent the knee and got my foot underneath me so I could shove up from the hip, putting the power of my leg against the boulder along with my arm and shoulder.

I pushed and I pushed, demanding more of my muscles than I ever have. They quivered, they trembled, they shook like leaves in the wind, but the boulder inched toward my right, a little more, a little more—

—and finally, it rolled off of me enough to free my right side, leg, and arm.

I gave one more mighty shove and as the boulder teetered right, I skittered left. The boulder fell back down and settled where it had been, but I wasn't under it anymore.

I was off to its left, a sweating, trembling mass of spider-nerves and exhausted muscles. From this angle, finally, I could see that two sides of the boulder were crusted with orange and green lichens. So Carrion hadn't telekinetically controlled solid rock after all—he had controlled the organic material that enveloped the rock, and the rock just went along. I was glad to have that mystery solved, even though I would have been happier if he had skipped the whole thing.

I stayed there on the grass for almost another hour. The sun would be coming up soon, though, and I had to get moving. Simply standing up was almost as hard as budging the boulder had been. I thought about hailing a cab instead of webslinging home, but it was Manhattan, shortly before dawn, and I really, really wanted one—so of course, there were none to be seen. Until I had only two blocks to go, at which point I saw a pair of them, idling beside the curb, their hacks having a spirited conversation about municipal politics.

I gave them a wave and went home to my wonderful, soft, empty bed.

I didn't really care if I never got up.

24

MJ CALLED AT seven-thirty.

"Mornin', Tiger," she said brightly. "Getting ready for work?"

Work. Nuts. "I guess I'm calling in sick today."

"Sick? Peter, are you all right?"

I resisted the impulse to make a crack about my crushing workload. "I just had a rough night," I said. I was pretty sure it was worse than that—a lot of bruising and a cracked rib or two, at best. I'm tough and durable, like a good tool, but even the sturdiest hammer can suffer some damage now and again. "And I have to get after Carrion again before he hurts anyone else."

"Take care of yourself," Mary Jane said. Concern was evident in her voice. "I don't want to sound like Aunt May, but you're too important to too many people to risk getting seriously hurt. I know taking chances is what you do, but make sure they're the right chances for the right reasons."

I yawned, stretched, and winced, holding the phone away from my mouth in hopes that MJ wouldn't hear the squeak. "I know, MJ. I will."

I didn't like hiding anything from her, and if she was there with me I would have told her everything, even let her tape up my ribs. But at the moment she had problems of her own, and since she would want to rush to my side—which was the worst possible place for anyone to be until Carrion was dealt with—I didn't let on how much punishment I had taken.

In the shower a few minutes later (the water stinging my bruised spots—which was all of me—like whips) I allowed myself to think about yet another problem, one I had kept putting off but knew I'd have to face at some point.

My best bet for containing Carrion was getting him back into S.H.I.E.L.D. custody. They had cages they could throw him into from which he couldn't escape—although I'd have to remind them not to let him out even for research purposes, as they had done with William Allen—and considering what he had done to Julia and her team, I had no doubt they'd be happy to put him away someplace safe.

But this Carrion, like Miles Warren, knew my secret identity. To assume he wouldn't blab once he was in custody was like those risks MJ had mentioned, stupid and dangerous. Some of the S.H.I.E.L.D. brass knew my identity, but not everyone—and as Stan Carter showed, not everyone who joined S.H.I.E.L.D. remained loyal. Try as I might (and I had to admit my head was still a little fuzzy) I could only come up with one way around the problem, and it involved causing Carrion's death. I could almost justify that by reminding myself that this Carrion was (mostly, at least) Stanley Carter, who had been dead for years. Carrion also held the memories of Miles Warren, Malcolm McBride, and William Allen— all dead, as well. So would killing Carrion really be the same as killing a person? Or would it be simply restoring this Carrion's various personalities to their natural state, returning them to their interrupted rest?

Probably the latter was the truth—Carrion was an unliving creature carrying the memories of four dead men, and to even think about him in terms of being alive was inaccurate.

Even so, I couldn't see myself deliberately taking his "life." That went against everything I believed—about myself, about the world, about the sanctity of life. I fought to preserve and defend lives, not to end them. And in the worst-case scenario, the death penalty, judges and juries and lawyers and appeals were involved. I was none of those things. I was just one spider-powered do-gooder who didn't want to make those decisions about someone else's life. Or "life."

I turned off the water and toweled off—gently, even the nubs of cotton scraping like razor blades over my tender flesh. I hadn't come to any conclusions about what to do with Carrion, but I did have an idea about how to look for him.

The Cabal of Scrier clearly had some sort of pipe-line to him. I had spread the rumor of a trap in the park at their meeting, and he showed up—not by chance, but clearly expecting a fight. The only way to interpret that fact was that someone in the Cabal had told him.

So I was headed back to Queens, back to that old church. There I would find me some Scriers and knock heads, if necessary, until I learned how to find Carrion. Then I would . . .

Then I would . . .

Well, I'd just have to figure that out when the time came.

It being midmorning and bright daylight, I took the no. 7 subway across the river, dressed in my civilian clothes. In Queens, I got off at the Hunter's Point station and walked through the crisp, bright day, passing underneath the Long Island Expressway. When I got close to the church, I climbed to the roof of a deserted warehouse and changed, webbing my clothing into a secure spot. I covered the rest of the distance at the higher elevations, moving between rooftops and trees, until I had reached the deconsecrated church.

The church was quiet, as was the neighborhood. A few vehicles rumbled nearby, and birds chirped their good-byes before heading for Florida. If there was anyone inside the church, I couldn't tell from here.

I dropped to the ground and returned to the door I had used last time. No one threw it open for me. When I tried it, though, it swung open easily. Which told me two things—someone was inside after all, and the door was being watched, because the Cabal of Scrier didn't let people just wander in off the street.

I was wrong.

Probably there had been someone watching the door. At the moment, though, all eyes were on Carrion. Except those that were on something else, behind Carrion. There were probably twenty or twenty-five Scriers in the nave, but I didn't take time to do a head count.

Beyond Carrion, a group of them had huddled together around a small table. Others were on hands and knees, painting something on the floor. They all wore those hoods and masks, so I couldn't tell if any of them were the ones I had seen here before.

But my quarry was there, so I didn't waste any time. I shot a webline to the arched ceiling and swung over the heads of the first few Scriers (their attention riveted inward, away from the doorway), the soft *thwipp* sound alerting them to my presence.

Midswing, I blasted some webbing at Carrion's eyes just as he turned toward me. "Stop him!" he cried, or started to, but when the webbing hit his face "him" turned into "hmmphhh!" His arm seemed to have recovered from the punishment I gave it the night before.

Some of them grabbed for me, even jumped into the air, but I was high and moving fast. I only had eyes for Carrion, and not in the romantic way.

Which was almost my undoing. I shouldn't have counted on the Scriers treating their church like . . . well, a church. One of them drew a gun and shot at me. My spider-senses warned me as he was pulling the trigger, and I released the webline, dropping low enough fast enough that the bullet sailed over my head and crashed into one of the fluorescent lights hanging from the ceiling. Minute shards of glass and dust wafted down like a momentary, localized snowstorm.

I landed in the midst of some Scriers. Immediately they swarmed all over me, clutching at my arms, my neck, my aching sides. I elbowed one in the side of the head, kicked another with my right leg, put my left hand on top of someone's head and pushed off, going for some height. That Scrier collapsed beneath me, but I kicked up and rode the others like the hero of the game being carried off the field.

The webbing I'd blinded Carrion with had already decayed, and he stared at me with his mouth open and those nasty yellow teeth exposed. "You're dead!" he finally managed to say.

"Look who's talking."

The Scriers had figured out that I was skating across them toward Carrion, so they moved away from me. More guns came out, but when I hit the end of the line and dropped to the floor again, they formed a loose circle around me. Anyone who opened fire would be more likely to hit their comrades than me.

Still, MJ had asked me to be careful, so I snatched the guns with webbing, then blasted them up to the ceiling where the webs would secure them until long after I was finished here.

Or so I devoutly hoped.

Some of the Scriers threw punches at me. They landed, and since I was still sore from the night before, I felt them. But they were human, so their blows didn't have any lasting effect. I waded through them, swatting Scriers aside right and left.

Finally there were none left between me and Carrion, and only Carrion between me and whatever the Scriers who had paid me no attention yet were doing.

I was starting to have a bad feeling about them.

They had finished painting on the floor. A couple of them had lit candles and positioned them at what appeared to be precise locations around the image they had drawn. Greasy black smoke gave the church a profane odor. I could tell now that the object around which some of them stood was a book, open on a podium, and one of the Scriers read from the book, his voice growing louder by the moment. A cairn of rocks had been piled in front of the drawing, with a human skull set on top of it for good measure.

I've always been good at math. When I added up Carrion plus book plus Cabal, the answer I reached was *Darkhold*. And that could only be bad news.

"Kill the intruder!" one of the Scriers standing around the book commanded. Another one, a spectator standing just to the side of the drawing on the floor, drew a .357, pointed it at me, and squeezed the trigger. He handled the big handgun like a pro. I sprang off the floor, nine feet into the air, performed a double front flip, and while I was there his bullet sped past where I had been and hit a Scrier in the sternum. The victim went down on his knees, blood bubbling up from the mouthpiece of his mask and through the fingers he clamped over his chest. He swayed there for a moment, then plunged forward.

Suddenly the only sound in the room was the droning of the Scrier reading from the book. He was reading syllable by syllable, and I doubted if his pronunciation of ancient Sumerian, or whatever language the book was written in, was that great. The other Scriers all fell silent for a few long seconds, then there was the rush of feet and rustle of robes as some went to their fallen fellow's side and others came after me.

"Don't you people ever learn?" I asked. I slugged a couple of them, then grabbed one under the arms and spun around, swinging him so his feet cleared the space around me. When I had backed them off again, I released him and he flew into some others, taking them all down in a jumble.

Carrion hadn't left, had hardly moved. He watched, probably hoping some Scrier would get in a lucky shot and he wouldn't have to tangle with me again. I felt the same way—I would rather have left and gone straight to the dentist for multiple root canals than have to fight him.

It wasn't my decision to make, though. Or my decision had been made long ago. Either way, I was committed.

I started toward him, stiff-arming the last Scrier who tried to intercept me.

And behind him, the Scrier reading from the book

got louder, head back, throwing his words out toward the sky. *"Enamorath!"* he called. *"Emmoreth!"*

He wasn't reading anymore, I realized. His hands were bunched into fists in front of his chest, his eyes squeezed shut, and he bellowed the ritual up into space. Which meant he was no longer staring at the text and working out the pronunciation of each syllable as he went. Something had taken him over.

Around him, other Scriers bellowed strange words in response to his. *"Ia! Ia! Cadelerath shrii Chthon!"* they cried.

As if answering their call, he shouted again. *"Ba'al Set Elianath!"*

The candles flared, turning into Roman candles that shot streams of flame and sparks a dozen feet into the air. The temperature inside the church shot up, too—suddenly it must have been in the nineties, approaching a hundred, like those blast-furnace days in the summertime when even the flies are too hot and lazy to move. I smelled something that reminded me of a sewage spill I had covered for the *Bugle* once, out at Brighton Beach, only worse—that combined with the stench of dead bodies, hundreds of them, or thousands. The kind of stink I imagined one might have found on a Civil War battlefield three days after the fighting.

Overhead, the remaining fluorescent tubes exploded, one by one, showering sparks and glass down on us.

Something was happening here, and even Carrion was enthralled by it.

I took advantage of the moment.

I slammed into him from behind as he stared into the air above the drawing, the space where smoke from the flaring candles was beginning to coalesce into something else, something solid. When I hit him, he let out a grunt and he fell down. I landed on his back. The Scriers ignored us. I looped an arm around Carrion's neck, trying to choke him into unconsciousness before he teleported away or killed me or repelled me off him.

He did none of those, but my arm relaxed anyway. I realized the danger of kneeling on his back, and got off him, but my focus, like his, was glued to that place before us, above the design painted on the floor. The smoke and air and sparks and the very fabric of reality seemed to be twisting and writhing there. I thought I had gone insane, that I was hallucinating, because in that space I saw thousands of golden spires gleaming in the sun, a city that had never existed on Earth, then creatures like giant iguanas, bright blue and pale pink and Easter-chick yellow hurtling across an unfamiliar landscape. I saw Neil Armstrong stepping onto the moon turn into John F. Kennedy taking an assassin's bullet and that morphed into Hitler spitting and gesticulating through a speech, into Lincoln in his box at the Ford Theatre, and then the images flickered faster, so all I had was a sense of the rush of violent human history, going back, back, and then the Earth spinning alone in space. Then it was surrounded by distant suns with planets of their own, then those suns disappeared into galaxies, into universes, and if Earth was still somewhere in there it was invisible among the multitudes, a small, lost, place inside universes of death and despair and corruption and horror.

The images whirled faster and faster still, coalescing more, solidifying, until they were one, no longer an image but now an object, albeit an insubstantial one. He was formed of swirling, oily black and red smoke, but as I watched he took the shape of a being, huge and dark and sinister (it—he—somehow stood taller than the skyscrapers in Manhattan but also fit beneath the old Gothic church's arched ceiling at the same time). I thought I knew what he might be, but the voice of the Scrier who had summoned him confirmed my worst fear.

"Behold," he shouted, "the arrival of Chthon!"

And I thought, *Holy crap*.

25

His pronouncement was a tad premature.

Chthon hadn't reached full solidity yet. But he was getting close.

My attention still focused on the great, terrifying rebirth of Chthon, when Carrion hurled me off his back, I went sprawling on the stone floor. A handful of Scriers tried to take advantage of the moment to pile on top of me. Like *I* was the threat, now that they had successfully returned an evil elder god to Earth. I snapped out my fists. Grunts and whimpers of pain were like sweet music. An elbow shot here, a knee there, and then I forced myself to my feet, scattering masked freaks all around me.

Carrion stood with his back to me, watching Chthon. I had to remove him from the equation first. I had no idea how to go about battling Chthon, but I knew I didn't want to have to worry about Carrion while I did so. One at a time.

With the Scriers either rapt at the appearance of

Chthon or picking their teeth up off the floor, no one came between us. I stepped lightly behind Carrion, reached out . . .

. . . and tapped him on the shoulder.

Startled, he spun around. If there was one guy in the room I wished would put on a mask, it was him. I forced myself not to grimace or squint. "Carter," I said. "I know you're in there. You've got to listen to me."

"I don't have to do anything except t-tear your insect head from your b-b-body."

"There's still some humanity left in you. I know there is. Especially in Stan Carter, but also in Allen, McBride, and Warren. No matter how much you may all hate me, you've got to see that letting Chthon return is just not a good idea."

"Away from me," Carrion said. His voice had changed, become deeper, and the stammer was gone. His face, too, seemed slightly altered, his chin a little more pronounced, jaw firmer. Was I imagining it? I couldn't tell. "Before I squash you again."

"B-b-but he's right," Carrion said. His face had changed again.

"He's our enemy!"

"N-no! We only th-think he is!"

I didn't know which was stranger, the fact that Carrion's ugly mug kept shifting in barely perceptible ways, or the fact that he was arguing with himself. "Listen to Carter," I urged. "He's right."

"Carter is a fool!" Yet another voice, and face. Dude was creeping me out.

"If Ch-Chthon gets a toehold in our w-world, we're d-d-doomed, too!"

"Carter makes sense," I said. "The Scriers obviously couldn't even control you! What makes you think they'll be able to handle Chthon?"

"We are powerful! We are—"

"Sorry to break it to you, pal, but compared to that?" I gestured toward the demon, still gathering mass and presence. The Scriers had taken up a chant in a language I didn't recognize. "You're small change."

"We—"

"Face it, Carrion. Compared to people—even me—you're pretty tough. But up against Chthon . . . ?"

"Silence!" one of the personalities inside Carrion shouted. He was coiled like a spring, ready to snap me in half. He lunged at me, and I tensed to leap away.

But he caught himself. His face was changing faster now, faster than I could blink. I thought I was coming to recognize the features and voices of Warren, McBride, Allen, and Carter. "He's abso-abso-ab—he's definitely right! Chthon is the enemy, not Spi-Spider-Man!"

"Spider-Man must die!"

"At our hands, not those of some relic from ancient times!"

"We've got to st-stop Chthon!"

All the while, Chthon was gaining in mass, becoming more solid, more *present,* by the second. I had the sense that the churning red and black gunk was really the atoms that would go into his physical form, and if they could be kept from merging together . . .

"Carrion! You've got to act now!"

Carrion stopped battling himself and stared at me.

"He's coalescing," I said. "When his body fully manifests, it'll be too late! Until then, you can repel organic matter, right? Can you keep him from solidifying?"

"We can," Carrion said. He sounded whole again, as if the battle was finished. I hoped the right side had won.

"Get to it, then! There isn't much time!"

Carrion eyed me like he might swat me just for daring to speak in a commanding tone. But then he turned away slowly, almost haughtily, and stepped forward to face Chthon.

Chthon's voice roared from that roiling dark fog with a thunder like waves crashing over the deepest part of the sea. "I sense great power within you, and I also sense that you are not some puny mortal, but a being more than mortal and less than god."

"Th-that's right," Carrion said. "F-far more than m-m-m—human!"

"Perhaps you are, little thing," Chthon's voice raged. "Yet still not powerful enough to challenge me, and too late to do so even if you were able."

"He's lying!" I shouted. "If it was too late he wouldn't bother saying so!"

"You're r-right, Sp-Sp-Spider-Man." Stan Carter's stammer was becoming more pronounced. I couldn't tell if it meant he was nervous about confronting Chthon— although who could blame him?—or had some other cause.

Most of the Scriers who weren't bleeding to death

were watching the face-off. The one with the book, though, was still chanting something under his breath. "The ritual isn't complete, Stan!" I called. "You can still stop it!"

"The foolishly dressed mortal knows naught of what he yammers," Chthon said.

"Who writes your lines?" I asked. "Shakespeare's less talented cousin?"

"I will have a special punishment reserved for you, little man," Chthon said.

"I'm shaking in my webbed boots, Cloudy."

"Enough!" Chthon rumbled. "Already Chthon grows weary of these games. By the power of the *Darkhold,* writ in fire by my own hand, this world shall bow in obeisance to me at last!"

"We're not much for bowing anymore," I said. "We're more into a handshake or a hug." I gave Carrion a shove in the middle of his back, and he took an inadvertent step forward.

Chthon reared back. He started to coalesce into a human-like form again, black with red highlights. For an instant he looked like Miles Warren, then like Wanda Maximoff, then like Modred the Mystic, then faster than I could blink he had gone back to looking like an unfamiliar, emaciated, almost generic male. "Halt or perish!" he declared, pointing a finger at Carrion.

"I don't th-th-th-think so!" Carrion replied. He held up both of his hands. I recognized the gesture. He was trying my idea, hoping to interfere with the organic matter that Chthon was becoming.

It was a long shot and I didn't hold out a lot of hope.

But it occurred to me that the fact that a Scrier was still reciting part of the ritual might mean that Chthon still needed a final boost into our world.

Carrion's efforts seemed to be bearing some fruit. One moment Chthon had appeared on the verge of solidifying, and the next he was scattered again, puffs of thick dark smoke with no shape or evident connection.

"Keep at it!" I shouted. I took a running start, used a Scrier's hooded head as a springboard, and vaulted over him. I had to bounce off a couple more Scrier noggins to get there, but at last I performed a flip and came down feet-first into the guy with the book. We both crashed to the ground, but I got up first and was about to pound him into next year when three other Scriers grabbed my arms. Before I could shake them off, the Scrier lurched back to his feet, still reciting.

And another Scrier broke free from the pack, grabbed someone's .45 automatic, and tore off his own hood and mask. He had short brown hair and a thick face with small eyes, narrowed more in concentration. I kicked one of the Scriers gripping me in the side of the leg. He buckled and I swung him into the other two. They went down in a heap, and I started toward the gunman.

Too late. He shouted, "Everett, you've gone too far!" Then he pulled the trigger.

But he wasn't aiming at me.

His bullet flew into the open mouth of the reciting

Scrier. It punched out through the back of his skull, geysering brain and blood, bone and cloth.

He collapsed, as if suddenly the robe and mask were empty.

"Scrier Sturtevant, no!" one of the other Scriers cried.

The one who had removed his hood and mask stood there, looking shell-shocked at what he had done. Other Scriers moved around him, some with guns in their hands. But no one made a move toward him.

No one human, anyway.

The smoke, however, streamed toward him—*into* him, black tendrils probing his eyes, nose, mouth, and ears. The effect was almost comical, or might have been if it wasn't so horrible. It looked as if he was sucking Chthon into himself.

From his tense, surprised body language, though, it was obvious that this was Chthon's doing, not his. The man trembled uncontrollably. I didn't think he could stand up without whatever rigidity Chthon gave him. The god was clearly possessing the shooter's body, and if there was anything I could do about it, I didn't know what.

But there was no one between me and the *Darkhold* anymore. I webbed the unholy book and flung it at the man. It spun end over end and one corner smacked into his forehead hard enough to stagger him. He didn't fall, though, and the smoke kept trailing into him, making his body jerk around like he'd grabbed a live wire.

For good measure, I kicked over the rock cairn.

Spotting the partially used paint can a Scrier had used to mark the pentagram on the floor, I upended it, blurring the pentagram's carefully drawn lines. I didn't know what this might do, ritual magic not being one of my specialties, but I didn't imagine it would help Chthon's cause any.

Carrion took a different approach. He shoved through the Scriers and latched onto the bare-faced man with both hands on the guy's cheeks. I knew what he was up to.

"Carrion, don't!" I called. "That's murder!"

That had never stopped him before, and it didn't now.

I could have interfered. There were a dozen or more Scriers between us, but I could have gone over or through them. I told myself I wanted to.

I hesitated, though. I knew what Carrion was trying to do. He wanted to deny Chthon refuge in the man. It made sense. For all I knew, the man wouldn't live through the trauma of Chthon's possession anyway.

And yet . . .

I couldn't just stand by and watch him kill again.

I started toward him. The Scriers were rapt now, watching the wordless struggle between Carrion and Chthon. They had forgotten about me. I forced my way between them.

Carrion was still, muscles bunched, willing the man in his hands to decay and his organic matter to separate. The man buzzed and quaked as the final tendrils of smoke streamed in through his openings. The closer I got to Carrion, the more I felt like I was trying to force myself through an electrically charged barrier. The air was thick, almost solid. It took all my strength to reach Carrion, and even when I did there was no strength behind my punch—the energy was dissipated before the blow landed.

He turned slowly to face me. As he did, the man in his hands blew apart. Smoke burst from the body, wafted toward the ceiling, and dissipated there.

Astonished and disgusted as I was, I barely noticed Carrion's condition. His gaunt yellow face had become positively skeletal. The flesh there had turned tissue-thin, and in spots it had been eaten away altogether. Moldering brown bone showed beneath it. He resembled one of his own victims, as if whatever he had done to the man Chthon had tried to inhabit—Sturtevant, someone had called him—had sapped his own life energy as well.

His hands suddenly empty (and dripping with gore), he slumped to his knees in front of me. "Sp-Sp-Spider-Man," he said, and with those words he sounded human again. His voice, and his eyes, sunken into the hollows of that awful head, were Stanley Carter's, and they pleaded for something.

"Stan?"

"Fo-forgive me, Spider-Man," he said.

His eyes rolled back and he pitched forward. I turned him over. His eyes were still open, but unseeing, and his flesh was already crumbling into dust. I released him, stepping back.

"Keep away from him!" I said.

The members of the Cabal had no problem obeying that command.

Chthon was gone. I believed that, unable to get a solid foothold in our world, the power of Carrion—magnified by his own contact with the *Darkhold*—had been enough to send him back to whatever dimension he dwelled in. Maybe I had helped, too, by interrupting Scrier Everett, throwing the book away from its altar, and kicking over the cairn. Scrier Sturtevant had probably played a role by shooting Scrier Everett.

Stanley Carter was no doubt wise to seek forgiveness. He had done much evil, hurt many people.

But he didn't need to seek it from me.

As far as I was concerned, at the end he had repaid his debts and more.

26

EMORY CARTER WOKE up with a start. His heart was pounding so hard he thought it would snap his ribs, part his flesh, and go for a run. *Is this a heart attack?* he wondered. *Is this how it feels to die?*

He sat up. Sweat ran down his sides in rivers, stung his eyes. His sheets were soaked with it. Willing his body to relax, his trembling hands to steady, he stayed there several minutes and tried to discern what had frightened him so. Finally, he remembered his encounter with his nephew, Stan, or the ghoulish thing claiming to be him.

Was it in the house with him now? He listened intently, trying to discern the sounds of it breathing or moving about. But every sound came from outside: the angry roar of a motorcycle, the chuff and hiss of a city bus, the plaintive wail of a distant train whistle. Emory turned on the bed so his legs hung over the side, located his open-heeled brown slippers, and slid his feet inside them. When he stood up, his legs quivered and threatened to give out, but he caught the wall and steadied himself. He didn't feel much like the Surgeon at this moment, more like a man with whom age had finally caught up.

Hunger gnawed at his stomach, but he didn't think he could eat if that thing was still in the house. He didn't even want to stay there—was surprised he had managed to fall asleep, much less sleep so soundly, and for so long. Daylight rimmed the closed curtains of his room with brilliant blades that stung his eyes.

He went down the hall to the spare room, the one he had thought, in his delusion, he was letting his nephew use. At the door, he stopped, listened again. A breeze blew against the outer wall and the house itself seemed to breathe, but no sound came from the bedroom. Using every shred of courage he could muster, he tapped at the door. "Stanley?" he whispered.

No one answered. No one moved inside. He tried the knob, found it unlocked, and turned it until the latch clicked. With three fingers, he pushed the door open, just a crack, and peered through.

More closed curtains, those same bars of light at their edges like strips of the sun had adhered there. But the ghoul, the Stanley-thing, was gone.

Its absence emboldened Emory. He pushed the door open farther, walked in. This was his house after all, his guest room. He was the one who said who stayed in it and who didn't. When that thing came back, he would just tell it to take a hike, to get lost. He didn't mind helping out family, but he wasn't opening his door to a stranger.

He wondered if he could get by with washing the bed linens, or if they would have to be burned. The thing had been pretty badly injured when it came in last night, bleeding and scraped and broken. Emory turned down the blanket and found drying bloodstains on the bottom sheet, rust-colored and already turning powdery. He scraped at one with a fingernail, brought it to his nose, and sniffed. The metallic smell of blood had always been a favorite aroma, an old friend. This stuff had a strange undertone, but it was definitely blood. Almost definitely. He touched his finger to the end of his tongue.

Yep, that's blood, he thought. *Maybe burning's the best thing for it. Not sure washing will get all these stains out, and I'm not sure I'd want to sleep in these sheets myself now.*

He bent over to grab the corner, to tear the sheets from the bed (hoping the blood had not soaked through to the mattress, because no way was he buying a new mattress), and a wave of dizziness washed over him, nearly knocking his feet right out from under. He braced himself on the bed with one hand, hoping it would pass.

Instead it got worse. The room tilted this way and then that, the floor spinning around, the ceiling dipping below his feet and then soaring into the sky, and he wondered once again if it was heart attack time, and then he fell facedown on the bed, his nose and mouth landing in the biggest of the stains. He knelt like that,

knees on the floor, face on the bed, as the world went
dark around him.

I dragged myself home from Queens, thinking maybe
I'd just go to bed until spring or early summer. Some
victories feel positively triumphant, but not this one.
I was relieved that the battle was over, that MJ could
come home and Aunt May could return to her life, but
I didn't particularly feel that I had won anything. I had
secured the surviving Scriers with webbing, pinned the
Darkhold to the roof so even if the Scriers could get to it,
they'd never be able to get through the webbing, used
someone's cell phone to alert S.H.I.E.L.D., and then
headed out just before they came.

But when I got home there was a message from
Aunt May on my phone. "Peter," she said, her voice
tight with worry. "I'm sorry to call so early, but you've
got to talk to Yselda Slown right away. Someone's attacked Vincent."

I called Yselda and got her voice mail. Some days
it seemed like no one actually answered telephones
anymore, including me. Yselda's outgoing message
said that she was at Lee Memorial Hospital in Soho. I
hurried there and asked for Vincent at the front desk.
Finally, after employing both puppy-dog eyes and some
fairly transparent flirting, I was directed to a room on
the third floor. Vincent shared it with a family of loud
talkers gathered around the bed of someone who had
been hurt in an industrial accident.

Yselda was there, eyes rimmed with red. When she saw

me she offered a wan smile, then fell into my arms and started crying with her head against my chest. I held her. "How are you doing, Vincent?" I asked over her head.

"Peachy," he said. His face had turned several different shades of blue and purple. When he opened his mouth I could see gaps in his teeth. "They worked me over pretty good, Pete."

"I'm so sorry," I said. I meant it. Unprovoked attacks happened in New York from time to time, but chances were good that this one had something to do with the trouble I had convinced him to stir up. "Do you know who did it?"

"They didn't announce themselves or anything," he said. He didn't have to worry about whispering with the shouters on the other side of the curtain. "But I have a pretty good idea. They warned me to quit what I was doing. Since I don't think they were hired by my competitors at Pretty Penny Printing, I was guessing they were talking about the demonstrations. And then when I knocked one of them down the stairs—"

"You knocked hired muscle down the stairs? You go, Vinny."

"Well, more or less. We fell down the stairs, anyway. But I tore his suit and—well, show him what you found, Yselda."

She released me, still sobbing gently. "Okay," she said. "When I heard the noise, I pulled the girls out of the tub and put them in their cribs, soaking wet, then ran into the hallway. I saw Vincent on the landing. But outside the door, on our floor, someone had dropped this." She took a blue plastic-coated card from her purse. It said VISITOR on it in white letters, and beneath that was the logo of New York Health & Life.

"Wow," I said. "I'm astonished they would have a thug come to their offices to get instructions on working someone over."

"Me, too," Vincent said. "But whoever did it is probably pretty low-level management, right? I don't think the big shots would go in for something so blatantly illegal. And the way I hear it, crooks are pretty stupid most of the time."

"You could be right." Crooks did tend to be among the least intelligent people I had met, with a few notable exceptions. And just because someone had worked his or her way up to a position of some minor influence at an insurance company didn't mean they had crawled very far out of the gene pool. "Are you stopping the demonstrations?"

"Of course," Yselda snapped. "Look at him."

"I am, but it's making my teeth ache."

"I guess for now," Vincent said. "Because I can't really walk a picket line with an IV tube in me. But this just makes things worse for us—more medical bills, and I can't even work. So when I get out I'll probably have to start the demonstrations up again. I'm afraid now if I can't get a settlement out of them, we'll have to declare bankruptcy. As it is, we might get evicted from our place."

"I don't know what I can do," I said. "But if I think of anything I'll let you know."

"Thanks, Pete," Vincent said. "You've been great, really. I appreciate you coming by. I'd be even more effusive if I wasn't on all these painkillers."

"No problem. I hope you feel better fast." I gave Yselda a quick hug, bumped knuckles with Vincent, and left them there with the loud talkers still doing their best to shatter windows up and down the building.

I did have one idea, but it wasn't something Peter Parker could do. Spider-Man had to do it—and it involved getting physical, which was the kind of thing he did best. I found an empty space behind the building, in an enclosed pen where two Dumpsters were stored, and took off my Parker clothes. Then I webslung back uptown, to the NYH&L building. It's not a universal thing, but it's common for CEO's to be given the highest offices in the building, with the best views, and I decided to start there and work my way down if necessary.

It wasn't necessary. Carlton Wicklin, a Globitek VP and Chief Executive Officer of New York Health & Life, had almost the entire penthouse floor to himself. Through one window I could see his executive assistant sitting at her desk, furiously typing something. Or playing an online game, for all I knew. But through the floor-to-ceiling glass walls surrounding most of the penthouse office, which was as luxurious as any high-roller's suite in Las Vegas I had ever heard about, I saw Wicklin, whom I had photographed a few times during my photojournalist days. Usually he was handing a giant check to some charity or other. Those giant checks were usually for a few thousand dollars, which was about what it cost to power the elevator to run all the way up to his floor every day. He was a true humanitarian.

When I tapped on the double glass doors leading from his private balcony into his office, he looked up from a sheaf of papers—probably documenting his successful bid to deny coverage to the elderly and the physically disabled—and blinked twice. To his credit, he made the surprised look vanish quickly from his face, and replaced it with a welcoming grin, as if he had invited me over for coffee and it had just slipped his mind for a moment.

"Open up," I said, "or I'm coming through the glass."

Wicklin cupped a hand over his ear. I repeated myself, louder, and added pantomime. He reached for a phone on his desk and I wagged a finger at him. He looked at me, looked at the phone, looked at me, and came to the door. I nodded.

When he opened the door, he gave me that grin again. "You could have made an appointment, Spider-Man, and come in through the front door."

"Not my style," I said, pushing past him into the office. "I prefer the unexpected drop-by."

He crossed his arms over his chest, showing me defiant. He wore a blue silk dress shirt with cuff links and his initials monogrammed on the pocket. And suspenders. I didn't think anyone still wore suspenders, and had to fight the temptation to snap them. "I'm a little busy just now."

"Putting widows and orphans out on the streets will just have to wait a few minutes."

"Listen, Spider-Man, I don't know what you think we do here, but this is an insurance company. We take care of people."

I crossed the plush carpeting to his desk. It was sleek and modern, made of highly polished wood. There wasn't much on top of it but the telephone, the papers he had been looking at, and a laptop computer. "I understand insurance," I said. "It's like if I warned you that something might happen to this nice desk and you didn't want it to happen so I said, well, if you pay me now, then in case something happens to it later I'll pay you back a little of what you gave me up front."

"Do I need to call security?"

"Depends. You like your desk?"

"Are you making threats here? Has the *Bugle* been right about you all along?"

"I guess you're not interested in insurance." I picked up one end of his desk. The thing had to weigh three hundred pounds. When I tilted it up, everything slid off the other side. The phone and computer made crunching noises.

"You *are* a maniac! I'm warning you, Spider-Man—"

"No, I'm warning you, Wicklin." I hoisted the desk up over my head and held it there, locking my elbows. It looked impressive, I'm sure. Wicklin's executive assistant looked impressed, anyway, when she came into the office to see what had made the racket and froze in the doorway, her eyes as wide as lawn mower wheels.

She was Asian, slender, her hair short and stylish in a cut that had probably cost about a grand.

"Should I call security, Mr. Wicklin?" she asked.

"Yes, Kristen."

"No, Kristen," I said. "You should stand right there so you can be a witness."

"Kristen," Wicklin said.

"Don't go anywhere, Kristen."

Kristen stayed put.

"You're in the insurance business, Wicklin," I told him, still holding the desk above my head. "Not the noninsurance business. Every person you turn away, every claim you deny, is *not* doing your business. You need to start doing it. I'm talking about all of New York Health & Life, top to bottom. Stop looking for ways to deny claims and start looking for ways to help the customers who keep you in business. You might be surprised—a little good word of mouth can go a long way, and if you start behaving like a company that cares about people, you might actually see profits increase."

"What do you know about the insurance business? We have risks, we have expenses—"

I was in no mood to let him talk. In another hour or two, that desk might start to feel heavy. "I know about people," I said. "I know what they need and what they want. They want to know that if they pay in premiums over the years, you'll be there for them when they have needs. That's pretty simple."

"I don't think—"

"I'm not interested in your opinion. You like those

big windows?" I nodded toward the floor-to-ceilings, since my pointer fingers were otherwise engaged.

He didn't say anything. He didn't have to. I got the answer from the way his cheeks blanched.

"Here's what I want you to do. Lose the words 'pre-existing condition' from your vocabulary. Just forget about them, because they're meaningless. If someone's sick, they need medical attention, and they're paying you so that you'll pay for that medical attention when it's needed. In general, you need to speed up the pro-cessing of claims—you don't let your customers pay their premiums late, so you need to pay their claims on time. You should be investing in the health of your cus-tomers, encouraging them to seek preventive care rather than only seeing doctors after the worst has happened. Got all that? You need Kristen to take notes?"

"No, I got it," he said. He was breathing heavily, as if he'd just come back from a run around the block. Or was holding a three hundred pound desk over his head.

I put it down, careful not to set it back in the right place so he'd have to move it himself, or have it moved. Petty, but so what? "One more topic we have to discuss," I said, moving toward him. My fists were clenched. I looked as threatening as a guy in a skin-tight red-and-blue spider suit can look. "A man named Vincent Slown was beat up by thugs hired by your company, because he dared to protest the fact that your company was stealing from him, accepting his premium payments with no intention of paying out his claims. He's in the hospital."

Wicklin shook his head. "No, you're wrong about that. We don't—"

I kept heading for him, and he backed away from me, hands up in front as if he could fend me off if I came at him. "Don't bother denying it. Even if you didn't know about it, I've seen convincing evidence and I'm telling you now. Someone in your organization hired a couple of bruisers to work over a sick man. I hope you or Kristen made a note of his name, because you're going to take a personal interest in his case. You, personally, will pay for all hospital expenses related to the beating. New York Health & Life will cover all the medical expenses associated with his illness."

Wicklin had backed up as far as he could, against the big windows. Behind him the city continued doing what it does best, ignoring the concerns of individuals while humming along on its own business. I moved in closer, leaving only inches between us. He tried to become one with the glass. "Are we straight on this, Wicklin?"

"You don't know what you're asking, Spider-Man. You don't understand this business."

"I think I do. I also understand theft. And either you follow through on your promises to people—and I mean the ones you make openly, not the dodges and deceits concealed in the fine print in the back of a forty-page policy booklet—or you're effectively robbing them. It's not entirely unheard of for companies to show some small bit of social conscience, and you're about to start. Who knows, maybe business will improve and other insurance companies will follow your example." I put my hand on his chest, fingers spread, and pressed him against the glass. "I'll be paying attention. And I'd hate to have to come back here."

"I'm sure that won't be necessary."

I had to give him props. He stank of flop sweat, which had coated the sides of his expensive shirt, but he didn't stammer or hesitate when he spoke. I was tempted by his suspenders again, but showed uncommon restraint.

I started for the door through which I'd entered, and paused just inside it. "One last little thing. If there's a demonstration tomorrow, which I think is a good bet, it wouldn't be a bad idea for you to show up with some milk and cookies for everyone, and to talk to them about the change of heart you've had today. You don't have to mention what spurred it, just describe the revelation that came over you. I think you'll find talking to those people and hearing their stories very enlightening. Kristen, you might want to schedule some time for that."

"Yes, sir," Kristen said.

"She's good. Think about a raise."

"Milk and cookies?" Wicklin said.

"What a good idea." I went onto the balcony and jumped over the side. I like to think Kristen applauded my dramatic exit.

But she probably didn't. At least, not out loud.

27

I WAS ALMOST home when I heard sirens screaming in the direction of my building. I poured on the speed. Before leaving for the hospital, I'd left a message on MJ's cell phone telling her it was safe to come home. I wanted to believe that it was, but if anything had happened to her . . .

No. I had to stop thinking like that. It was self-destructive, not helpful. I pushed that idea from my head and spun my webs.

A block away, I saw the reason for the sirens.

There was a woman on the sidewalk, surrounded by a pool of bright red blood. She had been split open from her stomach to her sternum, and even from several stories up I could see wet, glistening organs on the ground beside the open cavity.

Worse, on the wall beside her was a message written in red dust. It said simply, #1.

Only one guy left notes like that. And he was dead again.

Trouble was, he never seemed to stay dead. A new Carrion couldn't become infected by the virus as long as the last Carrion lived. If the Stan Carter Carrion had died fighting Chthon, that might have activated a new one.

But who? And where was he now?

This was starting to look like a never-ending battle.

And if Carrion was back—and this one, like the last, knew my identity—then MJ was definitely at risk if she had beat me home. Paramedics and police had reached the woman on the ground, so I kept going. One more building stood between me and my goal. I went up and over.

And on the street, directly outside my building, was another woman, split open like the first. I looked for the message and there it was, drawn on the sidewalk. #2.

I launched myself into open air, tucked into a forward roll, fired webbing at the roof of my building and came out of the roll, swinging right for it. Right before I slammed into it I put out hands and feet and broke my momentum. Clinging to the wall, I scampered to the window I'd left cracked open and hurried inside. "MJ?" I called.

She didn't answer.

The apartment had that empty feeling to it. I rushed from room to room. "MJ, you here?"

Still no answer.

I covered every room, and found no sign of her, or of Carrion. I snatched up the phone, dialed her cell. Voice mail again. I hadn't spoken with her all day and suddenly that worried me. "Call me as soon as you possibly can," I said. "And if you're on your way home, stop. Don't come here. I'll let you know when it's safe. I love you."

I hoped she was on a subway and had no signal. Just in case, I looked out the window, down toward the street. What if she was walking toward the building right now, on the same sidewalks from which Carrion was taking his victims?

The authorities had reached the second victim now. As they surrounded her, backing away the onlookers and taping off a perimeter, I realized something about both of the women he had just killed. They could have been sisters. Young, slender, with dark brown hair. It was only a sample of two, but if it was a preference rather than a coincidence, then MJ, with her red locks, wouldn't be of interest to him.

Unless, of course, he knew she was with me.

Then another awful thought hit me. MJ wouldn't be his type, but our downstairs neighbor, Robin Siegel, would. She had long brown hair she usually kept in a ponytail. She was athletic, running and playing regular tennis and squash, and she worked out in the building's gym at least three times a week.

I hadn't changed yet, so I let myself back out the window and shot a webline up to the overhang of the roof's edge, then lowered myself to Robin's window.

Peering inside, I saw Carrion facing Robin in her living room. She was backing away from him (giving me a flashback to the way I had terrorized Wicklin less than an hour before), and he was stepping toward her, maintaining the distance between them.

He held a gleaming scalpel in his gloved fist.

I kicked off from the wall to get some momentum, then shifted just enough for my feet to crash through the window. Glass showered them both. I landed on my feet, in between them.

"That's enough, Carrion," I said. "Get out of the apartment, ma'am. I'll deal with him."

"Oh my God, thank you!" Robin said, running toward the door. I was ready to blind Carrion if he made a play for her.

"Spider-Man." This Carrion's voice was as gravelly as the others, but carried a hint of age as well. "We meet again at last."

"You know who I am?"

"I know you're our enemy. And you're preventing us from helping that young lady."

"You have a strange idea of helping."

"You have no concept of what we can do to help. What we have done. Over the course of many, many years."

Now he was confusing me. Whoever was inside that unpleasant head had just become Carrion, literally in the last few hours. The other Carrions had never, to my knowledge, claimed that their murderous ways were a "help" to anyone. Who was this new guy, and what was he after?

"I don't need to know what you can do to know that

you're not really helping anyone. It's enough to know that you're finished, as of now."

"What is it you imagine you can do to us that you haven't already tried?"

"I'll think of something." He had a good point. What I needed, I decided, was another bolt of inspiration, like when Amber Collier's simple question about magnesium in class had given me the idea for the demonstrations against New York Health & Life.

And almost as if remembering that triggered something that had been locked in my brain, an idea came to me almost full-blown. Would it work?

That, I would just have to find out.

But not right away. Apparently tired of chatting, Carrion used his telekinetic power over organic matter to hurl a wooden dining table at me. It was lighter than the desk at Wicklin's office and I batted it away.

While it obstructed my view, though, he launched other objects—the chairs that went along with the table, some wood-handled knives in a wooden knife block, and the heavy wooden sideboard the knife block had been sitting on. The chairs crashed into me. I dodged most of the knives, but one glanced off my left shoulder. Then the sideboard hit me, and I staggered back a few steps, feet crunching over broken window glass.

I decided to let momentum carry me. Carrion lunged at me with his scalpel just as I flipped out the window, and he sliced empty air. "Don't go anywhere!"

"Come back!" he called.

"In a sec!" I caught the same webline on which I had come down and climbed it back up to my window. I couldn't tell if this Carrion knew that I was Peter Parker—he hadn't given any indication of that in Robin's apartment, but he had been drawn to my building, and not just because I happened to have a slender brunette neighbor.

I had to hurry. He could decide to teleport after Robin, or out of the building altogether, and go into hiding again. Or he could beat me into my own apartment and catch me there before I was ready.

The place was still empty. What I needed was tucked in a drawer of my desk, where I'd stashed it when I brought it home from Midtown High, before the combination of Carrion and Vincent Slown had distracted me so much that I'd forgotten all about it. Amber hadn't brought it up again, so maybe she had forgotten, too.

I grabbed the zipped plastic bag from my desk, snatched a paper towel off a roll in the kitchen, and crossed the room in two strides, aiming for the open window.

Carrion stood there, blocking my path, and I ran headlong into him. He took a couple of unsteady steps back but wrapped his arms around me before I could move away.

His touch burned, even through my costume. He was decaying the fabric, and my flesh would follow. I pounded his midsection with jabs, but I couldn't get my shoulders or back into them.

Then I felt the blade of his scalpel, cold for an instant, then hot. It sliced through my costume just beneath my left shoulder blade, dug into skin and muscle. "Yaaaah!" I screamed. I writhed out of his grip and stumbled backward, dropping my plastic bag. If he touched the open wound I was done for.

He chased me, slashing the air with the bloody scalpel. Blood ran down inside my uniform. His foot narrowly missed the bag. I still had a paper towel wadded in my left fist, for all the good that would do me. I could threaten to wipe him up, I supposed.

"We have decided that you must die," he said. "Only then can we continue helping those in need of our services."

"I have a slightly different agenda," I said. I needed to get back to the plastic bag without coming in range of his scalpel or his grasp. "But what say you tell me about these services? I could use someone who does carpets and windows."

"Joke all you like, Spider-Man. You have precious little time left to laugh."

I kept backing away, maintaining a safe distance between us. "You can do better than that, Carrion. That's a standard-issue super villain threat, and there's nothing standard about you, is there?"

"Not at all."

"So how many people have you helped with your services?"

"Counting today? Twenty. We have been busy today."

"How many today?" I asked, afraid of the answer. He seemed to want to talk about it, though, and as long as he was talking, I was breathing.

"Two today. So far. You interrupted number three, but then, she was just a way to pass the time until you arrived."

"You handle that scalpel like a pro," I said. "You a doctor?"

He smiled. I wished Carrion would never do that again, because it was just nasty to see. "In a manner of speaking. Once people called us the Surgeon. In our prime." He sliced at me again. "Our first prime, that is. But even then we didn't have the energy and the powers that we do now."

"I'll bet not." Something about what he had said rang familiar, but I didn't have time to sit down and puzzle it out. I just wanted to get to the plastic bag, which was still on the floor behind him. "Stan, you in there? I could use a hand here."

"Stanley is part of us," Carrion said. "But Stanley respects his elders. Our brother raised—" He cut himself off midsentence and snarled at me. "Enough talk!"

"Your brother?" I repeated.

With his left hand, he reached into his pouch. I knew what came next, the killing dust. Time to blind him. I blasted his face with webbing and he brought both hands up to block it, strewing dust in front of himself. I went to the ceiling and clung there, above the dust cloud.

Temporarily blinded, he staggered for a few steps, touching the webbing with both hands to decay it faster. I went over him and dropped down behind him, grabbing the plastic bag. As I tore it open, I remembered two things.

There had been a serial killer in New York, decades before, whom the newspapers called the Surgeon, because he sliced his victims open and removed their internal organs with surgical precision. Using something like a scalpel. Could this Carrion be the Surgeon, still alive after all this time?

The other thing was a more recent memory, from when I was trying to run down possible places that the Stan Carter Carrion might have been hiding. He hadn't had any living family in the city, but he had an uncle— Emory Carter, I recalled—somewhere in New Jersey. If Stan's father was Carrion's brother, then this Carrion might have been Emory. Maybe Carrion had visited him, and infected him with the virus, which hadn't taken effect until the last Carrion was dead.

That all raced through my mind in the split second it took to grab the lighter from the plastic bag. Carrion's eyes were clearing and he was turning around to locate me again. I could tell from his wordless roar that he was furious.

"So you're Emory?" I asked. "Emory Carter?"

"*We are Carrion!*"

"Yeah, well I'm Scrooge McDuck, and you're making a mess of my money bin." He came toward me, mouth open, rage making his horrific face all the more frightening.

Now or never.

I lit the paper towel, shoved it into the plastic bag, and threw the whole thing toward him. He reached out to catch it.

I shut my eyes.

I could hear and feel the reaction, could see the flare even through my mask and eyelids.

When it's ignited, magnesium powder burns fast, hot, and bright. It may not be like staring right into the sun at close range, but it's not far from that.

Carrion let out a wail that tore at my ears, a cry that I still hear in nightmares sometimes. I opened my eyes in time to see the last bits of magnesium and plastic bag pattering to the floor, still burning with that brilliant white intensity.

Once again, Carrion put his hands to his blinded eyes. But this time, his gloves were still burning from catching a bag full of flaming powdered magnesium, and he wasn't pressing his hands against webbing. That, he was used to by now.

Which was what I had counted on.

With nothing between his bare hands and his eyes, instead of decaying webbing, he was literally decaying himself, beginning with his eyes. The more they burned, the harder he pressed, locked in a circle of agony that blotted out everything else, including reason.

He stumbled around the room, knocking over a table, a chair, bumping into a bookcase. The whole time he was screaming from the pain, and interlaced in the screams, I thought I could hear the individual voices of

McBride and Allen, Warren and Stan Carter and Emory Carter adding to the din, a whole chorus of agony.

As he flailed blindly, I could see his flesh changing, drying out, turning color, yellow to green to black, tightening against bone and then withering away altogether. Bone gleamed through the taut skin, then came out into the air as the skin vanished. Then the bone yellowed and browned and began deteriorating as well. His screams stopped when his vocal cords were eaten away, and then there was only an awful clicking as his jaw tried to work. Finally his bony hands fell away from his face. His brown hood slipped from his naked skull and his eyeless sockets turned toward me as if seeking me out and his jaw swung open and I thought he was going to say something to me.

Instead, he collapsed in a heap on the carpet. His bag landed beside him, dust spilling from its flap. I stood a safe distance away and watched while his bones became powder.

Not knowing what else to do, I yanked up the carpet from the floor, folded it over the mess, and called Clarence Shields of S.H.I.E.L.D. I gave him Parker's address and told him what he'd find there, and that he needed to get there in a hurry with a way to contain the mixture of red powder and white.

That done, I found Robin Siegel outside and told her it was safe to go home again.

The last thing I did was call MJ, to tell her the same thing.

28

"So Carrion could still come back," Mary Jane said. "Or another Carrion, anyway."

"I can't definitively rule it out. It seems unlikely, though. S.H.I.E.L.D. contained the remains in our apartment, and they went to Emory Carter's home in Tappan and contained that, and they cleaned out the buildings the Cabal of Scrier had been using. I think they've located and contained the virus everywhere it might have been living, but I guess we won't know for sure unless another Carrion turns up at some point."

"Nothing like a life of certainty."

"Some things are certain," I said.

"Death and taxes?"

"Not as certain as they once were, apparently. I was thinking more about love."

"Love is good."

Because our apartment still stank from the fire and the rotting flesh and removing the carpeting had left a bit of a mess, we had gone out for dinner again, leaving windows open to let in some fresh air. When we got back, things had improved, but not enough, so we had gone up to the roof. The evening was cool but not yet uncomfortable, and I could tell the truly cold nights weren't far off.

We had been sitting on a bench some previous tenant had left up there, but MJ stood and walked close to the edge, gazing out at the lights of the city. I rose and followed her, not because I was afraid she would fall but because she smelled so delicious that I didn't want to be out of range. I reached for her hand and she took mine in her warm fingers. "Love is good," I echoed. "Especially when you're involved."

MJ turned away from the city, which was good because it meant she turned toward me. She put my hand on her hip and moved in close, her arms snaking around my neck, and as she did, someone in one of the lower floors started playing music, something Latin with a slow but driving beat. MJ started moving her hips, then her feet, and I went along with her and then we were dancing together, holding each other close, there on the roof of our building with only stars for an audience.

"Remember when I said it would be cool if you could fly?" she said.

"Yeah?"

"It would be. But this?" She took her head off my shoulder long enough to grace me with a smile I could feel down to my toes and nodded at the way we moved in graceful unison. "This, Tiger, is pretty damn cool, too."

I held her tight, squeezing her against me. "I wouldn't trade it," I said. "Not for anything."

"Nothing? All the money in the world? Eternal youth? Free cable?"

"Not for anything," I said again. "That doesn't come with qualifications. Or conditions."

I felt her lips against my neck, and her warm breath. "I like the sound of that," she said, between kisses. "A lot."

"I'm glad."

"You know how our apartment is kind of smelly?"

"Yeah," I said. "You want to sleep in a motel tonight?"

She kissed me again, this time between my lips and chin. "Not a chance," she said. "I'm tired of motels." Her lips found mine, lingered there a while. When she broke the kiss, she added, "I was just thinking we could probably ignore the smell. Especially if we leave a window open. And if it gets cold, we could cuddle. I'm sure we can find ways to warm each other up."

I started dancing toward the door leading onto the staircase. "You know what I love about you? Besides all the other things I love about you, I mean?"

"What's that?"

"Your problem-solving skills. Smell, window. Cold, cuddle. That's some seriously sharp thinking."

We were almost to the door. The music swelled to a crescendo and I pirouetted us around, and as we spun I held her familiar and comfortable and thrilling shape close and lost myself in the aroma of her hair and the depths of her eyes. All the bad guys went away, all the crime and violence and pain and poverty, and there was only us, only Mary Jane and Peter, dancing under a ceiling of stars in the midst of the world's greatest city, swirling and spinning and swaying in the New York night, and holding her tight I leaned toward her ear and spoke a single word, breathed it, really, and it made her smile, and her smile, as it always, always did, made me smile, too.

The word was "Forever."

She said it back to me, and her breath on my ear was like a whisper of summer cutting through the sharp autumn air, and at that moment I couldn't think of a sweeter sound in the world, or a sweeter possible word.

"Forever."

ABOUT THE AUTHOR

JEFF MARIOTTE is the award-winning writer of more than thirty novels, including *Missing White Girl* and *River Runs Red* (both as Jeffrey J. Mariotte), horror epic *The Slab*, teen horror quartet *Witch Season*, and more, as well as dozens of comic books. He's a co-owner of specialty bookstore Mysterious Galaxy in San Diego, and lives in southeastern Arizona on the Flying M Ranch. For more information, please visit www.jeffmariotte.com.

Not sure what to read next?

Visit Pocket Books online at
www.simonsays.com

Reading suggestions for
you and your reading group
New release news
Author appearances
Online chats with your favorite writers
Special offers
Order books online
And much, much more!

POCKET BOOKS
A Division of Simon & Schuster
A CBS COMPANY

POCKET STAR BOOKS
A Division of Simon & Schuster
A CBS COMPANY

13456